G000131356

I never dreamt I could
Deborah Fortin

Praise for Maria Grace

"Grace has quickly become one of my favorite authors of Austen-inspired fiction. Her love of Austen's characters and the Regency era shine through in all of her novels." ***Diary of an Eccentric***

"Maria Grace is stunning and emotional, and readers will be blown away by the uniqueness of her plot and characterization" ***Savvy Verse and Wit***

"Maria Grace has once again brought to her readers a delightful, entertaining and sweetly romantic story while using Austen's characters as a launching point for the tale." ***Calico Critic***

I believe that this is what Maria Grace does best, blend old and new together to create a story that has the framework of Austen and her characters, but contains enough new and exciting content to keep me turning the pages. ... Grace's style is not to be missed. ***From the desk of Kimberly Denny-Ryder***

30130505048864

THE *Trouble*

TO *Check Her*

Maria Grace

White Soup Press

Published by: White Soup Press

The Trouble to Check Her
Copyright © 2016 Maria Grace

All rights reserved including the right to reproduce this
book, or portions thereof, in any format whatsoever.

The characters and events portrayed in this book are ficti-
tious or are used fictitiously. Any similarity to actual
persons, living or dead, events or locales is entirely coinci-
dental and not intended by the author.

For information, address
author.MariaGrace@gmail.com

ISBN-10:0692647988
ISBN-13:978-0692647981 (White Soup Press)

Author's Website: RandomBitsofFaascination.com
Email address: Author.MariaGrace@gmail.com

Dedication

For my husband and sons.
You have always believed in me.

❧Chapter 1

*If you, my dear father, will not take the trouble of check-
ing her exuberant spirits, and of teaching her that her
present pursuits are not to be the business of her life, she
will soon be beyond the reach of amendment. Her character
will be fixed, and she will, at sixteen, be the most determined flirt that ever made herself and her family ridiculous.*
~Jane Austen, **Pride and Prejudice**

LYDIA STAGGERED OFF THE public coach in front of
Summerseat's coaching station and drew a deep
breath. So many people crammed into the coach! Had
she breathed since their last stop?

What a horrid way to travel—packed in with the
fetid odors of her unwashed companions. Mr. Darcy
might have transported her in his private carriage. He

had more than one, after all.

She pulled herself up straight and retied her bonnet strings. Her back might not ever be right again.

How glimflashy Darcy had been—a perfect match for Lizzy with her back up—ordering her this way and that, deciding where she should go and what she should do. What did either of them know about anything? What right did they have to ruin her life?

And nosy Aunt Gardiner, with all her intrusive and personal questions. Why did she need to know what transpired between her and Wickham in the privacy of their room?

A sharp breeze whistled past. Lydia pulled her shawl tighter over her shoulders.

Why had they made her leave anyway? Lady Catherine's opinion hardly counted for anything now, since Papa was moving the family back to London.

She dodged the huffy old woman who had been crowding her the entire journey. The fussock snorted and glared down her nose as she passed.

Crosspatch.

Papa had a new patron now, the Earl of Matlock. How wonderful it would be to rub shoulders with an earl! An earl with unmarried sons was even better.

But now, because of Mr. Darcy, she would never meet any of them. She stomped. Papa declared he would take no chances with an unruly daughter jeopardizing his new position.

Oh, this was so unfair!

She wove through the stale-smelling crowd, elbowing several young men out of her way, so she could climb up on a bench to scan the crowd. No one seemed to be looking for her.

Why did they make her travel alone? Mama would

be appalled that she traveled without a chaperone. But Papa would not pay for a maid to accompany her. Neither would Mr. Darcy, though he might have easily afforded it.

It was all so cruel! Everything she had known was lost to her—Wickham, her home, her friends, her sisters—and it was all Lizzy and Darcy's fault.

She jumped down from the bench. Had she ever been so alone?

She rubbed away prickles on the back of her neck. A rainstorm must be on the way. Might as well wait more comfortably. She sank down on the rickety looking bench, whipping her head this way and that.

Oh, this was so very, very vexing! Someone was supposed to meet her and take her to the school—where were they?

Perhaps the coach driver knew. She hurried back to the coach.

"Sir, excuse me, can you—"

The driver and another man untied the ropes that held the trunks to the coach.

"Out of the way girl." The driver grunted and shouldered her out of his path.

"But I need—"

"What you need is not my concern." He heaved a trunk to his shoulder.

How rude! He stank like a farmhand. Perhaps the other—

"You're gonna get hurt, girl. Outta the way." He trudged past, arms laden with luggage.

Oh! How could they ignore a lady? Did they not recognize she was a gentlewoman?

She looked around. No one noticed her, no one cared. Her hands trembled and her insides knotted beneath a welling scream.

"Miss Bennet?"

She whirled so fast the world spun.

A girl, slightly older than herself, in a plain, drab gown stood just behind her.

"Yes … that is me." Lydia gulped air to force the world to stop moving.

"I am Miss Annabella Fitzgilbert, from Mrs. Drummond's school. There is a chaise waiting for us."

At last!

"What took you so long? I have been waiting simply for ages. You should have been on time. I will inform your mistress."

The girl shook her head and smiled the same sort of smile Jane used to: lips pressed tight into a firm line, eyes narrow with lots of creases beside. She was not nearly as pretty as Jane though—quite a plain thing really. And she had freckles on her nose.

"My trunks. I do not know where they are. See to them." Lydia waved her hand toward the coach and scanned the street for an elegant chaise and handsome driver to carry her away from this nightmare.

"My name is Miss Fitzgilbert, not 'abigail'. I am neither your maid nor any servant at all. If you want your trunks, you best see to them yourself."

Lydia stomped. "You cannot talk to me like that."

"I can and I did. What is more, I suggest you become accustomed to it soon. You will find whomever you think you are matters little here."

"But—"

Miss High-and-Mighty Fitzgilbert lifted an open hand. "Stop it. I do not wish to hear. I do not care. Now attend to your things before they are stolen."

She pointed toward the baggage piled near the public coach.

Lydia swished her skirts and hurried to the pile of luggage. She wrestled her three trunks into an awkward stack.

"Is that everything?" Miss Fitzgilbert crossed her arms and tapped her foot.

"Oh, I left my bag on the coach!"

She pinched the bridge of her nose. "Well, you best hope you can find it. I shall watch your trunks. Go, now. Quickly!"

Lydia scurried back to the coach. Miss Fitzgilbert was horrible. Who was she? What if she were one of the school mistresses? Oh, that would be dreadful indeed. What kind of awful place was this school?

There—tucked under the seat she had occupied. She snatched her bag and jumped down, almost atop Miss Fitzgilbert.

"Hurry along now. Our driver has loaded your things. We must not keep him waiting." She grabbed Lydia's elbow and propelled her through the crowd.

She pulled her arm away.

Miss Fitzgilbert stomped off.

Would the chaise leave without her? It just might.

Lydia ran.

The hack waited near the street corner, dusty and plain and obviously worn, just like the driver. He grunted at them. Miss Fitzgilbert pushed her into a seat and climbed in after her. The chaise lurched into motion before Lydia was even settled.

Soon the coaching inn was out of sight, replaced by the dingy, dreary buildings of Summerseat. This place was nothing to London. It was not even much compared to Kent. Did it even have assembly rooms?

Not that she would get to see much of them. Regular balls and parties were probably not going to be part of Mrs. Drummond's curriculum of improvement.

She fell into the hard seat. "Is it far … to the school, I mean?"

"Not very, the house is on the edge of town. We would walk except for the trunks, of course."

"Of course," Lydia murmured.

"You are arriving from London, but are recently from Kent, I understand." The freckles on her nose twitched when she smiled that Jane-ish smile.

Jane had sense enough not to have freckles.

"Yes, my father—"

Miss Fitzgilbert turned her face away. "Mrs. Drummond requires that we do not speak of our previous stations."

"Why ever not? That must be the stupidest thing I have ever heard."

How dare Miss High-and-Mighty roll her eyes!

Had they not been in a moving coach, Lydia would have stormed away.

"You know why you have been sent here, do you not?"

"Because my sister is high-handed and her husband very cruel indeed."

"And your loss of virtue and reputation is their fault, I imagine?"

What did she know of that?

"Indeed it is. I would be married now apart from their interference."

Who would have expected such an unladylike snort to explode from such a prim little thing?

"If you are as the rest of us, you should count your

good fortune not to be married right now. He was probably a scoundrel—a blackguard of the worst sort."

"How would you know?"

"You regard yourself unique? Let me assure you, you are not. Every one of us shares a similar tale of virtue lost. Not one of the men in question has been worthy of the moniker 'gentleman'."

"You do not know—"

"I do not need to. Every girl who comes to this school has virtually the same story. Any man who would put you in the position to be sent here is no gentleman."

Lydia tossed her head and sniffed. "Well, you are wrong. I am not like any of the others."

"I have heard that, too." Miss Fitzgilbert squeezed her temples.

Now she looked like Lizzy.

"Some of us have come to appreciate our own folly and are grateful for Mrs. Drummond's intervention and that our future is much improved by our attendance here. But there are those who do not see it that way. I think you might be that sort. You should know those of us she has helped have no patience with those too proud to recognize their good fortune."

What a dreadful sort of superiority she displayed. Who did she think she was?

The carriage turned down a short drive leading to a large quaint house set off the road. The sign in front read: *Summerseat Abbey,* and in smaller letters, *Girl's Seminary.*So this was Mrs. Drummond's school for girls.

Covered in dark vines, it might have been cheerful in the spring when everything was green and blooming. But with autumn's approach, everything was drying brown and crunchy. Messy looking and imposing.

Who would want to enter such a grumpy sort of building, much less live there? Was everyone there as disagreeable as the edifice? If Miss Fitzgilbert was any indication, they were.

If only she might go home.

Miss Fitzgilbert jumped down from the chaise, smiling as though this were the most wonderful house she knew. Proof indeed she was a fool.

Lydia stepped down lest the bossy girl pull her out by force.

"Do not dawdle! Miss Drummond waits for you." She beckoned and led Lydia inside.

The vestibule was unremarkable, giving way quickly to a short corridor and a closed oak door upon which Miss Fitzgilbert knocked, thrice.

"You may enter." The voice was old—not old and frail, but old and overbearing like Lady Catherine's.

The room was polished and tidy and so proper it might scream out in pain if one breathed wrong.

Had the temperature suddenly dropped? Lydia ran her hands over her arms.

The woman behind the desk matched the room, starched and stiff. The curls peeking beneath her mobcap might have been lacquered in place and her tiny eyes flashed like jet beads.

Was there anyone more formed by nature to be a harsh school mistress?

"Miss Lydia Bennet?"

"Yes, madam." She curtsied, knees quaking.

Compared to this harridan, Aunt Gardiner was positively gracious.

"You may sit." She pointed at a hard chair. "Miss

Fitzgilbert, pray see her things are taken to Juliana's room."

"Yes, madam." She curtsied and left, closing the door behind her.

The room was so quiet. Was it possible to hear someone blink?

Mrs. Drummond blinked very loudly. "I suppose you think you have been sent to me because your benefactors are heartless and wish to spoil your fun."

Why did it sound so awful when she said it?

Lydia stammered sounds that refused to shape into words.

"I thought as much." She drummed her fingers upon her brightly polished desk. Not a paper out of place, nor a bit of dust marring the surface. "So we may add ungrateful to your list of sins."

"My … my … list of what?" Lydia's eyes grew wide.

"I am hardly surprised that you would be completely insensible to your blessings." She pushed her glasses up higher on her nose.

"My blessings?"

"You are sitting there, feeling sorry for yourself, missing your home, family and friends, and I suppose, your paramour as well."

"I … I … I suppose."

What was so wrong with missing the things and people she wanted?

"Have you forgotten your father cast you out? You have no home."

"That is not true." She slammed her hands on the arms of her chair.

"I am afraid it is. You may see it in his own hand."

"But … but …"

Mrs. Drummond shoved a piece of paper at her lined with Papa's thin, spidery letters.

In all matters regarding her future, refer to Mr. Darcy. We wash our hands of her.

"He cannot mean that!"

"I cannot judge what he does or does not mean, only what he has written."

"I am his daughter. He cannot turn me out."

"Again, I can only follow the instructions I am sent."

Papa allowed Lady Catherine to carry Lizzy off without protest. Her face turned cold and tingly.

"My sisters! They surely will not abandon me. Jane and Mary are to be married …"

"It will be their husbands who decide if you are received in their homes or not."

Mr. Bingley was willing to invite Lizzy into his home. Surely he would accept her, would he not?

"Jane will, surely she will." She gripped the unyielding edge of the desk.

"Perhaps that is true, but unless you have means to travel, you shall stay here until you are sent for."

"There must be some way for me to leave if … if…"

"You may see the letter your benefactor, Mr. Darcy, sent me."

"Stop calling him that! It is his fault—"

"That you are not married?"

"Yes, exactly. I should be mistress of my own home right now, not in some horrid school for girls."

"Then you are free to go." Mrs. Drummond gestured to the door, her voice as calm and level as when Lydia first walked in.

"I have no money."

"That is your concern, not mine."

"Mr. Darcy paid you—"

"To accept you as a student. If you leave my establishment now, I will return that money to him. That sum is not yours, nor has it ever been." She met Lydia's gaze with a steely, Lady Catherine glare.

Cruel woman, she had no feelings! Lydia rose and paced around the room.

"So, Miss Bennet, will you be staying?"

She wrapped her arms tightly around her waist. "I have no choice."

"Yes you do—you always have a choice. You may not prefer the alternatives, but you are making a choice."

Lydia harrumphed. "I will stay—for now."

"Do not make the mistake of thinking your presence is any boon to me. If you leave, I have sufficient applications that it would not be a week before I would have another girl in your place. Your family knows what a difficult, disagreeable child you are. It will be no reflection on my school. Realize, though, if you run away, no one will go after you. I will, of course, send a letter to your benefactor and he may mount efforts for your recovery. But you will not be permitted within these walls again."

"I cannot believe—"

"That is what happened to the girl whose place you are taking."

"No, surely, you—"

"Yes, and she was the daughter of a viscount."

Lydia clutched the back of the nearest chair.

"If you intend to stay, sit down. Otherwise, you know the way out."

Knees trembling, Lydia perched on the hard chair.

"You have made a wise choice, Miss Bennet. The first in what I hope will be a long series of wise choices. Now, let me acquaint you with our ways."

Why did she look like a cat about to deliver the death bite to a mouse in her claws?

"All of your fellow students are like you, gently bred females who do not deserve the title of lady. Every one of you has given her virtue and her good reputation away. You are also blessed with someone who cares enough to attempt to restore you to some level of decency and thereby offer you a future you are unworthy of."

"But … but I am—"

"I do not care, Miss Bennet. No one here does. Most of the girls here come from positions much higher than yours. By your actions, you treated your status as meaningless, so we shall do likewise."

"My actions?"

"Need I remind you?"

Lydia looked down and pressed the back of her hand to her mouth.

If only she had been allowed to marry! She would be the guest of honor at balls and parties and would be serving tea in her own parlor right now. Some day she would pay Mr. Darcy back for sending her here.

"Our first rule is that students neither refer to their rank nor their family's status. Special privilege here exists only to those who earn it. Do I make myself clear?"

"Y … yes madam."

"I do not enforce many rules with my cane, Miss Bennet, but this one I do. I offer no warnings, no second chances on this point. If you are in violation of this directive, you will be punished."

"But I have never—"

Mrs. Drummond flashed a brief, strained smile that might have cracked her face had she held it any longer. "Shame that, it might have kept you from your current dilemma. Nonetheless, you would not be the only girl who received her first licks of the cane by my hand."

Lydia blinked rapidly, eyes burning. What a horrid woman.

"Do not look so distressed, Miss Bennet. You merely need obey the rule to avoid punishment."

"Yes, madam."

"Now for the rest. While we intend to provide you with the necessary accomplishments for a young lady, due to your circumstances, we find it necessary to add additional components to your education. As it is quite possible you will fail to improve, we must prepare you for the options that will be open to you."

"Options?"

"A life of service, and possibly poverty—but hopefully not crime."

Those were options?

"What are you saying?"

"Every morning, you shall rise and see your room properly tended to. Afterwards, you shall report downstairs. We keep only a minimal staff, so you shall be assigned to one of them to assist in her chores."

"I am to be a maid?"

"Perhaps when you leave here, you will. I do not know. Regardless, you should have household skills, either to use for gainful employment or in preparation for managing your own home."

"I have not—that is I do not know how—"

"I expected as much. My staff has trained many

ignorant girls, and they shall train you. Following chores, you will report for breakfast, then lessons. We teach reading, writing, drawing, arithmetic, geography and French. I have just employed a new music master, so music lessons will be scheduled as well. I expect diligent application to your work. You might not be a scholar, but all my girls can and will work hard."

Driven like farm mules was more like it.

"After a brief respite for luncheon, afternoons are assigned to our charitable efforts."

"Charitable efforts?"

"On Mondays, we visit the foundling home. Tuesdays, we bring succor to the women in gaol. Thursdays, we provide lessons for the children in the work house. Fridays, we visit the parish alms houses to assist the unfortunates living there. Wednesdays and Saturdays, we sew and mend garments for those in need as well as anything that needs mending in the house."

"Is there no free time?"

"Since you have made very poor choices during idle time, Miss Bennet, I see little need for it. Still, the time after dinner and half a day Sunday, after holy services, is allowed for rest."

How could she possibly survive such demands? Mama had not even required she be awake to attend breakfast at ten o'clock.

"Do you still desire to stay? You may leave at any time; just remember, my door will not be open to you again." Mrs. Drummond gestured toward the door, the same indifferent expression on her weathered face.

"I … I will stay."

Mrs. Drummond rose, but barely stood as high as Lydia's shoulder. It was probably a good thing, for had she been any taller, she would have been unbearable.

"Follow me then. I will show you to your room. You will share Juliana Morely's room. She will become your elder sister here and aid you in settling in."

A sister sounded nice. Was it possible she might be like Jane?

Their shoes clattered on the hard wooden steps, clean, but scuffed by scores of footsteps. The banister was worn smooth by many hands. Were they all as shaky and miserable as hers?

The house was larger than any she had ever lived in—but nothing to Rosings Park. A few student paintings decorated the walls and some inexpertly embroidered cushions and screens caught her eye as they hurried past. The furnishings she could make out were what Mama called serviceable.

They may as well have sent her to a workhouse.

"We have twelve pupils, including yourself, at present. All the students reside in the east wing of the house. The teachers and I are quartered in the west wing. You are not to go there, unless in company of the staff. Neither are you to enter another student's room, except that you are invited by both the room's residents."

She had never been forbidden in so many places all at once. Was she to be welcome anywhere?

Mrs. Drummond paused and pointed. "There you see the school room and the music room, both of which you will have free use of. Downstairs, the morning room and back parlor are for students. The drawing room is not, unless you are receiving a visit from someone outside the school, which I think highly unlikely. My study is likewise prohibited unless I have called you there."

Why would she ever want to go there otherwise?

Mrs. Drummond continued on her way. "The dining room is for meals only; do not linger there. No trays will be sent to your room unless there is verifiable illness. Meals are served promptly. If you are late without acceptable reason, you will not be admitted."

Mrs. Drummond seemed the type to starve young ladies.

"This is your room." She pointed to an open door on the left side of the hall.

Lydia peeked in. The chamber was bright and tidy, but colorless. A few pencil drawings and magazine fashion plates were pinned up on stark white walls. What a wonder that Mrs. Drummond allowed such a luxury!

Two plain beds filled most of the room, neatly clothed with sturdy coverings. The edges of a thick wool blanket peeked out from the coverlet—perhaps she might not freeze.

A dressing table with a tarnished mirror, a utilitarian chair and writing table near the window, and a chest of drawers near the closet completed the furnishings.

"The room is not to your liking?" Mrs. Drummond glared every bit as imperiously as Lady Catherine might have.

"No … not … it is …"

"Better than you deserve. I hope you will come to understand that soon." She strode to the pile of trunks near the window. "Now, show me what you have brought. We shall determine what is appropriate for your station as a student here and if there is anything else you might need."

Now her trunks were to be searched? Would the humiliation never end?

"Do not dawdle girl! You are not my only concern today." She clapped sharply. "Move along now."

Lydia jumped and scurried to her trunks. The first held her body linen, stockings, night dresses and dressing gown. Mrs. Drummond inspected every one of the pieces Jane and Aunt Gardiner had carefully packed.

"You are fortunate to have been provided with so much. Fold them and put them in the bottom drawers of the dresser." She handed over a chemise with a pretty lace trim along the edge.

Lydia laid it on the bed and folded it into quarters.

"Not like that."

Of course.

"I see we must begin at the beginning. Your mother truly did you a disservice. I hope you are quick to learn. Watch." Mrs. Drummond smoothed the linen garment and drew it up into neat, regular folds that no doubt would fit perfectly into the drawer. "Understand?"

Lydia nodded.

Mrs. Drummond shook it out. "Now you."

Lydia's hands quaked as she tried to force the stubborn linen into the required shapes. Folding linen has always been a servant's job.

"Better," Mrs. Drummond flicked the chemise in the air, shaking out all her efforts.

No! That was unkind!

"Again."

Three more attempts and the chemise was deemed

accepted.

"Now this." A petticoat took the place of the chemise.

Lydia attempted to groan, but a raised eyebrow from Mrs. Drummond stopped her cold. The harridan would probably not hesitate to beat her for a badly folded petticoat.

It took five attempts to please her captor.

"Finish the rest of your things. I will examine your gowns. Have you brought any other wraps?"

"The ... the larger trunk has the gowns and the other has wraps and warm things."

Mrs. Drummond would probably confiscate her nicest frocks away and leave her with only a single dress. Her eyes blurred, but she blinked fiercely. She would not give Mrs. Drummond the satisfaction of seeing her cry.

A pile of body linen appeared on the bed. Lydia turned her back to the trunks. Watching would only make it worse.

"Day dress, day dress, morning, walking. Whomever packed for you saw you were well equipped. This—" She walked to Lydia holding a white muslin dinner dress.

She would be holding that; Lydia's favorite garment and the only truly pretty thing stuffy Aunt Gardiner had allowed her to bring.

"—is unnecessary. We do not dress for dinner here."

She held her breath and fought the urge to snatch the dress away.

"But I shall allow you to keep it, for there is the rare occasion it may be appropriate."

"Thank you." She took the dress with trembling

hands. Mrs. Drummond would probably not approve if she clutched it to her chest.

Mrs. Drummond carefully laid out her dresses on the end of the bed. "Put these in the closet when you have finished the linens. Now for the rest." She opened the final trunk and laid out the shawls, bonnets, gloves, spencers and shoes.

A flash of red! What was that?

Lydia whirled.

Her red cloak—the one her Wickham had bought her.

A sob welled in her throat. She stuffed her fist in her mouth, but it was not enough to contain the despair of the day. She sank onto the thin carpet, fighting to silence the cries wracking her chest.

A warm hand soothed her back. "There, there now girl. It has been a trying time for you no doubt. Let yourself have a good solid cry, and you will feel much better for it."

She could not have done otherwise had she been of a mind to. Gut-wrenching sobs tore through her. All the while, Mrs. Drummond crouched beside her, hand on her shoulder, muttering soothing sounds.

At last, she hiccupped and lifted her head. Mrs. Drummond pressed a handkerchief into her hand. "Dry your eyes now, and we will finish settling you in."

Lydia folded linen while Mrs. Drummond arranged her things in the closet.

"Finish the rest on your own. The girls will be returning soon, and I shall inform Juliana of your arrival."

Lydia sniffled. "Yes, madam."

She pulled something white and fluffy out of her

pocket. "One final thing. Put this on. All our new girls are required to wear one."

"A mobcap?"

"You will have no maid to do your hair. Best you are not distracted by it as you learn your place in our society."

"Miss Fitzgilbert did not wear one."

"She did when she first came. She earned the privilege to remove it. In time, you might as well. I very much hope that will be the case. Until such time, you will be addressed by your Christian name, and you will address other girls of your station thus. When you earn release from your cap, you may be Miss Bennet once again." Mrs. Drummond nodded and left, closing the door behind her.

Horrid woman! Lydia threw the cap at the door. It floated daintily to the floor, well short of its intended target.

Dreadful, awful, terrible place!

She kicked the cap. How could Mrs. Drummond demand she wear such a thing—to dress as a servant, or worse, as though she were on the shelf? She was only seventeen—she was not a spinster, and she would not be one either. But how could she find a husband when she was confined to this … this asylum?

Two years, Mr. Darcy said, two years—that was nearly forever. But he said he wanted to see improvement. If she 'improved', perhaps he might commute her sentence. If Mrs. Drummond wrote him of her virtues, he might permit her release.

It would require a great deal of effort to make Mrs. Drummond believe her improved, but it was her only choice. But what did improvement mean?

She snatched the cap off the floor and paced like a caged creature.

A horse wore its traces; a dog wore its collar. She would wear the dreadful thing; slave like a servant over chores; study her lessons and make charitable visits with a smile. That should be enough. Enough to convince Mrs. Drummond anyway. The stupid old cat.

She might not be as clever as Lizzy, but she was determined. That should count for even more; enough that she might even be free in just six months.

She folded the remainder of her linen with great care.

Chapter 2

A SHARP RAP ON THE door made her jump. The door opened and Miss High-and-Mighty Fitzgilbert poked her head in.

"Are you unpacked now?"

"I … yes …"

"Good. I am to help you store your trunks in the attic, then we may go down for dinner."

She opened her mouth, but shut it quickly. Miss High-and-Mighty would probably report any complaints to Mrs. Drummond.

The attics were surprisingly airy and tidy, and their task completed in short order.

"The house is so quiet," Lydia muttered, fighting to keep her steps soft on the stairs.

"Do not become accustomed to it. With so many young ladies in residence, that is rarely the case."

"Then why—"

"Did you not notice? Everyone has been out. You really must pay attention to something beyond yourself."

Perhaps someone should tell her more of what was going on. It was, after all, only her first day.

"Where have they all gone?"

"Usually, we would be visiting the alms houses, but once in a while, the vicar's wife invites all of us to tea. I missed it because of your arrival."

No wonder she was in so foul a temper.

"Do you hear that? They are returning. Come along—you can be introduced in the parlor before dinner."

If they were all as bossy as Miss High-and-Mighty, she would just as soon keep to herself. But Miss Fitzgilbert had been punished by missing the tea, perhaps for being so disagreeable. It was entirely possible some merry girls awaited her in the parlor. She brushed the dust from her hands and hurried downstairs.

Soft voices and the rustling of moving bodies filtered through the hallway. Miss Fitzgilbert paused at a doorway, allowing Lydia to peek into the parlor full of young ladies, most sporting ugly mobcaps like hers.

A hard hand on her back shoved her inside. Lydia nearly tripped over the edge of the rug.

The noise in the room stilled, and every gaze turned to her. Reflex dropped her into an unsteady curtsey. From the corner the room, Mrs. Drummond nodded, though her severe features bore no evidence of approval. Two women sat beside her. Other teachers, perhaps?

Mrs. Drummond rose. "May I present our new

student, Lydia Bennet."

"Good afternoon, Lydia," the entire room intoned.

Lydia curtsied again.

What else was one to do in such an awkward circumstance? Hopefully, it would be enough to hide her cringing at hearing her Christian name.

The round, softish woman to Mrs. Drummond's right stood. A heavy chatelaine at her waist clattered. She must have every key to every lock in the school on those chains.

Just like a jailor.

Did she lock the students in their rooms every night?

"Miss Honeywell teaches sewing, writing and drawing."

Miss Honeywell's chubby face sported the closest thing to a smile Lydia had seen all day.

"Have you had any instruction in my subjects?" Her voice trilled high and sweet, not nearly so awe inspiring as Mrs. Drummond's.

"A little."

"And you have practiced?"

"Not very much."

"I expected as much." Miss Honeywell sat down with a sigh. She folded her hands in her lap, a mild look of disappointment on her face.

Crosspatch!

The other woman took to her feet, tall and gaunt. Her hollow cheeks and prominent collarbone lent her a skeletal air that fit her thin raspy voice. "I am Miss Thornton, and I guide my students in reading, geography and sums." She sat down, not seeming to care for Lydia's potential accomplishments.

"Dinner is ready. You girls may introduce yourselves at the table." Mrs. Drummond led the teachers out.

So they would be permitted conversation at dinner. Happy thought indeed.

Miss Fitzgilbert preceded the students, three other capless girls immediately behind. Lydia hung back. Though it was fitting for a newcomer to lead the procession to the dining room, it did not seem to be a good idea to insist upon it now.

The last two girls in the room looked at her.

"I am Joan Colbrane," the blonde girl with a beauty mark on her cheek said.

"And I am Amelia Easton." The dark-haired girl with a foreign look and vaguely French accent curtsied.

"You can sit with us." Joan took her arm.

"The dining room is this way." Amelia gestured down the hall.

Joan lifted her head, nose in the air. "We are the lowest—"

"I thought there was no talk of rank here."

"Not rank in society you silly thing, rank in the school," Joan said.

"When you are a good little girl and do everything as Missus says you should, you rise in rank." Amelia touched her own mobcap.

"Hurry, they are waiting!" Joan dragged Lydia into the dining room and propelled her toward a chair at the center of the long table, the most ignoble spot in the room.

Lydia nearly stumbled, but caught herself on the back of the chair. She moved to sit. Amelia hissed at her.

Oh botheration, no one else sat. She pulled herself

back beside the table.

Mrs. Drummond nodded. She and Miss Thornton at the head of the table, and Miss Honeywell and Miss Fitzgilbert at the foot sat down. The students followed suit.

How odd, two seats, one at Mrs. Drummond's left and one near the foot of the table, remained vacant.

Amelia handed her a bowl of roasted potatoes. "Serve yourself, dearie; we have no footmen or gentlemen. Do it quickly and pass the plate. None of us like to wait."

She dumped a spoonful on her plate and handed it to Joan.

"The food here is decent enough," Joan whispered.

"Mercy that it is, you know." Amelia handed her a dish of peas and lettuce.

"We work hard enough most days. I dare say we would starve to death quite easily if it were not for the cooking here."

"Do not be late for meals. Missus does not tolerate that. You come late, you do not get food at all," Amelia said.

"How cruel! Is that why those seats are empty?"

"The one by Missus is odd indeed. I do not know why Miss Long has moved down. She is not wearing a cap, though, so she cannot have fallen too far from favor. The other is Juliana Morley's seat. She has special permission to be late on Saturdays. She is the only one." Amelia cast a knowing look at Joan.

"Why?"

"You will see." Amelia smirked.

Lydia chewed the inside of her cheek. "You do not like her? I am to share a room with her."

"You poor dear." Joan patted her arm.

"You may come visit in our room whenever you like."

"Is she so very terrible?"

"Oh, not at all. Dear little Juliana is very, very good. She is the sweetest, nicest, kindest girl among us." Joan batted her eyes.

"I do not understand."

"You will." Amelia handed her a bowl of oat pudding.

Just her foul luck to have a horrid roommate who was some favorite to Mrs. Drummond. She would probably be some sort of moralizing tell-all who bent the headmistress' ear with reports on all her fellows.

Why could she not share with gay companions like Joan and Amelia?

Mrs. Drummond rang a dainty crystal bell, and the room stilled. "You will have noticed an extra place at our table tonight. Tonight, we welcome a new member of our staff. Pray, come in." She looked over her shoulder and beckoned to someone just beyond the doorway.

A lean, almost awkward young man, all elbows and knees, with pale skin and a shock of black hair ambled in. His face was very plain, not worthy of note at all, except for his eyes which were a rich, deep, vibrant blue.

He stopped beside Mrs. Drummond.

"Mr. Amberson has taken the position as our music master."

"Old Mr. Clearly died last month," Joan whispered.

"He will teach you, as well as taking other students from the village. He is my nephew and shall have the quarters across the hall from mine. The staff shall manage the maintenance of his rooms without your assistance. Any of you found in his quarters will be dismissed from school immediately. Am I understood?"

"Yes, Mrs. Drummond."

"He's probably a gentleman of good reputation, but meager fortune. His dearest aunt does not want us tainting him." Amelia snickered behind her hand.

Mr. Amberson bowed. "A pleasure to make your acquaintances. After dinner, I should like all of you to play for me that I might take a measure of your proficiency." He sat down beside Mrs. Drummond.

Ill-ease descended upon the room like a summer thunderstorm. A few girls basked in the news: Miss Fitzgilbert and Miss Long and two girls wearing caps. Obviously, they were proficient and happy to show off.

The rest turned aside or squirmed in their seats. The awkward ginger-pate across from Lydia sniffled and blotted her eyes with the back of her hand.

"That is Emma Greenville." Amelia rolled her eyes.

"She is quite the dunce at music. Made Old Clearly ever so cross. He would always cane her hands when she fumbled, but it made no difference. She plays no better now than before. We are quite certain it was her playing what gave him the apoplexy that killed him." Joan tittered. "I bet she will fall into a grand swoon or have a hysterical fit to get out of playing."

"Not likely—remember what Missus did to Constance over her last fit?" Amelia turned to Lydia. "Let us just say we do not recommend it."

Papa had little tolerance for hysterical fits in his

own daughters, though he was happy to treat them in other families.

"Will he be so terribly strict?"

Joan shrugged. "There is no way of knowing. But he is young, and that is to our material advantage."

"I have heard that they grow stricter with age and bad pupils. Perhaps we might be very lucky and he might fall in love with one of us." Amelia threw him a sidelong glance.

"Do not let Old Lady Drummond hear that. I wager she would cane us for the very thought!"

"Does she do that often?"

Joan shrugged. "Not so much—"

"Not so much! Do not fabricate tales to make her feel better. It happens most every day I should say. There is a reason why the chairs in the dining room are padded."

Lydia shuddered.

Joan leaned in close. "Do not listen. She is a dreadful tease."

Perhaps, but Mrs. Drummond did look ever so mean—just the type who would find great pleasure in punishing a girl for almost no reason at all.

How would she ever survive?

Amelia elbowed her. "You will get used to it. It is not so bad after the first eight or ten times."

"Stop being so mean!" Joan hissed.

"Oh, look!" Amelia sat up very straight and twitched her head toward the door.

A young woman in a dull grey dress, cap, and apron waddled in. Her face was pudgy-round, and she was very fat. She took the remaining open chair.

"That is Juliana Morley."

What joy was hers. She would share a room with

the ugliest girl in the school.

Juliana kept to herself and ate only a few bites during dinner. Mrs. Drummond must have her on some sort of restrictions. There was no way she could have become so fat eating the way she did, not even partaking in the sweet course when it arrived.

Mrs. Drummond signaled the end of dinner. She and the teachers led the girls to the parlor. Miss Greenville tried to hang back, behind even Lydia, but Mrs. Drummond noticed and insisted she resume her proper place near the head of the line. Did their headmistress miss nothing under her command?

Mama had never been a particularly watchful woman. A gay story or delightful bit of gossip distracted her easily enough. Lydia had used her mother's peculiarity to her advantage and rarely had to give account for anything. Somehow it did not appear that tactic would be nearly so effective with Mrs. Drummond.

In the parlor, the girls gathered around the pianoforte. Those Lydia presumed proficient beamed with looks of smug satisfaction, obviously expecting praises and petting from Mr. Amberson.

Haughty little chits.

He might be the only man in their midst, but he was too plain to be worth the effort of impressing.

Most of the rest appeared mildly disinterested while Miss Greenville sniffled and averted her gaze.

"Miss Fitzgilbert, as head girl, you shall begin." Mrs. Drummond pointed at the piano bench.

The girls shuffled to make way for Miss High-and-Mighty. Someone really should remove the vile, smug look from her face. Perhaps her fingers would tangle over the chords. That would serve her right.

"Do you need music?" Mr. Amberson asked.

"May I play a piece that I know?" She sat down, head bowed.

What a good play she made at looking humble.

Lydia caught herself just before she rolled her eyes and wrinkled her nose. Joan elbowed her a moment later. Confound it! If she were that obvious, Mrs. Drummond might have seen her as well. She would have to be far more careful lest she incur the head-mistress's ire.

"Certainly." Mr. Amberson positioned himself slightly behind Miss Fitzgilbert. He clasped his hands before him and closed his eyes.

She began to play, so softly at first it was difficult to tell she had begun. The music surged in undulating swells, filling the room with liquid sound that ebbed and flowed from gentle ripples to pounding thunder-ous waves and back again.

For all her disagreeable qualities, Miss Fitzgilbert was indeed a proficient. Even Miss Bingley would have conceded that.

Miss Greenville was called upon to play next. Poor girl, to have to follow such a performance! Her pale complexion was blotchy, and her eyes full of tears. A true shame indeed—for when one was a ginger, tears hardly improved one's looks.

"I cannot sir," she mumbled, standing beside the piano bench. "You may as well just cane my hands now as Mr. Clearly did." She extended trembling hands and squeezed her eyes shut.

"I do not think that necessary. No, not at all." Mr. Amberson blanched and turned wide-eyed to Mrs. Drummond. He reached for a portfolio beside the piano and pulled out a sheet of music. "Now, sit down."

She perched on the seat like a bird ready to take flight. He pulled an armless chair in beside her.

"Can you tell me what this is?" He pointed to the music.

"A note, sir." Her voice trembled.

Lydia held her breath. Somehow, it did not seem humor would be welcome right now and possibly not ever. Amelia and Joan appeared to do the same.

How ridiculous could Miss Greenville be?

"What kind of note?" he asked.

"A whole note?"

"Good. Do you know which whole note this might be? What would a musician name it?"

"No, sir. I have no idea."

He studied her. "Were you not taught?"

She squeezed her eyes shut and gasped something like a sob. "No … no sir. Mr. Clearly said a girl of … of my advantages should already know, and he would not … not indulge my demands for special treatment." She dragged her sleeve across her face.

"I see." His countenance grew dark. "And had you any musical instruction prior to coming here?"

"The guitar, sir."

"Very well." He rose.

Miss Greenville cowered.

Heavens, what did she expect?

Mr. Amberson disappeared though the door, and the room erupted into whispers. Miss Fitzgilbert handed Miss Greenville a handkerchief and laid her hand on the nearly sobbing girl's shoulder.

Mr. Amberson burst into the room carrying a large leather case. He placed it on top of the piano and withdrew a beautifully polished guitar.

Miss Greenville's eyes grew so wide they might have fallen out of their sockets.

He plucked the strings and fiddled with the tuning keys. "There, that is right now. Play for me."

Miss Greenville took the instrument and stroked it almost reverently. "It is beautiful. I have never seen one so fine." She whispered, arranging the guitar on her lap.

She strummed one chord tentatively, the next with greater purpose, and a third with an air of confidence and decision. With two nods, Miss Greenville transformed from pathetic to proficient. A melody, as complex and compelling as Miss Fitzgilbert had played, filled the room.

Miss Greenville finished and handed the guitar back to Mr. Amberson, ignoring the astonished expressions trained on her.

"I imagine Mr. Clearly thought the pianoforte the only instrument worth learning." He said.

"Yes, sir. I … I mentioned once … and he said he would … would …"

"I understand." He glared at Mrs. Drummond.

He dared glower at her? Someone actually challenged the harpy in her lair!

Lydia snuck a peak at Joan who hid a smirk behind her hand.

"I bear no such preconceptions. I brought a practice instrument with me and shall place it in the music room. We shall continue your lessons on the guitar as we begin your training on the pianoforte."

Miss Greenville rose and dipped in a fragile curtsey. "Thank you so very much, sir."

He nodded and gestured for the next girl to take her place.

He was not effusive with his compliments, but neither was he hasty with criticism. No disappointment crossed his face when girls fumbled over their music, only the same patient nod and injunction to perform their best.

Was it possible—a patient music master? Had ever such a creature been born?

Lydia's belly fluttered as her turn came. How humiliating to be the very last one.

"Have you had any instruction, Miss Bennet?" he asked.

"A little."

"How little?"

"We saw a music master for a year, I think."

"Play this for me." He placed a sheet of music in front of her.

Lydia bit her lip. That piece—her old music master had tried to make her learn it. How she had hated it—somber and dull and difficult with all the sharps and flats.

"Play, Miss Bennet."

How stern he sounded. Where was the kindness he had shown Miss Greenville?

She forced her fingers across the keys, pausing to stare at the music and start over each measure she fudged. By the time she finished the meager five lines, sweat beaded her upper lip, and her shoulders were so knotted she could barely move.

"And in that time, were you apt to practice?" He asked, lips pressed into formidable lines.

She dropped her chin to her chest. "Not very much, sir."

"It shows, Miss. It shows. You have the potential to play very well indeed, if you only discipline yourself to practice." He glanced over the girls. "We will get on very well in our lessons. There is one thing, though, that I have very little tolerance for, and that is laziness. Not all of you are musical. I cannot change the gifts of Providence. Not all of you will be masters of the art, but there is not one among you who cannot improve herself by diligent application. I expect improvement from all of you." His gaze fell upon Lydia.

She turned her face aside and struggled not to fidget. Why did he single her out so? He was every bit as disagreeable as his horrid aunt.

Mrs. Drummond dismissed her and insisted Mr. Amberson play for them. He was, of course, very good, both on the piano and the guitar. And he sang.

Oh, what a voice, low and molten, like a rich cup of chocolate. It would have been far more wonderful had he not been so much like his aunt.

Mrs. Drummond permitted them a quarter of an hour to talk and otherwise amuse themselves. Then she herded them off to bed, like a nasty, biting dog chasing lambs into a pen.

Lydia climbed the stairs with Joan and Amelia.

"I shall like music lessons now." Joan said, "Mr. Amberson is ever so much nicer—"

"—and better looking—" Amelia waggled her eyebrows.

"—than Mr. Clearly."

"I wonder if he is sympathetic to gingers. He certainly favored Miss Greenville." Amelia's upper lip curled into the barest hint of a ladylike sneer.

"He was very kind to her, especially seeing how upset she was," Lydia said.

"Too kind if you ask me." Amelia whispered. "I

do not trust him—why should he be like that if he did not have some dark plan in mind?"

"Dark plan?"

Amelia leaned in close and whispered in her ear. "Seductions."

Lydia stumbled on the next stair.

"You and your flights of fancy." Joan hissed. "Pay no attention to her. She sees seducers everywhere, and not once has she been right."

"How would you know? Just because Old Clearly could not bring it up does not mean—"

"And how would you know about his—"

"I heard from the girl at the grocer that she had heard from his scullery maid that his wife said—"

"Enough chatter. To your rooms, now." Mrs. Drummond nipped at their heels and drove Lydia to her dismal cramped chamber.

Two candles lit the room, one near each bed. Mrs. Drummond shut the door behind her.

"It is nice to meet you, Lydia." Juliana tried to curtsey, but it was an ugly awkward thing to watch. "I am glad you will be sharing my room. It has been lonely since Constance left."

"Has she been gone long?" Lydia turned her back and began her toilette.

"A few weeks. We were not very good friends. But still, I think company a nicer thing than not." Juliana waddled to the drawers and pulled out a night dress. She untied the fall front of her gown and pulled it over her head. "It is a great deal to ask, but would you help me with my stays?"

Now she was to be a lady's maid, too? Lydia turned, her curt reply fading on her tongue. Juliana wore old fashioned long stays, encasing her body like a sausage.

"I know they are worn and ugly, but they are all I have."

"You father sent you here with only those ratty things? Are the rest of your clothes rags?"

Juliana bit her lip, eyes downcast and shrugged.

Even if Juliana was fat and ugly, that was too cruel. At least Aunt Gardiner and Mr. Darcy made sure she had decent clothes.

"Come, I will untie them."

She shambled toward Lydia, and they met in the middle of the room.

Lydia fumbled with the knots. "You do not have these laced very tight. You know if you—"

"The midwife says I must not—"

"Midwife?"

Juliana wrestled the stays off and turned to face Lydia, one hand on her very pregnant belly.

"Oh!"

"I am surprised one of the others did not tell you. I serve the midwife on Saturday."

"Whatever for?"

"That is how I am paying her for her services. Each Saturday, I go to her in the morning and assist her with whatever she needs, then she bleeds me—" Juliana touched the bandage on her elbow.

"Bleeds you? Why? My father, he is a doctor, thinks it a questionable practice. He says it is used far too often and to the detriment of many patients."

"I have never seen a doctor. The midwife has said I have hard-pulse disease. If I am not bled then I may collapse and have fits."

"And you are pleased with her advice?"

"She showed me, and I could feel my pulse is

harder than hers." Juliana dabbed her sleeve over her eyes. "Besides, hers is the only help I have. I must trust her."

"Your father—"

"He does not believe that a case like mine is deserving of assistance."

"That is—"

"Do not think him so bad, though. If the baby is a boy, he has found a cousin of his, a farmer and his wife who have only daughters. They will raise him as their heir." Juliana smiled, but it was the same smile Jane wore when she disagreed but did not wish to be disagreeable.

"And if it is not?" Oh, that sounded rather heartless. She bit her lip. "You see, I am one of five sisters and no brothers."

"Then … then … Mrs. Drummond and the midwife have promised we will find a way." She shrugged and turned away to put on her night dress. "You are wondering about the father, no doubt."

"I … I …"

Of course she was! Who would not?

"Thank you for being kind enough not to ask. For that, I will tell you the truth."

"There is no need … truly …"

"Yes there is. You deserve to know the kind of girl you share a room with."

Heavens, would she not cease her prattle?

"Not so very long ago, I was a gay miss with my cap set at a particular young man. He was the favorite of the neighborhood. Every girl sought to catch his eye."

"Was he an officer?" Lydia giggled.

"So you like a red coat? I did too, but he was simply a dandy, quite dashing in his blue coat and buckskin breeches. He wore them very well, you know."

Lydia sighed. Wickham showed such a well-turned calf in his.

"I thought I stood no chance with him. I am not nearly so pretty as many of the others, nor so well dowered. My family was—is—respectable, but not of the first circles." She sat on the bed and plucked pins from her hair. "When he began to pay attention to me—I was all astonishment. I could not believe my good fortune."

Wickham had made her feel that way, too. Would she ever feel that again?

"The others were so jealous of me. I liked that, though I knew it was wrong. I enjoyed their envy being included in all their calls and parties."

"Why was that so wrong? Is not such a thing to be savored?" Lydia perched on the edge of her bed.

"It led me into great foolishness. I thought myself above them, above all I had been taught. I agreed to things I knew were wrong—"

"Like what?"

Juliana seemed to study the ceiling. "He wanted to be alone with me. We would meet out in the woods and talk—at first."

"But where is the harm? I do not see—"

"Perhaps that in and of itself was not so bad, but it led to more and more intimacies. Each one seemed trivial enough—and he said he loved me ever so much. At last he said he wished to marry me and would speak to my father of it very soon. So … so … I allowed him … he gave me a green gown."

"A what? Why would he—"

"He lay with me, there in the fields in the green

grass."

Lydia blushed. Wickham had always insisted upon a proper room and furniture.

"It made him quite happy and did not hurt so much as I had been warned." She shrugged and brushed her hair. "It even became pleasant after a while. We did it nearly every day for weeks, waiting for the right time to talk to my father."

She and Wickham had done something similar. "Did your father refuse the marriage?"

"No. Something happened. I know not what, and his father sent him away to the continent. When I learnt of my condition, my brother concealed a letter from me in one he wrote."

"Did he not write back?"

"He did." Juliana blinked rapidly and squeezed her eyes shut.

"He refused to marry you?"

Lydia rubbed her temples hard. Wickham's harsh words echoed in her ears. How could he have abandoned her? If only—

"I am not sure of the truth of the matter. He may have wished to, but his father refused him. Then again, he may never have loved me at all and only seen me as a cheap bit of muslin to exercise his urges upon." Her voice broke.

That is what Lizzy and Aunt Gardiner said of Wickham ... and herself.

"My father was furious when he discovered I had 'sprained my ankle'. He has not spoken to me since. I am fortunate he sent me here instead of casting me into the streets."

"He would not—"

"Yes, he would. It was only the intervention of my

mother and brother that prevented it. He has entirely cut me off, denied me the money that was to have been my dowry. He paid Mrs. Drummond for two years of keeping me, then I must make my own way. Me and the baby, if it is a girl." She stroked her belly, lips pressed tight.

"Have you no other family?"

"I am dead to them."

"What … what will you do?"

"Mrs. Drummond is trying to prepare me as a governess or a companion. It would be difficult to find a position with a baby, though. So, if the baby is a girl, the midwife has consented to make me an apprentice as soon as I have recovered. Mrs. Drummond will pay for the apprenticeship from the unused portion of my tuition here. So, it is possible you may not have to endure sharing a room with me very long."

"I … I …"

"I could see it on your face when I came in to dinner tonight."

Lydia tried to say something, but only managed to stammer.

"Do not apologize. Joan and Amelia despise me, and several of the others do not like me very well either. Miss Fitzgilbert is very kind though. You will like her very well, I am sure. And Mrs. Drummond, too. She treats me far better than I deserve."

"She...better than you deserve? I think her quite horrid."

"I did too when I first came. I hope you might be, in a way, my friend, since you must live with me as long as I am to remain here."

"Perhaps …"

"I am pleased to hear it. That is enough for now. Good night then." Juliana blew out the candle nearest her. She slipped into bed and rolled onto her right side, away from Lydia.

Lydia followed suit, but lay staring at the ceiling for a very long time.

Mrs. Drummond treats her well? Miss Fitzgilbert, very kind? Juliana must be daft. Could she not see how very awful they were?

Lydia stared into the darkness towards Juliana's side of the room. No—it could not be. In addition to everything else, the girl snored! How was this to be borne?

No wonder her father put her out. She must have been beastly to live with—utterly beastly.

But to send her away with nothing, to cast her into the streets—

Did Papa truly mean to do that to her? He said she had no place with them. At least Mr. Darcy said if Mrs. Drummond was pleased with her, he would find her a situation.

Her stomach knotted. A 'situation'? Did that mean she was to be a governess like Juliana? Would she not live with them and find a rich husband?

She curled into a tight knot and covered her face with her hands. Mr. Darcy said if Mrs. Drummond were not satisfied with her, she would be Papa's problem.

Would Mama truly let him cast her out? She had done nothing when Lizzy was taken. Aunt and Uncle Gardiner had turned their backs and walked away when she had begged them to let her stay.

Her belly grew tight, and she fought back bile. Perhaps they meant what they had said, and she was truly abandoned to this wretched place.

Chapter 3

BRIGHT MORNING SUN streamed into her room. She pulled the sheets over her head.

Why did it have to taunt her misery?

"Did anyone explain our Sunday routine to you?"

Why was Juliana so cheerful?

"No." Lydia peeked above the covers.

Whatever it was, she was not going to like it.

Juliana waddled into the sunlight and stuffed her feet into a pair of worn slippers. "I will go downstairs for some wash water and explain it all when I return."

She padded away.

Lydia groaned and ducked under the bedclothes. Perhaps if she fell back to sleep before Juliana returned, she might be left in peace.

The doors squeaked open.

"We were very lucky today. Cook had a kettle steaming when I got to the kitchen."

She huffed a bit as she placed a ceramic jug on the wash stand.

"What good fortune." Lydia rolled out of bed.

"You have the first turn—only pray, leave me some warm water." Juliana shuffled aside.

Lydia sloshed water into the wash basin and then added a bit more. What right had Miss Waddles-About to tell her how much to use?

She washed her face and hands and turned to find Juliana in her chemise and stays, wearing a hopeful look.

"Could you help me with these again?"

Lydia huffed and flung a hand in the air. "I suppose so. Shall I do your hair as well?"

"Thank you, no. It is all hidden under my cap so there is little point." Juliana turned her back to Lydia.

Gah! Was the girl too stupid to recognize sarcasm?

Lydia pulled at the laces. "These are near to breaking."

"Do not pull them very tight. I cannot afford new ones."

Lydia nearly dropped the laces.

Not able to manage so minute an expense? Surely she exaggerated … but why else would she wear such ridiculous stays?

"That is perfect. Thank you. I am sorry to keep bothering you with them." Juliana trundled off and began to wash.

Lydia dressed, appreciating her own short stays as never before.

"Now we must clean our room."

"Excuse me?"

"Each Sunday before holy services, Mrs. Drummond requires we clean our rooms." Juliana slipped her apron over her head.

"She … I … but …"

"It will not kill you. And we never know, one day we might have to find employ as maids."

"I shall never be a maid." Lydia tossed her head.

"I hope you are correct, but it is a better fate than starving in the streets. Either way, we must clean the room."

She was serious? They were actually going to do this?

"No matter, I will show you. It is not so bad once you get accustomed to it. Go downstairs and get a kettle of boiling water and a pail for the slops. I shall start on the beds whilst you are gone."

Who was Miss Waddles-About to order her around?

"Would you rather work on the beds and I get the water? I have already fetched water once today, and only thought it fair we should share the job. But, if you disagree, here is the dust rag."

"Why would I need that?"

"To dust the chairs before you turn the sheets on to them."

"Oh, I suppose I will get the water." Lydia hurried out lest Juliana invent another chore for her.

Joan met her on the stairs, water jug in hand. "So you have been sent to fetch water, too?"

"I am to bring boiling water." Lydia wrinkled up her face into a mockery of Juliana's expression.

Joan choked back a laugh. "Did you not have hot water to wash with?"

"Juliana brought some up."

"Why do you need more? We always use it for cleaning, too. What is the point in climbing the stairs more than we must? She's just seeing how much work she can make you do."

"I thought she was demanding far too much." Lydia stomped into the kitchen.

Mrs. Drummond presided by the stove near Cook, adding kettles and pots to heat.

"I need wash water," Joan said.

"And a boiling kettle and slop pail," Lydia added.

"Provide Miss Bennet with her request whilst I have a talk with Miss Colbrane." Mrs. Drummond took Joan by the elbow to a far corner.

Cook wrapped the handle of the kettle in a towel and handed it to Lydia. "Mind yourself not to get burned."

Lydia could just make out Mrs. Drummond scolding Joan's attempts to take short cuts in their cleaning. It sounded as though they would be cleaning the teachers' bedrooms as well. Amelia would be so angry!

Perhaps it would be best to listen to Juliana for now. She seemed to have garnered some favor from Mrs. Drummond. If she played Juliana's friend, she might share in it as well.

She trudged back upstairs, burning herself twice along the way.

Juliana met her at the door. She took the kettle and set it on the hearth. "I have the windows open and the beds stripped. Empty the wash basin and chamber pot into the slop pail, scald the vessels, along with the water jar and tumbler and empty them into the pail."

"Why am I to do all the work? I brought up the water."

Juliana turned aside as though she had not heard. "I will cover the large furniture with the dusting sheets and fetch the supplies to clean out the fire-place. Just be happy we do not have a carpet to drag outside and beat."

Unpleasant though it was, emptying and scalding the vessels and discarding the slop pail did not take very long. So, she was sent to fetch damp sand for the floor and a fresh pail of scrub water.

Just how many times had she climbed the stairs this morning? Surely Juliana was inventing errands.

Juliana finished the fireplace and ordered her to dust the windows and furniture while she did the walls and ceiling.

How often had the lazy girl stopped, huffing and panting, unable to catch her breath? A clever way, indeed, to leave Lydia with all the work.

Dusting finished, Juliana took the sand jar, leaving Lydia to drag all the small furniture to the center of the room.

Lydia shoved the broom at Juliana. "You sweep. I am utterly fagged."

She leaned on the doorjamb to watch. How droll was Juliana, maneuvering the broom around her belly.

"Oh!" Juliana staggered and caught herself on the chest of drawers. The broom clattered on the floor.

"Juliana!" Miss Fitzgilbert rushed in.

When had Miss High-and-Mighty arrived? Proba-bly sent by Mrs. Drummond to snoop on them.

"The midwife told you not work too hard. Come, lie down in my room whilst I fetch Mrs. Drum-mond." Miss Fitzgilbert took Juliana's arm. "You need to finish sweeping and scrub the floors."

"By myself?"

"Can you not see she has made herself ill? Had you been a bit more considerate, she might still be able to help you." Miss Fitzgilbert tossed her head and disappeared with Juliana in tow.

Lydia stared after them. How could she possibly be expected to do so much alone? She grabbed the broom and flung it from side to side. That only threw dust upon the furniture she had just cleaned.

Gah!

Mama was very particular about how the maids did their work. What did it look like when the maid had done this at home? She closed her eyes and mimicked the motions she remembered.

Yes, that was more effective.

"Do not forget to sweep under all the furniture." A voice called from the door.

How kind of Miss Fitzgilbert to stop and offer advice.

Lydia snatched a flannel cloth and reached under the chest of drawers. There was hardly anything under it. Underneath the beds was similarly clean.

What a waste of time.

Dust pail filled, the only thing left was to scrub the floor. Wretched task, on her knees, her hands in the cold water, by herself. She turned her back to the door and dunked the cloth in the chilly, soapy bucket. How she hated the feel of it on her hands, slippery and dry all at the same time.

Soon she would sport chilblains and cracked fingertips! How then would she be able to sew or practice the pianoforte?

She sat back on her heels and dragged her sleeve across her forehead. Only in spring and fall, when Papa demanded everything be completely cleaned did she ever work this hard. And then only if Mama did not have enough extra household money to hire an additional girl for the duration.

"I see no one has taught you to scrub floors."

She jumped to her feet, slipping in a soapy puddle.

Mrs. Drummond loomed in the doorway behind her.

"Ah, yes, I mean no, madam."

"Then I shall show you, but pay attention for I shall only do it once." Mrs. Drummond minced over the sopping floor, leaving footprints in her wake. "Bring the sand. You have some stains."

Lydia slipped and nearly overturned the sand jar.

Mrs. Drummond dropped to her knees near the far corner and beckoned Lydia down. "First, you must always begin farthest from the door and work toward it, lest you trap yourself inside with a clean, wet floor between you and the way out." She pointed to the messy footprints.

Lydia winced.

Mama's maid started from the far side, too. Who knew it should matter so much?

"Now to begin, soak the cloth in the soapy water and wring it a bit. Too much only makes a mess. Now rub it along the length of the floor boards, not across. This is especially important if you must scour a stain. Here, give me the sand." She sprinkled a generous pinch on a dark spot. "Scrub with the grain of the wood until it is gone. Do not rub in circles or across the grain." She looked up at Lydia. "I will not have my floor boards ruined."

"Yes, Mrs. Drummond."

"Now, when you are finished, you must use fresh water—where is your rinse pail?"

"I … I … do not have one."

Had Juliana told her to get one? Perhaps … oh

bother, she did not remember now.

"Go downstairs and fetch one. Quickly, now!"

Lydia almost tripped over her own feet as she dashed to the kitchen. Several buckets waited near the door. The cook signaled her to take one.

One never realized how heavy water was until it needed to be carted about. No wonder charwomen were so disagreeable.

Lydia staggered into her room. The pail sloshed out splashes as she skidded toward Mrs. Drummond.

"Down here with me." She passed a clean rag to Lydia. "Dip a fresh rag in the clean water and wring it well. Rinse the soap off the floor or it will leave ugly marks and the dirt will stay behind. Like that. Finally, use a dry cloth and sop up the rinse water."

Side by side, they wiped the clean patch dry.

"Now you have a clean floor." Mrs. Drummond rose and dried her hands on her apron. "Finish up, and you may go to the morning room for breakfast." She left Lydia to stare at the empty doorway.

How cruel, to leave her to this huge dirty floor all by herself.

Lydia shoved stray hair out of her eyes. Perhaps— she tucked it under her mobcap and it stayed. That was useful.

Hunkered down on sore knees, she whimpered. Why had Mrs. Drummond not brought Juliana back to help her finish? No, no such work for the headmistress's pet. She muttered under her breath and set back to scrubbing.

An hour later, she swabbed the last bit dry and backed out of the door, dragging her pails and cloths with her.

Miss Fitzgilbert bustled past. "Bring all that down

to the scullery, the rags too. You will see a great basket for them as you enter."

Oh, how she wanted to speak her mind, but she was far too weary—and now too hungry—to do so.

She trudged behind Miss High-and-Mighty, and left her burdens in the cramped, dark scullery.

How very good it felt not to be stooped over a bucket of dirty, frigid water.

She straightened her back and stretched. Other girls with their burdens pushed past her, and she dodged out of their way.

What was that? Something smelled very good indeed.

She followed the scent to the morning room. All manner of good food graced the table. Plain to be sure, but hearty and plentiful.

Amelia waved at her to take the seat between her and Joan.

"I am so fagged!" Lydia fell into the chair and threw her head back.

"I hate Sunday mornings!" Amelia muttered through a mouthful of potatoes.

"At least we get to eat before she drags us off to hear the vicar."

"Oh I detest the sermonizing." Amelia rolled her eyes. "And Mr. Weatherby is so long-winded—"

"And holy!" Joan sat up very straight and folded her hands before her, eyes cast skyward.

Amelia giggled. "Very, very holy. Can you imagine being a vicar's wife?"

"What a horrible fate, particularly with one like him. How can one do anything right in his eyes?"

Amelia leaned low to the table and whispered. "It is truly awful when Mrs. Drummond has him to dinner with us."

Lydia covered her sigh with her hand. "Does she do that often?"

"At least once a fortnight." Joan pouted. "I expect he will be joining us sometime this week."

"How he likes to remind us of how very wicked we are."

"And how grateful we should be for our situation here."

"As if anyone could be grateful for this workhouse." Lydia piled a slab of ham and several potatoes on her plate and reached for a platter of scones.

The girls filed upstairs to dress for church. It would be a relief to remove the damp, dirty work gown for something fresh and—dare she even think it—pretty.

Juliana leaned heavily against her bedpost, breathing heavily. Both beds were fully made and the rest of the furniture back in place.

"I am so sorry I could not join you scrubbing the floors. I thought perhaps I might—" she gasped and grabbed the headboard.

"You are so pale!" Lydia ran to her.

"I am … so dizzy …"

"Lay down. I will fetch help."

"I only just made the beds—"

"Well, the floor is clean if you insist on not mussing the blankets. Do get off your feet before you fall." She helped Juliana to the bed and dashed out.

Miss Fitzgilbert caught her in the hall. "Why are

you not ready for church?"

"Juliana is most unwell. She can barely stand."

Miss Fitzgilbert looked toward Lydia's room, forehead creasing. "Go back to her. I shall get Mrs. Drummond."

Lydia ran back. Juliana lay, curled on her side, face ashen.

"Please, some water?"

Lydia fumbled with the water jar and tumbler, nearly dropping them twice before she separated them.

"Here."

Juliana propped herself on her elbow and swallowed a few sips. Her color changed and her eyes grew wide.

Lydia sprinted for the wash basin and returned in time for Juliana to cast up her accounts.

Mrs. Drummond rushed in. "I told you to rest. Why did you make the beds?"

"It would not have been fair …"

Mrs. Drummond brushed sweat-matted hair back from Juliana's brow. "We need the midwife." She looked over her shoulder at Lydia. "Find Miss Fitzgilbert and tell her. Go with her to fetch the Mrs. Harrow."

"What of church?"

"You are excused for today."

"Yes, madam." Lydia managed a hurried curtsey and ran off.

Miss Fitzgilbert hovered just outside the door. "I heard. Get your bonnet and wrap. I will meet you downstairs."

Lydia raced back to snatch up her things and dashed down the stairs again.

How many times had Lizzy rushed out on some emergency with Papa? Had she been this anxious? She had never seemed so when she assembled Papa's bag, set out his coat, and waited patiently for him by the gig.

Miss Fitzgilbert pelted out the door. Lydia ran to keep up through unfamiliar scenery.

Heavens! She did not know her way around Summerseat. Should she become separated from Miss Fitzgilbert, she could lose her way entirely.

Lydia increased her pace, keeping one eye on Miss Fitzgilbert and the other on the landmarks that flew past.

After half a mile, Miss Fitzgilbert slowed a mite and finally spoke. "I am surprised you are not complaining I am walking too fast or that this is a pointless errand."

"I know you think me a stupid little thing, but my father is … a medical man. I am well acquainted with the haste those situations call for."

"How gracious of you."

"Why are you so cross with me? I did not make her ill. This is not my fault."

"You think not? I beg to differ." Miss Fitzgilbert pumped her arms and strode still faster.

"How can you blame me?"

"Any fool could see she was ill."

"Perhaps you could, but she looked quite fine to me."

"Because you were too selfish to see—her color, her difficulty breathing—did you not notice any of it?"

"No … I did not."

Miss Fitzgilbert tossed her head. "Too concerned

about your own hardship to care or see anyone else's."

"What would you know of hardship, of what I have suffered?"

Miss Fitzgilbert stopped short.

Lydia nearly ran into her.

"And what do you know of the rest of us?" Miss Fitzgilbert set off again, faster than before.

"What has everyone else lost compared to me? I have been—"

"I do not care to know."

Gah! The wretched girl did not deserve to hear about her dear Wickham.

"There is the midwife's house." Miss Fitzgilbert pointed to a narrow, rock-strewn lane that wandered off the main road.

Old trees reached their gnarled limbs above the path, casting cool shade beneath. She ran toward the vine- covered stone cottage, Lydia lagging behind.

A plain, serious woman opened the door. She looked like the woman Charlotte Lucas might be in twenty years.

"It is Juliana, Mrs. Harrow. She has taken quite ill." Miss Fitzgilbert's words tumbled out in a panting rush.

"Is she having fits? What about bleeding?"

"No, I do not think so, or at least Mrs. Drum-mond said nothing about it."

"That is good then." She stepped outside and cupped her hands alongside her mouth. "Boy! Hitch up the cart. Be smart about it. I'll fetch me things." She shut the door.

"Now what?" Lydia stared at the closed door.

Should not Mrs. Harrow have asked them in?

"We go back. Mrs. Harrow knows the way to the school."

A donkey brayed, followed by muttered expletives not fit for a young lady's ears.

"I think it very inconsiderate for her not to drive us back." Lydia rubbed her hands along her shoulders against the deep shade's chill.

"She has not room for two, and it would not do for one of us to walk alone."

Lizzy often went out alone, particularly on errands for Papa—though Mama had never much liked that.

They walked several minutes in exhausted silence. Mrs. Harrow's donkey cart passed them, the ungainly animal hurrying at a fair clip.

"Donkeys are such stupid looking creatures." Lydia kicked a small rock skittering into the dust.

"Their long ears are quite ridiculous, especially that one, with the ear that falls to the left. Sometimes her boy puts a straw hat on it. The creature looks like an old gossip standing by the fence."

Lydia tittered—a gossiping donkey? What a lark!

The cart disappeared down the road, and the awkward silence returned.

"Has Juliana been ill long?"

"She was much better when she first arrived. She has grown sicker as she increased. You are fortunate to share a room with her." Miss Fitzgilbert retied the strings of her bonnet and straightened her gloves.

"She snores abominably."

"Perhaps, but she does not complain. Some of the others do naught but whinge when they fancy themselves unwell, but Juliana says nothing, often for far longer than she should."

Lydia turned aside and bit her lip. "My father said

MARIA GRACE

those patients were among the most difficult to tend; sometimes even dying without giving him a true picture of what was wrong. He resented being denied the chance to treat them properly."

"Poor thing insists it is her penance for acting so wickedly. It is not fair that she should be so stricken. She is the sweetest, kindest girl among us."

"My father says sickness makes little sense, striking where it will. Our vicar once said it was the hand of divine punishment. That made Papa very angry. He went on to tell the vicar so. It caused quite a row. Papa insisted it could not be so simple; the issue had to be far too complicated for mere men to comprehend."

"Perhaps he is right … Look, there are Miss Honeywell and Miss Thornton, leading everyone back from church." Miss Fitzgilbert hurried away.

Naturally the head girl would need to appraise the teachers of every detail.

Lydia inserted herself into the back of the line with Joan and Amelia.

"How did you get so fortunate as to miss out on service this morning?" Amelia asked.

"Mr. Weatherby was in rare form today." Joan wrinkled up her face.

"Indeed he was: long, holy and boring. The very epitome of a churchman."

"At least we shall be spared his company at dinner this week. He has been called away on some business and," Joan lifted her nose in the air and folded her hands before her chest, "regrets he must decline the invitation."

Lydia giggled.

A cluster of women, children in tow, crossed the

street as they approached. Two young dandies on the corner stared at them, something unsettling in their eyes.

"Why do they gawk so?" Lydia glanced over her shoulder at the women whispering amongst themselves.

"Oh, them." Amelia made a terrible face at the gawkers. "Ignore them; they are stupid, arrogant, biddies who think their marriages make them better than us."

Were not married women considered above the unmarried? Did they not have some right to regard themselves superior?

"But why must they stare?" Lydia pointed at the men with her chin.

Joan snorted. "They are horrid and think far too well of themselves. They like the look of us well enough, but are far too fine to tip their hats."

Joan and Amelia giggled.

"They call us Mrs. Drummond's Lady-birds. Can you imagine their cheek?" Amelia cast another foul expression at the dandies.

Lydia fought the urge to run over and shake them. She was a gentleman's daughter and fitting company for anyone—probably too good for those jealous old hens.

Wasn't she?

"Just ignore them." Joan elbowed her.

Mr. Amberson walked behind them, a very somber expression on his face. He saw the gawkers too. What did he think of them?

Why did she care?

❧Chapter 4

BACK AT THE SCHOOL, the girls were dismissed to their own amusements for the afternoon. Lydia tried to go to her room, but the midwife chased her out.

Dear Juliana had to rest and must not be disturbed.

Mrs. Drummond told her she could not even sleep there that night. If one of the other girls would not share with her, she might sleep on the daybed in Mrs. Drummond's office.

That would give anyone nightmares.

Lydia secured an invitation from Joan and Amelia, but they shooed her away for the time being as they intended to have a long nap.

Strains of music filtered from the music room.

Miss Greenville was quite good with the guitar. It sounded like the other top girl who played so well—Miss Long perhaps—was there with her and maybe one other singing. They must be putting together a performance.

Even if she wanted to practice, she would not have been welcome to intrude on their gathering.

In the parlor, several girls worked on fancy projects, though it made no sense. Mrs. Drummond certainly would not allow them to wear anything so fine. Why bother working so diligently on something that would never be seen?

Several others played games: spillikins, knuckle-bones, cards. Lydia was good at knucklebones. Maybe … no, they had already started and the very blonde girl without a cap—Penelope was it?—glowered at her as she approached.

How cruel.

Lydia wandered away.

Soft voices drifted from the morning room. Miss Honeywell and Miss Thornton discussed something in serious tones. If she stopped and stayed very still, she might be able to hear. She held her breath and listened, but eavesdropping for gossip required too much effort right now.

A breeze wafted in.

A walk in the modest garden behind the house might do well. Lizzy always took walks when she was out of sorts.

Lydia tiptoed to the back door. She did not have to sneak about—it was allowed after all. But boldness did not feel natural in this place.

She slipped into the garden. A few faded autumn blooms greeted her amidst the mostly dry stems and spindly stalks.

The cramped gazebo in the corner might be appealing in the warm months, but it looked so—

undressed now. Like Juliana padding about in her stays and chemise.

She giggled.

"Oh, Miss Bennet." Mr. Amberson sat on a painted bench in the shade, a newspaper in his lap. He tipped his hat.

What was it men found so endlessly entertaining about a newspaper? Papa was forever reading his.

"Excuse me sir. I did not mean to intrude."

"Not at all. By all means, avail yourself of the fresh air. I am a proponent of the restorative powers of fresh air and a turn about the grounds." He returned to his paper.

It was nice that someone in this dismal place acknowledged her.

A narrow path at the edge of the house led into a dainty copse. She followed it.

Gardens were so much pleasanter in the spring than in the autumn when everything was turning all crunchy and crumbly underfoot.

The gardens at Rosings often presented surprising trifles if one looked carefully. Lady Catherine had a fondness for nasty, miniature, stone dwarves that the gardeners tucked in among the plants. It was jolly fun to see polite guests shocked to discover them. They would wonder if they had seen them at all and be far too well-mannered to remark.

What a good joke! Mama encountered one once and nearly screamed.

This garden was dull and needed something equally lively. But she was no stone mason.

A gnarled bit of fallen branch caught her eye. It had something of a face, if one looked at it right—all drawn up on one side, a bit like a sailor with one eye put out.

Lydia picked it up and brushed off the dirt. A few properly shaped pebbles would make it perfect. She strolled along the path, scuffing her toes in the gravel.

Oh, that one would do very well for an eye—it even had a dark patch in the right spot!

She giggled and picked it up.

And that one resembled a tooth! Even better, that mound of heather would shelter him well enough that few would make him out clearly—just like Lady Catherine's garden dwarves.

She skipped to the heather and gently separated the stems.

"Might I inquire as to your occupation?"

She jumped and almost dropped her creation.

"Forgive me, I did not mean to startle you." Mr. Amberson gazed at her hands, the corners of his mouth turned up just a mite. "What is that?" He reached for it.

Her hand trembled as she surrendered it to him. Would he be cross with her meager spot of fun?

He turned it round until he had it right way up. "He is an excellent fellow indeed, but he needs a bit of something—a kerchief tied round his head."

She tittered. "I think you are right."

He tucked into his pocket and pulled out a tattered rag. "It is not good for polishing instruments anymore." He tied it around the face where it might have kept hair from its eyes, had it hair.

"How perfect!"

"Now what did you propose to do with it?"

"I know a lady who keeps such things in her garden ... to make it more interesting to her guests. I thought that clump of heather quite dull."

He pressed his lips hard, but a stifled chuckle still escaped. "A first-rate thought. Might I assist you?"

"It would be much easier with someone to hold back the heather for me."

"I am at your service." He parted the thick plant enough for her to tuck their creation well into the stalks. When he released the plants, one could barely see it. Perfectly situated to give polite strollers a start.

"Do your duty, Mr. Birch." Mr. Amberson touched two fingers to his forehead in salute.

"Mr. Birch?"

"The name does suit, I think."

"It does. I just had not thought to name such a thing."

"All artists name their creations. They are not complete until named."

"I have never known an artist."

"They are unique and peculiar creatures, much like Mr. Birch. Are you an artist Miss Bennet?"

What a very odd question.

"I do not know. I have never been taught."

"You might be. What you did with Mr. Birch is very clever indeed. You may find Miss Honeywell's drawing instruction quite liberating."

"Liberating?"

"When one is an artist, there is something inside that must be released. Penned up, it can be destructive, like a caged animal searching for escape. But once expressed in one's art, it is freed, liberated if you will, and the character changed into something generative and remarkable."

She peered up at him, brow knotted.

"If you are an artist, it will, in time make sense to you. And if not, you will determine that I am a queer, but harmless fellow, best left to his music for he makes little sense otherwise. Good day." He tipped his hat and sauntered back to the house.

What an extraordinarily peculiar man—all elbows and knees as he walked. A bit grasshopper-y. It was a wonder he did not fall over his own feet.

Yet, he seemed kind, certainly kinder than anyone else in this place. And he had not made fun of her over Mr. Birch.

There was much to be said for such a person, even if he was, by his own admission, rather peculiar.

She strolled several more circuits around the shrubbery, passing by the heather each time to relish Mr. Birch's lopsided grin. Somehow it made the dreary plot just a bit more inviting.

Perhaps she would tell Joan and Amelia about him … perhaps not. They might not keep her secret as well as Mr. Amberson.

That night Lydia joined her friends in their room. Joan and Amelia fashioned the bedclothes into a tent to contain their giggles over stories told in hushed whispers.

Both girls had been very wealthy and enjoyed so many adventures before being consigned to Mrs. Drummond. Amelia had lived in France and visited the court with her mother, a French noblewoman. Joan had been presented at court and had danced with the Prince himself. None of her own stories could compare.

Their admirers made Wickham drab and ordinary by comparison. Might she have met someone far more dashing, too? Wickham had seemed so splendid at the time. But Amelia's lover promised to seek her out to the ends of the earth when her father denied his suit.

Why had not Wickham done that? He had not tried very hard at all to stay with her. Instead, he had demanded money from Mr. Darcy.

How unromantic was that?

The horrible noises coming from Amelia's side of the room insured many sleepless hours to contemplate Wickham.

Amelia sounded like Lady Catherine's sow. Juliana was positively dainty by comparison.

After a few days, the midwife pronounced Juliana improved and Lydia returned to her own room. Naturally the privilege came with the admonition that Juliana was not to exert herself, but being able to sleep at night was well worth it.

Days blurred into weeks and the routine, though dreary and difficult, became familiar. Mr. Amberson had been right, though. Miss Honeywell's drawing lessons emerged as the high points of her existence. She even found solace in practicing her writing—creating her letters so perfectly even Mrs. Drummond praised her hand.

Why did those words of praise raise such warmth in her chest?

Papa and Mama were not apt to say such things. She was pretty and gay and that was all that mattered to them.

On her fourth Friday at the school, she wandered into the music room. A large oak tree grew in front of the window. Its bare branches made the most entertaining places for imagined fairies and sunbeams to hide and play. One day she would draw them, but for now it was pleasing to just imagine their antics.

She sat at the piano stool. The music she was supposed to learn had been left on the music stand.

Why did everything nag her to practice?

Mr. Amberson was an excellent music master. He had no apparent favorites and was patient in nearly all things, even with indifferent musicians. What was more; he never raised his voice, ever.

Only disrespect seemed to rouse his ire. More than that, it made him angry, almost frighteningly so. But his anger was different to Papa's. He did not spew cruel, harsh things, nor did he tend toward violence.

No, Mr. Amberson was entirely calm. She had never seen a man so calm and controlled in his fury.

Not knowing what to expect was frightening.

Ruth Sommers discovered what his anger meant and would not be likely to test him again. She had foolishly thought her considerable talent would shield her from his displeasure as it had with Mr. Clearly. Twice he cautioned her to mind her tongue. But she failed to heed his admonition.

When he came across her mocking Miss Thornton he took her directly to Mrs. Drummond who applied her cane to the matter. How Ruth screeched!

Lydia trembled.

What a dreadful thing, to be struck like a servant.

Though Papa might have become angry with her and her sisters, he never struck them. His heated words and the shunning afterwards were brutal enough to do the job sufficiently.

By all rights, she should feel wary of Mr. Amberson now, but he had warned Ruth before he acted. Moreover, he did exactly what he said he would.

He had never warned her of anything, so, perhaps she was safe, for now.

Lydia swallowed hard and played the first notes.

It was a pleasing country tune that sang of dancing and spring. The fingering flowed easier now, too.

The melody might do very well for a jig, if one changed the tempo a mite. She played the chorus through again, imagining herself and Kitty dancing to it.

Oh, but the last line did not fit the dance. Perhaps repeating those measures from the verse?

She played thorough it again, skipping the complex fingerings Mr. Amberson insisted she try.

Yes, that would make for a very agreeable dance.

"A very interesting interpretation, Miss Bennet."

She snatched her hands back from the instrument.

Why was he forever startling her, lurking in doorways like that?

"I … I was only fiddling about, sir, not really playing anything."

"I beg to differ. You were indeed playing something."

"I was not doing as you asked." She wrung her hands in her lap, beneath the keyboard. "I can do it the way you taught—"

"No, I should like to hear what you were playing again."

"But I cannot manage the left hand—"

He sauntered in and stationed himself to her left. "Then I shall play that part. You just do the melody. Begin and I shall follow."

She drew a deep breath and played the opening notes. Her fingers quivered just a bit. Hopefully he would not notice.

Mr. Amberson's long fingers added a bass line that fit the melody she played, but did not match the music as it was written. It was close, but much prettier.

They ran it through twice. How pleasant to play with someone else who could manage all the difficult places.

"Very nice, Miss Bennet. Very nice indeed. The arrangement is still rough. The dynamics and transitions require further attention, but I imagine you have only just begun composing?"

"Composing?"

Is that what she had done? What a singular thought.

"Continue to work with it. We shall revisit this at your next lesson."

"I cannot write music."

"I believe you just have." He tipped his head and left.

Why did he always simply disappear like that? Why did he say such queer things? He was so peculiar.

At least he had not disapproved.

Papa became quite cross if she did not play music just as it had been written. It made practice dreadful, but this might even be considered fun.

She returned to the keyboard.

An hour later, scuffling in the hallway broke her concentration.

Lessons! Oh, Miss Thornton was ever such the stickler about tardiness!

Lydia jumped off the piano stool and dashed out. She scooted into her place in the school room just as Miss Thornton shut the door against latecomers.

"We thought you were not going to make it!" Joan whispered.

"Whatever were you doing to make you so late?" Amelia asked.

"Practicing."

"You, practicing?" Amelia sniffed.

Miss Thornton strode to the front. "We shall begin with your ledgers today, continuing where we left off last time, considering household accounts."

Lydia opened the ledger, now filled with tidy numbers, sitting politely in orderly lines.

Miss Thornton paced before her students, droning on about the need for accuracy and precision in one's record keeping. Careful plans must be made, and good regulation must be maintained at all times when it came to monies and spending. Mrs. Rundel—whose book every young woman must have—suggested maintaining separate purses to manage monies allotted to various purposes.

On this point, Miss Thornton became very animated; her color heightened, hands waving with a flourish. What a laughable expression she wore, a bit like a toad with glasses balanced on the end of its nose, curls stuck to its forehead.

Lydia bit her lip and held her breath to avoid laughing. Miss Thorny Patch had no sense of humor … and did not seem to want anyone else to have one either.

Now she was blathering about preserving vegetables. Why should anyone care how many wide mouth bottles were required to store peas grown in a particular size plot?

Lydia stared at her ledger page.

How many peas would grow in the plot Miss Thornton described? She sketched the garden and sketched tiny pea plants in the intervals recommended. If they were to bear peas, they needed to flower. What did those flowers look like?

She closed her eyes a moment. Yes, that was it. She moved her pencil to a fresh spot on the paper and drew a fair likeness of the pea flowers she had seen in Mrs. Collins' gardens.

Whilst she did not have stone dwarves in her gardens, Mrs. Collins had an abundance of toads. A toad took shape next to the pea blossom, sheltering in its shadow.

Oh, it looked like Thorny Patch! She added glasses and curls—and a wee wart on the chin just to prove it was not—

"That is her!" Joan pressed into her shoulder, peering at the image. "Amelia, look." She pulled Lydia's ledger toward her and pointed at the drawing.

"Oh, you have captured her at her best," Amelia whispered a mite too loudly.

"Give it back. That was not—" Lydia snatched her book but Joan slapped her hand on it.

"No, I want to see."

"It is mine and I need it!" Lydia shoved Joan's hand away and grabbed the book.

"Lydia Bennet." Miss Thornton did not have to shout. Her voice penetrated every corner of the school room that had gone silent as a church yard.

"Yes, Miss." Lydia barely choked out the words.

"What is the disturbance in my classroom?"

"My ledger … she was looking at it, and I needed it back."

"And upon what were you so intent upon examining, Joan Colbrane? Are you unable to do your own work?"

"No, madam. Lydia draws pretty pictures, Miss, and I was looking at them."

Lydia turned to Joan, eyes bulging. Would that she could shake the stupid girl!

"Come to my desk, Lydia, and bring your book."

Somehow her leaden feet carried her to the front, leaving her nearly breathless and panting when she reached the teacher's desk.

The tall, gaunt teacher looked more like a witch than a toad now. She held out her hand, eyes narrowed into frightening slits, like those archers used to shoot through in castle walls.

Lydia surrendered her book, hands quaking so hard she nearly dropped it.

What were they all staring at? Did they think it good fun that she faced the wrath of Miss Thorny Patch? Why were Joan and Amelia not called out too?

Miss Thornton leafed through the pages, huffing and muttering under her breath. "I see you have some confusion as to what subject you are studying. You have mistaken these lessons for Miss Honeywell's instruction in drawing. What precisely is *this* doing in your calculations?" She pointed at the garden sketch.

"I needed to know how many plants were in the garden," Lydia stammered.

Several girls, including Amelia, snickered. Juliana and Miss Greenville winced.

"And this?"

"That is a pea blossom."

"So you could calculate how many peas your plant might bear?"

Several laughed out loud.

Could one die of embarrassment?

Was this how her sister Mary felt when Mama required her to play before company then criticized her afterwards?

"And this—how do you explain this frog—"

"It is a toad, madam."

Miss Thornton twitched. "This toad … with glasses?"

"I … I … I cannot."

"I believe I can. I am not a simpleton, Miss Lydia Bennet. I full well recognize your creation." She set the book aside.

"It … it was not ... I did not intend …"

"I will tolerate a great deal, even sketching garden plots to count plants if you cannot cipher properly. However, I draw the line at one thing. Do you know what that is?"

"No, Miss …"

"Disrespect. Each one of you is here because you have failed in that very subject. You have all demonstrated disrespect for the morals and conventions of society, your parents and yourselves." She lifted the top of her desk and removed a worn wooden ruler.

The room wavered around her.

"Extend your left hand."

"No, miss! Please, I did not mean—"

"I am not interested. Extend your hand."

"I promise I will not—"

"Enough! Your hand." Miss Thornton pointed her bony finger.

Lydia trembled as she reached out her hand, palm up.

"Do not withdraw it until you are instructed, or I shall send you to Mrs. Drummond for her cane."

Lydia squeaked something unintelligible. Her vision fogged with scorching tears that burned their way down her cheeks.

Miss Thornton brought her ruler down with a resounding thwack that echoed off the walls.

Lydia yelped, palm blazing.

"Contain your unseemly outburst, girl."

The ruler came down again.

Lydia bit her lips and squeezed her eyes shut, barely containing her exclamation. The effort only worked until the fifth blow. With the final three she cried out.

"I'm sorry, I'm sorry, Miss!"

"I am certain you are. Now," she pushed Lydia's journal at her, "return to your seat and finish your work."

Lydia pressed her throbbing palm to her belly and trudged back.

"She's a terrible old hag," Joan whispered.

"You're lucky she was so easy on you," Amelia said without looking at her.

Lydia was the first one out of the door when horrible Miss Thornton dismissed them from their lessons. She dashed to her room and shut the door behind her. Casting her ledger aside, she threw herself headlong on her bed and dissolved into a heap of misery.

Why had Miss Thornton been so mean? She had

not meant to be disrespectful.

If that was how a mere ruler stung, what must the cane be like?

And why had Joan and Amelia sat idly by? It was their fault after all.

She clutched a pillow to her belly. Curling around it, she succumbed to great, wracking sobs until her throat ached.

"I am so sorry, Lydia."

She looked up. Through blurry, irritated eyes, she made out Juliana standing over her. But the sympathy only made the ache more poignant and the tears began anew.

Juliana sat beside her and rubbed her back, murmuring soft, soothing sounds.

Jane had done that when Lydia was a little girl hiding in the attic from the horrible, hurtful things Papa said.

"Miss Thornton can be very harsh at times, and her ruler is very hard. Let me see."

Lydia rolled to her side and extended her hand. Juliana gently traced the red marks with cool, pudgy fingers that looked like fat sausages.

"I dare say you will have a few bruises." She pressed a fresh handkerchief into Lydia's other hand. "Dry your eyes a bit. I will fetch a compress for you." She waddled out.

Lydia sat up and huddled over her lap, cradling her hand.

No one had ever intentionally caused her physical pain before. Hot tears trickled down her cheeks and dribbled off her chin.

The door swung open, and a vaguely vinegary-herbal smell wafted in. Juliana trundled in with a small basin.

"Here, give me your hand." Juliana a wrung out an old flannel cloth and wrapped it around Lydia's palm.

"I did not mean to be disrespectful. I was only sketching the toads that lived in Mrs. Collins' garden."

"A toad?" Juliana giggled. "You drew Miss Thornton as a toad? May I see?"

Lydia shrugged and pointed to her book on the floor.

"Oh my! This is just like her. No wonder she was so very cross. I am not sure I would like to see my face on a toad either."

"I would not draw you as a toad."

"How would you draw me?"

"Give me a pencil."

With a few careful strokes Lydia formed the image of a softly smiling duck with big eyes, wearing a fluffy mobcap.

Juliana turned it one way, then the other. "I like it very well. Much better than being a toad. I like that she smiles and has wee feathers peeking from below her cap. I think her very dear, indeed."

"Truly?"

"Yes, I have little reason to lie to you. After all, if I tell you I like it, you will be apt to draw more. Then you will ask my opinion and pin them up on our walls. Were I to tell you I like the drawing when I do not, I would pay a very high price for my falsehood."

"I never thought about it that way." Lydia closed the book and set it aside.

"I have spent a lot of time thinking about how consequences that seem surprising might have been foreseen had I but considered things first." She rested her hand on her belly.

"One cannot predict the future."

"No, but if I pause to think about things, or what others might think or feel, I am not scolded nearly so often."

"Scolded? You are Mrs. Drummond's favorite. I can hardly see her raising her eyebrow at you, much less her voice, or her cane." Lydia rolled her eyes.

"She does not have favorites among us. I have been so ill—she is generous in making allowances for that. But do not mistake that for favoritism. You can be quite sure when I first came, I was called to her office often."

"Did she …" Lydia glanced at her hand.

"Yes, and it was awful. I was stupid enough to provoke her to it more than once. And to apply her cane as well. I thought her horrible and mean and unfair."

"But she is."

Juliana shook her head. "The last time it happened, she was ever so severe with me. The hurt was awful. I hated her so! I could not sleep that night and went down to the kitchen for a compress. I heard Mrs. Drummond talking with someone. Foolish girl that I was, I thought she might have a gentleman caller. I was certain she was a terrible hypocrite; doing the very things we were forbidden. So I hid in the hall and peeked in, certain I would catch her in the act."

"And? Who was there?"

"The vicar and his wife. Mrs. Drummond was weeping. It seemed she had been for quite some time."

"I had no idea she could."

"Neither did I at the time. She spoke at length with them about 'her girls' … and about me."

"What did she say?" Lydia bit her knuckle.

"It was what she did not say that struck me. She did not say I was … any of those things my father called me. She did not insult me or complain about the burden I was to her. What was more; she said she hated to be so severe with me. That made her weep again."

Lydia sniffed. "I would have thought she enjoyed—"

"Well, she does not," Juliana snapped. "I had never considered she—or anyone else—really had feelings, none that mattered anyway. Seeing her seeking the Weatherbys' advice, it just made me think."

"What did they tell her?"

"That surprised me too. He said, 'Remember the parable of the shepherd, the Good Lord left the ninety and nine to search after the one. Bringing back a lost lamb is never easy, but when it returns home, that is cause to celebrate.' I thought how pleasing it would be to be a reason for celebration rather than tears." Juliana shrugged and padded to the window.

Lydia stared at her. Perhaps she should say something, but what?

"I am sorry. I have talked far too much about myself when you are the one suffering." Juliana turned to face her.

"No … no … it is quite all right."

"You wish to be alone?"

"We are to visit the workhouse soon and …"

"You need to gather yourself. I should have thought of that." Juliana tiptoed out.

Lydia wandered to the writing desk.

Maybe Miss Thornton was shocked to see her toady-portrayal. But was that any reason to beat her?

Old Thorny Patch could have just said she did not like it and not to do it again.

How was it Lizzy always seemed to know what someone thought or felt? Is that what she was supposed to do? Turn into Elizabeth?

She would never be able to do that.

She was only a silly little girl—that's what Papa always called her. Silly—and stupid and foolish and not capable of anything but being pretty—and maybe drawing teacher-toads.

She put her head down and wept.

Chapter 5

LYDIA KEPT TO HERSELF for the next week complete. Jane always sought her out when she did that at home, but here, no one bothered.

Sunday morning, Mrs. Drummond called Juliana away before chores began, leaving Lydia entirely on her own to clean. It was some small consolation that Juliana was sent to mend linens. The only chores she did anymore were those she could do sitting down.

Church was dull as usual, but the vicar was not as bad as Mr. Collins—at least he told amusing stories.

A chill breeze blew through the sunshine as they walked back from church. Lydia lingered as far back from the rest as possible without drawing additional attention to herself.

Joan and Amelia wove their way through the line to walk with her.

"Droll as ever today, the vicar was." Joan elbowed Lydia.

"I so hate his stupid tales, always trying to make his children sound so good. A parable for us to learn from." Amelia smiled beatifically and batted her eyes.

Lydia kept her eyes fixed straight ahead and walked faster.

"Do not be this way, Lydia." Joan slipped her arm in Lydia's.

Amelia did the same on the other side. "Do not vent your anger at Old Thorny Patch upon us."

"She would never have seen anything but for the fuss you made." Lydia pulled her arms away.

Joan held her fast. "You know she never misses anything—she would have seen it when she came along to check our work."

"I dare say she would have been even more cross then!" Amelia released Lydia and tossed her head. "At least she did not send you down to Mrs. Drummond."

"You should have told her the drawing was not of her."

"Contradicted her and had a taste of her ruler, too? What good would that have done any of us?"

"You know she does not listen when she is angry. It would have only made things worse for us all." Joan's voice thinned into an annoying whine.

Perhaps that was true. But Papa was far more unreasonable than Miss Thornton and Lizzy often changed his mind—or did she? It seemed like she did at the time, but maybe Papa turned his wrath toward her instead.

Joan tugged her arm, "Say you are not angry at us anymore."

"Oh do! It has been so dreadful dull with you snubbing us so. It is like being cut by the *ton* when you turn your back on us."

"Oh, all right." Lydia harrumphed. "But you must promise—"

"Oh, we do! We do!" Joan clapped and bounced on her toes.

"We will not look at your drawings in class ever gain. But you must promise to show us in the evenings when the teachers are not about."

"You want to see them?"

"Of course we do. They are so very clever." Joan said.

"I dare say your sketches might be the very high points of our week."

Could she truly bring so much enjoyment to her friends?

"Very well."

Joan and Amelia grabbed hands and cried, "How wonderful!"

Mrs. Drummond glanced back at them, a severe expression on her face.

Of course she would disapprove. She disapproved of everything.

Lydia peeked over her shoulder.

As usual, Mr. Amberson trailed behind them. He shared Mrs. Drummond's somber mien. While he often looked thoughtful, he rarely looked so … heavy.

What troubled him so?

"We are going to have a game of knucklebones this afternoon. Play with us?" Joan pressed her hands together, pleading.

Lydia won several games in a row, and Amelia declared herself excessively tired. She excused herself to go upstairs and rest. Joan pleaded boredom and insisted on choosing another game, but they could not agree. So they went their own ways.

Why did Sunday afternoons have to be so dull? She should work on her sewing, but the day was too fine for sitting.

The garden—she had not checked on Mr. Birch in some time. She should make sure he kept at his post.

The trees had lost what leaves remained, and the late afternoon breeze nipped at her neck and ears. Why had she neglected to don her shawl? Winter would be upon them soon. What were winters like in this part of the country?

Mr. Birch peeked out from the heather stalks, still well-hid by their bushy tendrils. No one had claimed to have discovered him yet, though she had heard Ruth telling Miss Greenville that she thought a creature was living in the heather. She pressed her hand to her mouth and giggled.

"I see our friend is still on duty."

She jumped.

Why was he forever doing that? How could so awkward a man walk so quietly she never heard his approach?

"Yes, he is, sir."

A small gust of wind danced past, rustling the plants and raising gooseflesh on her shoulders.

"Winter will be upon us," she said.

Mr. Amberson did not look at her. He stared first into the heather, then at the sky.

What was wrong? Was not the weather an acceptable topic for conversation?

"I do not think the winter is a very pleasant season, except where there is snow, for that is very pretty. Does Summerseat experience a great deal of snowfall?"

He clasped his hands behind his back and chewed his upper lip. "I am troubled, Miss Bennet."

Lydia blinked. Why would he tell her such a thing, unless—

"Miss Thornton spoke to me."

Of course the teachers would talk among themselves. Now he would think her disrespectful.

She could run, but she would still have to face him for music lessons. Might as well get the tongue lashing over with now.

She lifted her chin and stared over his shoulder.

"She told me of your drawing in class. It pained her greatly ..."

"I did not mean it."

"... to have to punish you so harshly."

Surely he was wrong.

"She thinks rather well of you, you know, and it distressed her to find you so ..."

"Disrespectful," she whispered.

"Easily distracted."

She traced circles in the dirt with her toes.

"I feel I am somewhat at fault. I encouraged you to draw, but offered no guidance, no structure."

His fault?

She stared into his eyes.

"One's art is a powerful thing, Miss Bennet, a gift, which by its very nature moves and influences others. It requires careful management or it has the power to wound both the artist and his audience."

"I do not understand."

"Are you familiar with the works of the great satirists of our day? Rowlandson, Gillray, Cruikshank?"

Could he see how hot she blushed?

Wickham had taken her to see the print shop windows with the scandalous prints in their windows. The prints had fascinated her, not just because they illustrated things she had never seen nor even imagined, but for their artistry.

"Their work often features unflattering portrayals of powerful people. Those who are so featured are rarely pleased. How would you like to find yourself portrayed in a shop window?"

Laughed and gawked at? How dreadful!

"Some say those artists serve a vital role, forcing us to look at the absurdities we otherwise ignore. But consider, in France, not so very long ago, such men might easily have met their fate at the national razor."

Lydia gasped. "Surely not."

"Inquire of Mrs. Drummond, perhaps when you have your next French lesson. She lived in France for a time and might be willing to speak of the experience."

"She never speaks of it."

"There is a reason." He chewed his lip again. "If you have been given an artist's gifts it is incumbent upon you to steward it well, for it touches the human heart and causes us to reflect. The process is not without risk to us all. But we must match the risk to the reward we gain."

"What reward? You speak in riddles."

"I am sure it seems so." He reached into his coat and removed a worn journal. He pressed it into her hands. "A book for your sketches. I used it for a time for my own drawings before I realized music was my true medium. I tore out those pages, so you might begin afresh."

She flipped though the blank pages, edges a bit tattered and dirty.

How could something so old and worn feel so precious?

"Collect your sketches here, not on your lessons. Then you may show them to me, and we might discuss them."

"I would like that very much. May I show—"

"Them to others? They are your creations, Miss Bennet. You may do with them as you will. But be careful, not everyone appreciates an artist's creations. Some are quick to criticize and such words wound with a poignancy few can match. Others would seek to use our creations for their own gain. Guard your heart wisely, for it is the well-spring of life."

"Thank you sir, I will." She pressed the book to her chest.

"I have faith in you." He tipped his hat and ambled off, heaviness sloughing off with each too long step.

What an odd, dear fellow.

And what a lovely gift. She turned the book over in her hands. Oh, a little pencil, well used, was tucked in the bindings.

She flipped to the first page and lowered herself to the ground. The image of Mr. Birch, as a man, not tree bark—took shape, dancing on the deck of his ship. He looked nothing like any person she actually knew.

The next morning, after chores and breakfast, the girls filed into the school room for Miss Honeywell's lessons. Lydia's stomach clenched as she sat down, and she rubbed her left palm.

Miss Honeywell would have them write today, so she checked her pen. The tip was still very fresh—she wrote with a light hand that did not spoil her pens quickly. Miss Honeywell approved.

Joan and Amelia rushed in, stifling giggles. Miss Honeywell shut the door and took her place at the front of the room.

"Today we shall begin by writing a letter. Select a passage from *Hints on the Gentle Art of Letter Writing* and use it in your letter, attending carefully to the elegance of your hand. Make it of interest to the reader, bearing pleasant tidings and no requests for money or complaints about your accommodations here." Her voice turned sharp.

Two girls near the front blushed and looked away from her.

"When you have finished, bring your letter to me."

The passage of choice was easy enough, a short writing on the changing seasons. But to whom should she write? If she did not come up with an acceptable correspondent, Miss Honeywell might well make her write to Papa or Mr. Darcy.

She chewed her lip. Mr. Darcy would probably return her letter overwritten with red ink to correct her errors. And Papa would likely burn it unread. That made it impossible to write to Mama and Kitty as well.

Jane then? Yes … no, not without her new directions. Heavens, where did Jane live now she was Mrs. Bingley?

Mary! She stayed at Mrs. Collins' house in Kent, waiting to be married. A letter to Mary it would be.

Dear sister Mary …

She dutifully copied the passage, changing a word or two to make it her own. What else, though? What might Mary be interested in? Chores, charity work and lessons; none were particularly diverting.

Mr. Michaels, her betrothed, would be a steward … perhaps accounts and ledgers and preserving peas?

Joan giggled and slid a piece of paper toward Lydia. It bore a rough drawing of a round little pig with hair drawn up in a knot so tight its eyes were pulled wide open. Underneath in tiny letters was 'Honeyham.'

Lydia' gasped and held her breath to suppress her initial giggle.

The drawing, while amusing, was not very good. Without the caption, she might not have recognized who it portrayed. The proportions of the face did not capture Miss Honeywell properly. The cheeks—

What was she thinking?

"Fix it; it is not quite right."

She thrust it back at Joan.

"Please."

"No, I will not draw teachers."

"Just this once …"

"Is there a problem?" Miss Honeywell pushed up from her desk and folded her arms over her chest.

Lydia rose. "No, Miss. I … I was wondering if … if I might include a sketch in my letter to my sister … of … of the garden?"

"Finished your letter already? Bring it here."

Lydia grabbed her letter with shaky hands and slid the sketch back to Joan. She swallowed hard as she made her way to the front.

Miss Honeywell snatched the letter, but the lines beside her eyes melted as she scanned it. "Why might your sister be interested in ledgers and accounts?"

"She is going to marry the steward of a large estate. She is very practical, not romantic at all. I ... I thought he must talk about such things very often."

Several girls giggled.

Miss Honeywell seemed ready to as well. "A fair enough reason, I will grant you. You may begin your drawing lesson with a sketch on this letter."

Murmurs spread through the room.

"Thank you, Miss." The words tumbled out in a heady rush. "May I sit near the window so I can look at the garden while I sketch it?"

"You may."

The desk near the window had a short leg, so it wobbled, but it was worth it to be away from Joan. She would be less of a sauce-box when Miss Honeywell discovered her likeness as a porker.

The garden looked different from above. It would be more difficult to render on paper this way.

Sometime later she felt someone staring over her shoulder. Miss Honeywell stood behind her, eyes narrowed, scrutinizing her paper.

"An admirable effort, but your perspective is flawed." She pointed to several spots in the drawing.

So that was the problem!

Miss Honeywell placed a fresh sheet of paper on the desk. "Your pencil please."

With several quick strokes, she created guidelines and roughly penciled in the fence and gazebo accordingly.

"I see! Oh, oh! I see!" Lydia took the pencil and began replicating the technique beside Miss Honeywell's example. "Please, Miss, might I begin the letter again, with a proper sketch this time."

"You wish to recopy what you have written?"

"Oh yes, I must. I cannot send the letter with such a flawed rendering."

"Very well, you may stay then and redo it after we have finished the reading instruction." An odd little smile crept across Miss Honeywell's lips. She turned to the class. "Now, we shall read aloud from Fordyce. Miss Bennet," she handed Lydia the tome. "Begin on page one hundred twenty two."

Lydia read her page aloud, barely aware of the words she uttered.

So many sketches in her notebook needed to be redrawn with correct perspective. It was so simple, so clear now. How had she missed it before?

Her fingers twitched with the need to complete her drawing correctly. At last Miss Honeywell dismissed the girls, and Lydia returned to her letter.

"Do hurry. It is nearly time for us to leave." Juliana peered from the doorway.

"Already?" Lydia set her pencil aside. "I have only just finished."

"You have missed luncheon. Mrs. Drummond sent us all to prepare to visit the alms houses. She will be frightfully cross if you dawdle."

"Must she always be cross about something?" Lydia placed her letter on the teacher's desk. "I am coming."

Missing luncheon was disagreeable, though not as troublesome as getting the perspective on the gazebo correct. It took three tries to produce a satisfactory effort.

"Here, I thought you might want these." Juliana held up Lydia's red cloak and bonnet.

Lydia swallowed hard and slipped the cloak over her shoulder. What would Wickham think to see her here? Would he like her drawings? He had not cared about much after Mr. Darcy refused to fund the settlement Wickham wanted.

She followed Juliana downstairs, tying her bonnet on the way.

They were the last ones to gather in the front hall. Mrs. Drummond reprimanded them with her eyes.

"I cannot walk fast," Juliana murmured.

Mrs. Drummond grumbled, but her sharp expression faded. "Go to the kitchen and pick up the baskets Cook has prepared and assemble outside."

Lydia found Joan and Amelia, who hung back, and ducked between them.

Amelia grabbed her arm. "Wait, do not be in a hurry."

"If we are fortunate, all the baskets will be taken before we get to the kitchen," Joan whispered.

"Cook always overfills them, and they are so heavy. I do not see why we should be bringing things to poor widows. The money paid to Mrs. Drummond for our upkeep ought to be spent upon us." Amelia turned up her nose.

She had a point. They might hire another maid or eat nicer food if Mrs. Drummond spent her funds differently. But even Lady Catherine sent baskets around to the cottages and farms when there was sickness, and she was hardly the charitable sort

"I was right!" Joan elbowed Lydia. "All the baskets are taken. We are free of the burden."

The girls gathered outside the back door, and Mrs. Drummond led them off. Juliana trudged just ahead of Lydia, both hands clutching a heavy basket that kept bouncing against her belly. Not a quarter mile down the road, she lagged behind the group.

Lydia looked over her shoulder several times. Juliana kept falling further back, stopping every dozen steps to catch her breath.

"Botheration." Lydia ran back and intercepted Juliana. "Give me the basket."

"No, no, I should carry my share." Sweat trickling down Juliana's dangerously scarlet face.

"At this rate, you will not arrive before dark."

"Then you do not need to wait for me—go on."

"No, you are not supposed to do heavy work. Mrs. Drummond will probably punish me for allowing you to carry it at all. Just give it to me." She pulled the basket away from Juliana.

Gracious it was heavy! Why did she insist on carrying it alone?

"Thank you." Juliana stooped over and panted.

Miss Thornton came up behind them. "It is too far for you to walk to the alms houses. Go back to the house. Cook has charity clothes for you to sew."

"No, no, I can …"

"Do not argue, go." She pointed to the house.

"Yes, Miss." Juliana tried to curtsey but nearly lost her balance.

"Catch up with the others now," Miss Thornton said, her voice pleasanter than usual.

Lydia trudged back to Joan and Amelia.

"Clever of you." Amelia's eyebrows flashed up.

"Trying to gain favor with Miss Thornton or Mrs. Drummond?" Joan leaned close and winked.

"Oh, just help me carry this heavy thing."

They jumped back, hands in the air.

"I would not want to take away the favor for which you have worked so hard." Amelia sniffed and quickened her pace.

"And my hands are raw from scrubbing the steps this week. I have no wish to carry anything." Joan sauntered away.

Lydia grumbled under her breath.

The group stopped at a bend in the road near the parish alms houses. Her arms, shoulders and back screamed epithets learned from Mrs. Harrow's boy.

Mrs. Drummond arranged them in three groups to make their visits. Perhaps, if she were lucky she might be assigned with Joan and Amelia and not Miss High-and-Mighty.

She peeked at Mrs. Drummond. What luck, she was distracted by Miss Honeywell.

Lydia wove through the group to Joan. "Where is Amelia?"

Joan pressed her fingers to her lips and kept her gaze focused toward Mrs. Drummond.

Lydia peered over heads and between shoulders. "Where is she?"

"Stop that—someone will notice." Joan whispered. "She accompanied Juliana back to the school."

"No she did not—"

"Hush now!" Joan pinched her arm.

"Lydia, bring your basket, and join Miss Fitzgilbert." Mrs. Drummond beckoned her.

Would nothing go her way today?

She stalked toward Miss Fitzgilbert.

"Oh, you got the basket meant for two to carry. You should have had help. Let me …" Miss Fitzgilbert grabbed one of the handles.

"Can we set it down?"

"Not here, the road dirt is foul. Take my basket, and I will hold this one for a bit."

They traded loads.

"Why did you carry it alone?"

"Juliana had it first. I took it from her."

Miss Fitzgilbert looked skyward and shook her head. "She tries to do too much."

"Miss Thornton sent her back. I asked Joan and Amelia for help, but …"

That earned a snort and rolled eyes.

Miss Greenville and Ruth Sommers joined them.

"I think we are going to the House of Three Widows," Miss Greenville said.

Her basket was piled high with linens and a blanket.

"I do not like them very much." Ruth, voice low, glanced over her shoulder toward the teachers conferring with Mrs. Drummond. "Widow Barnes scares me."

"Why?" Lydia's eyes grew wide.

"The poor old woman is hard of hearing and nearly blind." Miss Fitzgilbert edged toward Miss Greenville who took one handle of the large basket.

"She stands very close to you and speaks very loudly, but she means no ill."

"At least her breath is not as terrible as Widow Randall. Her teeth are so rotten—do not let her breathe too close to you." Ruth snickered.

"Widow March and her granddaughter are very gentle and kind though. They always like it if we sing." Miss Greenville's eyes drooped a mite.

Mrs. Drummond waved. "Come along girls."

Ruth came alongside Lydia as they followed Mrs. Drummond. "Has anyone warned you not to ask impertinent questions whilst we visit?"

Lydia shook her head.

"I am not surprised. *They* think it amusing to allow others to wander into trouble, but I fancy no more encounters with Mrs. Drummond's cane. So, do not ask personal questions of their circumstances or their pasts. Mrs. Drummond considers it rude. If they wish to speak of it, listen politely and make the right and proper responses: 'indeed', 'is that so?', 'how interesting' and the like. Do not pry further than they volunteer."

"I am … am glad to know."

"And you must not stare. Widow Randall is excessively sensitive to it."

"Anything else?"

"Do not accept anything Widow March offers you. She is touched and does not realize what she is doing."

"Touched?"

"She is simple, like a child. You do not need to be afraid of her, though."

Lydia smacked her lips against the road dust that coated her tongue. A sharp breeze, carrying the promise of winter, cut between the girls. The dilapidated cottage awaited them, plain and dingy. Shutters hung askew, and weeds prevailed in the tiny unkempt yard. A tattered garden plot peeked around the side, as if not on speaking terms with the cottage.

Mrs. Drummond knocked sharply.

The door creaked open and a wizened raisin of a woman peered out. Her leathery face broke into a toothless smile. She cackled an indecipherable greeting and urged them all inside.

Dark, dank air hung heavy, pressed down by the low ceiling. Dust and dirt clung to the walls, the furniture and streaked the faces of everyone inside.

The smell!

Unwashed bodies, and rotting food, burnt rushes and stagnant water, woven with urine and waste.

It clung to her, creeping along her skin, wrapping tendrils about her neck, slowly closing down, strangling—

She bolted out of the door, and ran to the garden's edge.

Air! Clean air!

Her knees went soft, and she clutched an unsteady fence post.

"Lydia?" Mrs. Drummond appeared at her elbow, her face a mix of ire and something softer, but less clear.

Words it tangled in her tight throat and came out more like a sob.

"Take a deep breath, and another. Any better?"

Lydia nodded, more because she should than because she agreed. If she had to go back in that house, she might never breathe again.

"How … how can they live like that? The smells, the miasma. Is not the place full of disease?"

"Something you learned from your father?"

She gulped another breath. "He was most emphatic. He would not tolerate …"

"I see."

"Why do they not …"

"Because they cannot. They can neither afford to do differently nor have they the strength for the tasks if they could."

"But … but …"

"Housekeeping requires strength. Sand, soap, coal to heat water, it all costs money these women can ill-afford."

"Please, please do not make me go back in there."

Perhaps if she held the fencepost tightly enough, the shaking might stop.

"It is not fair to allow the other girls to do all the work. They are all inside helping to clean and mend and cheer the widows. Why should you alone be excused?"

Lydia cast about. "I … I might work out here perhaps? The yard is full of weeds … and the garden has not been prepared for winter. Have they any tools?"

"The rest are so engaged inside, the garden will not likely receive their attention. You may do the garden chores. If I find you have shirked your duties, though, the consequences will be most severe. Come." Mrs. Drummond led her to a ramshackle shed and pulled the door open.

It groaned and shuddered and threatened to come apart with the effort.

"The tools are here." Mrs. Drummond dusted off her hands and returned to the cottage.

Lydia rummaged in the shed. Dust swirled, and she sneezed. At least this place smelled of earth and growing things. A rake, a hoe, a shovel—worn and rusty—but they would suffice.

Mama had been a fine gardener. Her flowers drew admirers, but her true brilliance was in her kitchen garden. Every vegetable, every herb flourished under her hand. Although she kept a gardener for the heaviest labor, she did much of it herself, and insisted her daughters help.

Lydia picked up the hoe, a familiar, comfortable weight in her hands, breaking up tough roots and clods of dry dirt. She and Kitty and Mary had such merry times, laboring under Mama's tutelage, taming the unkempt garden into a thing of beauty.

She hummed a song under her breath.

Soft steps shuffled behind her. "That be a pretty tune, dearie." A miniature, crooked woman stared at her with tiny dark eyes. She leaned on a walking stick as gnarled as she.

"My … my mother taught it to me. We used to sing it when we worked in the garden."

"Did I know your mother?"

"I … I do not think so. She has never been to Summerseat."

"Nor have I." The old woman shook her head. "No I have not, and I have no need to either. I like my little village well enough, you know. Burlington is quite good enough for me. I have no need to go traipsing about the country, gadding about here and there you see."

This must be the touched widow. She looked of a mind to continue talking too.

"Winter is coming you know, and the garden needs much work. Do you mind if I work whilst you talk?"

"Not at all, dearie, not at all. I would not keep you from it. I could not live with being the cause of your wee ones to go hungry." She tottered closer.

"My what?" Lydia brought the hoe down a mite harder than necessary.

"Your little ones. How many do you have now? Is it is three or four? Your eldest is now big enough to be of some use out here. Dontcha go coddling the boy now—you hear? As soon as mine were short-coated, I set them to work, I did. Tied their leading strings to whatever were near and set them to something useful whilst I worked. No idle hands you see, no idle hands. Here, here, give me that rake. Cannot bear being idle now, neither." She pointed and held out her hand.

Lydia gave her a broken toothed rake. "I can manage. You should not—"

"I am sure you can. You are such a good girl, dearie. Do not deny an old soul her satisfaction." She scratched at the dirt with the rake.

At least she seemed pleased with her efforts, though she accomplished little, humming loudly as she did.

Was it—yes, the same tune Lydia had hummed earlier. Lydia began to sing the only verse she remembered.

A thin and raspy voice joined in the chorus, and her rake kept time. The widow continued on with a verse Lydia had never heard. They sang another chorus together, which led into yet another unfamiliar verse. After four new verses, the old woman insisted they sing the whole song again to be sure Lydia learnt them all properly.

Halfway through, several more voices joined them. Miss Greenville, a ragged woman who must be the widow's granddaughter and was that—yes, it was Mrs. Drummond. Her rich, melodious tones hardly seemed in keeping with her tiny frame. As they sang, each one took up a task, and the remaining work was finished in a final repetition.

As the last notes faded into the rapidly cooling evening air, Lydia gathered the tools and returned them to the shed. The widow followed her.

"Here, have this." The widow thrust a dirty pebble at her.

"I cannot."

"I know it is very fine, dearie, but I want you to have it, to remember our little song and the old woman who taught you."

"But I have nothing to give you."

"You have already given me enough. A fine afternoon with music—promise to teach the song to your wee ones, and it is enough."

"I promise."

The widow dropped the cold stone into Lydia's palm and folded her fingers closed around it. "Treasure it as I have." She tottered off toward the cottage.

Mrs. Drummond approached, her brow drawn into knots.

Lydia opened her hand and shrugged.

Mrs. Drummond picked up the stone and brushed some dirt away. It was pinkish with dark spots and shiny flecks. "It is only a garden stone." She handed it back to Lydia.

"Shall I put it back?"

"No, she would be pleased for you to keep it." Mrs. Drummond twitched her head toward the cottage.

The old woman stood in the doorway, watching them.

Lydia tucked the pebble into her apron pocket and waved at the widow. She waved back.

"Come girls, we must make haste if we are to return home before dark. The others have already left."

Miss Fitzgilbert handed her an empty basket and Miss Greenville pressed a handkerchief into her hand.

"You have dust on your cheek."

Lydia wiped it away.

"It was good of you to work in the garden." Ruth said softly.

"It was?"

"That is the worst job of all. We would all rather avoid it. Much better to toil in the house."

"I much rather be in the garden." Lydia returned the handkerchief.

"In that case," Miss Greenville nudged her with her elbow, "we shall have to make sure to pay our visits with you every time."

"You carry heavy baskets, tend the garden, and provide a sweet serenade. What more could we want in a companion to the Alms houses? In fact, for such companionship, I shall carry the basket home for you." Miss Fitzgilbert took back the empty basket.

How utterly unlike Miss High-and-Mighty.

"So what was the secret Widow Randall was so intent on telling you that she kept you in the house so long?" Ruth asked.

Miss Fitzgilbert rolled her eyes. "She has a special receipt to sweeten the breath. She thought I might benefit from it."

Miss Greenville laughed first, but soon they all doubled over, tears in their eyes.

Perhaps it would be pleasant to pay visits to the alms houses with this group again.

Chapter 6

SEVERAL DAYS LATER, Lydia sat in the music room at the pianoforte, plinking her way through yet another dreadful scale.

Why did he torture her with something so dreadful and tedious? Perhaps if she played it with a lively rhythm? It was a little better, but not much.

Gah! She brought her elbows down on the keys.

"That is most definitely not the next note in the scales, Miss Bennet." He glowered until she removed her elbows.

"I am sorry, sir." She hung her head.

Mr. Amberson pulled a chair close to the pianoforte and sat down. "You do not like playing scales very much?"

"No, sir."

"Nor learning them, I imagine."

"No."

"Why?"

"They are dull and unimaginative. They must be played just so and there is no room for anything pretty or gay. I hate memorizing them."

He held her gaze, steady, eyebrows rising slightly. "Why? It is not hard for you. You are not stupid."

"Yes I am."

"I can hardly agree. Why would you say that?"

"My Papa—"

"No, I did not ask why someone else might say so, but why would you?"

"I cannot cipher properly—I must draw it before I can understand. I get confused with directions and do things out of order. And I hate to read—I care nothing for history or geography, and I despise Shakespeare." She braced her elbows on the top of the pianoforte and covered her face with her hands.

Now he would scold her for certain.

"What has ciphering to do with being stupid? You search a table or work it out in a sketch, can you not?"

"Yes, but it is not the right way."

"What matters the way you come by the correct answer, if you are able to do so?"

"Papa does not agree."

"Is he always right?"

She peeked at him, into rich blue eyes, wide and kind and sincere.

"Pray forgive me, but I hardly think that one man can be right in all his opinions. And as to reading, I have seen you in the parlor with a novel, and you seemed very well pleased. So you do not prefer subjects dry and dull. How do such preferences render you without intelligence?"

She shrugged. "I never considered that."

"Perhaps you should. Now, as to scales …" He moved closer to rest his hands on the keyboard and began to play a scale. "I cannot argue. They are dry and boring. I have never known a single student who relished the study."

"Then why? It hardly improves one's learning to be tortured simply because the master can order it."

He played a sour note and stopped. "Think you so little of me, Miss Bennet? Do you honestly believe that of my character, my nature?" He folded his arms over his chest.

She bowed her head. "No, I do not."

"Then why would you say such a thing?"

"Because I do not understand why you do this."

"And?"

"And the only reason I can think is that it is fun to be mean." She cringed.

Pray let him not yell too loudly.

"You could ask me why—do not assume you know my mind."

Why did he have to speak so softly? It would be easier if he yelled.

"I … no … would that not be impertinent?"

"As impertinent as defaming my character with your flawed impressions? I hardly think so."

"And you would not be angry with me for asking?"

"Far less so than I am now."

She jumped away from the piano stool.

"I may be angry, but I hardly deserve that." A small scar on his forehead caught in a deep crease, like a tightly knotted shoe lace.

Why did he not just rail at her and be done with it?

"Whoever made you so afraid, I am not he."

She dropped her gaze and stared at her hands. "I know."

"Then show me that you can believe better of me. Ask me why I make you learn scales."

She bit her lip and screwed her eyes shut.

"Miss Bennet."

She peeked through her lashes. He extended his hand toward her, palm up, fingertips inviting.

Dare she?

His eyes, wide and so deeply blue, reassured her. She reached toward him, and he locked his fingertips with hers.

"Ask me."

"Why must I learn scales, sir?" Her voice broke over the last word.

"Every music student asks that question. I hated scales until I discovered their true nature. I have taught you chords, have I not? Consider them as words. You know but a few right now, correct?"

"Yes."

"So, like a small child, you can converse, but with only small words, and only small things. That is not enough for you, is it? You want to speak more. You need not just words, but an alphabet from which to form your words. Scales are that alphabet. They allow you to decipher what you are hearing and create it yourself."

His color heightened and his eyes lit. She tightened her fingertips against his.

"Scales contain the fundamental structure, the foundation of music itself. They will teach you how to set a mood and express a tone. If you find them dull as they are, then once you have committed them to memory, play them in patterns of thirds or fifths, in intervals, or interesting rhythms. Focus on hearing them like the guideline sketches you use when you draw. They set the directions, the boundaries, giving initial shape and form to what you create."

He waved her to place her hands on the keyboard next to his. They played the scale together.

Guidelines, as for perspective … of course!

"I had no idea."

"No student does. That is why you must trust your master."

"I … I do …"

He removed his hands from the piano. "You trust I am a better musician than you, and that I have something to teach you."

"Is that not trust?"

"I wish for you to trust my character, Miss Bennet. Trust that when I ask something of you, it is for your good, not mine. Trust that I would not knowingly hurt you."

She rose and walked to the window, a familiar, sick sense in her stomach.

"What have I done to make you so afraid of me?"

He sighed and played a soft, minor melody that mirrored her inner turmoil.

"You are in charge of me, and you get angry."

"So you expect I will hurt you, because I am in a place of authority?"

She bit her lip and nodded.

"Have I ever raised my voice to you? Spoken harshly to you?"

"You took Ruth to Mrs. Drummond."

"You are terrified that I might grow unexpectedly angry and you might suffer the same fate?"

She squeaked and clutched the windowsill.

"Am I so wholly unpredictable? Think on it. At what have I become angry?"

"Ruth was disrespectful … and Penelope lied to you …"

"Are those unjust moments for anger? Did I not give them both ample warning and opportunity to choose a different path? Even then, did I speak hurtfully to them?"

"No, sir."

He approached with soft, measured steps.

"Would you … would you take me to Mrs. Drummond?"

"Would you force me to do it? I do not see you intractable as that."

"You think far too well of me."

"Perhaps, you think far too meanly of yourself. Will you show me your drawings?"

She swallowed hard and nodded. "They are not very good."

He led her back to the pianoforte, and they sat.

She opened the book. "This is Mr. Birch in the garden, and this is Ruth telling of a creature she thought she saw there."

He turned the page. "And this?"

A dark image of faces, rooms, shadows and scribbles stared at her. She tried to flip past it, but he held the place.

"That is nothing, really—it is terrible. Pray do not look at it."

"It is very interesting. Something troubled you beyond words, and you were able to speak it here." He traced a tortured profile amidst the darkness.

"It is ugly."

"Not ugly, evocative. Not all art is beautiful, just as not all human experience is comfortable. It reflects the totality of our existence, pleasant and unpleasant. I am pleased you dared capture it. Was this after you visited the alms houses?"

She nodded.

He placed his hands on the keyboard and played a dark melody, haunted and torturous.

Her face flushed. He could not have seen her more clearly had he walked in on her toilette.

"You communicated something of the human condition without a single word. What have your friends said of it?"

"Joan and Amelia? I have not shown them. I do not think I shall."

"I see." He shut the sketch book. "Shall we have a go at the dance melody you were arranging? Perhaps you can show me how knowing your scales would influence the music."

"I should like that very much."

"Lydia!" Juliana called from the doorway. "Hurry! Miss Honeywell is nearly ready to begin lessons."

"Oh, goodness! Not again!"

"Go on, I will put the music away."

"Thank you, sir." She darted out.

"For one who dislikes practicing as much as you claim to, you certainly lose track of time easily." Juliana giggled.

"It is not so bad as I remember." Lydia shrugged and rushed to her seat between Joan and Amelia.

"Girls," Miss Honeywell paused until the room stilled. "I have just been to collect the post. A number of you have letters today. For our reading lesson, those of you with correspondence will pick an appropriate passage to read aloud. Miss Fitzgilbert, Miss Greenville, Miss Long, Ruth, Stephanie, Lydia and Amelia."

Lydia joined the procession of girls filing to the front. She took her letter, but did not look at it until she returned to her seat.

"Who is it from?" Joan whispered.

Oh, thank heavens!

"My sister—and you?" She elbowed Amelia.

"My friend Frances, in town." She cracked the seal.

"Those of you without a letter, come around my desk to read from Fordyce whilst the others read their letters."

Lydia bit her lip and opened the missive. Surely there would be something she could share from the letter.

Dear Lydia,

I am pleased to receive your letter.

You asked after our parents. As of her last letter, Mama, Papa, and Kitty were doing well in London. Discussions continue concerning Papa's new patron, but I do not believe any agreements have been reached. Mr. Darcy has refused all requests to intercede on Papa's behalf.

Mama says their house is not so comfortable as the one in Kent, and the Darcys denied them the use of their townhouse. She is most put out over that.

Lizzy invited Kitty to remove to Pemberley with them, but Mama insisted she stay in London—not enough society in the wilds of Derbyshire. Kitty enjoys the broader society in London, though it is a great deal different from the balls and parties every night that she expected. As I understand, some talk of 'events' has unfavorably impacted the invitations she receives.

Mary was always delicate and most politic in what she said, but a gloved slap to the face was still that. She could skip reading that bit aloud.

To answer your question, Col. Fitzwilliam has moved into Rosings Park now that he is master there. Mr. Darcy has been here to assist him several times. He assures me Lizzy is well, and if the expression on his face is any indication, they are quite well matched.

Lady Catherine has not recovered from her daughter's death. Mrs. Collins and I call upon her regularly, but little seems to lift her spirits. She has not hosted a dinner, tea, or even a card party since you left.

Mr. Michaels is much in London to deal with estate matters, so my own wedding has been postponed. I am a bit disappointed, but I am content to wait as necessary. It will all work out soon enough.

While I have little to do with ledgers and accounts right now, Mrs. Collins does include me in her planning. Her garden is still full of toads, especially the pea patch. That seems to be a favorite spot for them.

We just finished putting up vegetables for the winter, though no peas were among them. If you are interested, I would be happy to send you Mrs. Collins receipt to preserve peas.

The drawing you sent is quite lovely. The gazebo reminds me of a small one near the stream at Rosings. I had no idea you could draw so well. Perhaps in your next letter you might include a picture of your school or your room.

Those passages she might safely share. She took her pencil and underlined those bits that were best left private.

Amelia sniffled and rubbed her eyes with the back of her hand.

"Have you received bad news?"

"No … no …" She folded the letter clumsily. "It is only that I miss my friend and all the merry times we had together."

The knot of girls at the front returned to their places.

"Miss Long, rise and share your letter with us." Miss Honeywell said.

Helen Long was by far the tallest girl in the school. She moved like a willow in the wind, effortlessly graceful in everything. Were it not for her high, squeaky, little girl's voice, she would have been the envy of every girl in the school.

"It is from my aunt. She writes … It is so pleasant to hear from you, dear …"

And so dull.

Lydia clenched her hands open and closed under the desk. Why could people not write more interesting letters?

Miss Long sat back down. Miss Fitzgilbert stood and shared news of an impending visit from her eldest brother and his wife. They had news, most vital news, to be shared with her, and it could only be shared in person.

Why did she look so very troubled? Perhaps she disliked her brother, or his wife.

Miss Honeywell stopped her before she finished. "Mrs. Drummond should be informed of this news. Go to her office now."

Lydia's stomach made an arsey-varsey plunge through her chest. Though Miss Fitzgilbert was clearly not in any sort of trouble, the prospect of being sent to Mrs. Drummond's office still seemed quite awful.

"Amelia, you may share your letter."

"My friend writes: we all miss you so very much since you are gone away to school. The very light has gone out among us without your company, but we muddle on the best we can without you."

Miss Honeywell turned toward the window and rolled her eyes. How rude! She was the one who demanded they read from their letters.

"I am at sixes and sevens over the upcoming ball you know. My dress should arrive from the modiste tomorrow. I took your advice and chose the white silk. You were right; it is the most elegant fabric for a gown. The details are utterly delicious and I know you must approve …"

As Amelia described the gown, Lydia sketched it in the margin of Mary's letter.

Either the dress was a truly awful amalgam of awkward trims and design, or Frances could not properly describe a gown. No modiste would permit such a monstrosity to leave the shop.

"Thank you, Amelia. You have delighted us long enough. Lydia, you will share with us now."

Compared to Amelia's, Mary's letter was frightfully dull. But there was little to be done for it. She rose and read as quickly as possible without earning Miss Honeywell's rebuke.

After lessons, Miss Honeywell dismissed them to their sewing. The best light and the best company gathered in the parlor.

"That was a very nice letter you had from your sister." Juliana held up her sewing in the cheery sunlight.

It was a simple baby dress, probably for her own babe to soon wear.

Lydia stabbed her finger. "Botheration! I do not like to sew."

She sucked off a drop of blood. Bloodstained work would never pass Miss Honeywell's inspection.

"None of us do," Joan muttered, "But it is our lot, I suppose."

"When I leave this place, I shall never sew again." Amelia dropped the boys' shirt she hemmed and crossed her arms over her chest.

"Somehow I doubt that." Miss Fitzgilbert squinted at her whitework.

She really was quite good at it.

"Why must you always be so disagreeable?" Amelia harrumphed. "Perhaps you are willing to settle for a poor man or a life working your fingers to the bone. I shall have a rich man and servants to manage such things."

"I hardly see rich men knocking on the door for the likes of us." Miss Greenville shared a glance with Miss Fitzgilbert.

"The only man we have spoken to in months is Mr. Amberson. He is so odd and plain, and hardly rich." Miss Long sniffed.

Odd? Mr. Amberson was not odd. He was very nice and even pleasant looking, once one became accustomed to him. Why would anyone think him plain?

"Well, some of us still have friends and connections outside this dreadful asylum." Amelia turned her shoulder to them.

"There is no need to fuss at us because you are unhappy. It is not our fault."

Miss Fitzgilbert would make an excellent grumpy governess.

"Perhaps you should go elsewhere if my company so offends you."

"Perhaps you should find company who better appreciates your complaining. The light here is best for sewing. I shall not permit you to deprive me of it."

Amelia balled her fists. "Who do you think you are? Lording over us with your high and mighty attitude—you know that is what we call you—Miss High-and-Mighty. We all hate you."

"Then why do you not leave?"

"I will." Amelia threw down her sewing and stalked out, Joan following in her shadow.

Lydia set aside her sewing.

"Pray, stay with us," Juliana whispered. "She is in such high dudgeon. I do not think she will be very nice to you."

Amelia was rather horrid when she was in a temper.

"Your sister's letter mentioned an estate—Rosings Park was it? Is it a very grand place?" Juliana asked.

It would not hurt to stay a few minutes more and give Amelia a chance to finish railing.

Lydia picked up her needlework. "The house was very large and fine. Lady Catherine invited my parents and elder sisters every week, but I only saw it a few times. Lady Catherine frightened me. She knew everything about everything and wanted her share of every conversation. Her butler looked like a giant troll."

Juliana chuckled. "I cannot believe he was so bad, not if a lady hired him."

"Truly, he was fearsome! Long Tom he was called for he was so tall."

"Taller than Mr. Amberson?" Miss Long asked.

"By a hand span at least, and I am sure his face would crack if he ever smiled."

The girls giggled, even Miss Fitzgilbert.

"The midwife—I saw her come visit today. What did she say?" Miss Fitzgilbert asked.

"That I needed to be bled. I am so dreadful tired of being stuck and bleeding into her bowl. It makes me so lightheaded and so tired." She stroked her belly. "She believes the baby will come before the new moon, and thinks it will be a boy."

"That is excellent news. I do so hope she is right for then you could stay on at the school with us," Miss Fitzgilbert said.

"And he would have a proper family. That is the best thing." Juliana's voice thinned and broke into tiny sharp shards. "You said your brother and sister would visit soon. Are you much excited?"

"Truthfully, I do not know how to feel."

"I would dread my brother, Darcy, and Lizzy coming, even though I long for company."

"My brother and sister have never visited before. I dread the news they might bring. It must be something very horrible indeed. Who is reluctant to put good news in a letter?"

"When will they come?" Miss Greenville asked.

"The day after tomorrow, or possibly the next, depending on the vagaries of the weather."

"At least you will not have to wait very long." Juliana did not look up from her sewing.

"Waiting is awful, is it not?" Miss Long nodded vigorously.

"I am very bad at it—or so my sisters would tell me." Lydia chewed her lip.

Not just her sisters, Papa and Mama scolded her for it often.

"No, what you are very bad at is being at places on time. You are forever distracted by some drawing or piece of music." Juliana peeked up.

If Mama or any of her sisters would have said such a thing she would have reeled from the rebuke, but from soft, round, duckling-Juliana it felt more a friendly tease.

The other girls laughed, a warm embracing sort of sound.

Was this what Jane meant when she talked of laughing with someone, not at them?

"Oh gracious! The distraction must be contagious! Look at the time. We need to get ready for dinner." Miss Fitzgilbert folded her sewing.

The others followed suit with much giggling and the work baskets were tucked back on the shelf.

Lydia was the last to leave the parlor. Before she reached the stairs, Joan and Amelia stopped her.

"So did she tell you about her brother's visit?" Amelia grabbed her hand.

"We are just wild to know."

"No, not really. Only that she expected bad news. Oh, and that she expected the call the day after to-morrow or the next."

"I wonder what the news could be." Amelia's eyes grew wide and her mouth widened into something that might be called a smile had her narrowed eyes not hinted something far darker. "Perhaps her father is cutting her off, and she is being sent to a poor rela-tion."

"Or a position has been found for her as a gover-ness for nine horrid children."

"Or a companion for a cruel spinster who will beat her with a birch." Amelia snickered behind her hand.

"Or a teacher in a remote girls' school run by a woman worse than the old lady."

"Or maybe work as shop assistant or in a chop house."

"That's horrible!"

"Oh, do not be such a killjoy. What is wrong with speculating satisfying fates for her? We know you do not like her any better than we do." Joan glowered.

"We simply must find out what it is. I shall surely go mad if I do not know." Amelia dug her fingers into Lydia's arm.

"We will find out readily enough. There are few secrets here." Lydia pulled her arms free and edged back toward the stairs.

"She will not tell us anything. She can be full stubborn, you know. I have a much better idea." Amelia looked at Joan.

"Oh, yes, that is a splendid idea."

Amelia grabbed her hand. "We will show you."

They dragged her down the front hall to a dark side passage and pointed to a dusty door.

"So? That is the store room. What of it?"

Joan opened the door and pushed Lydia inside.

"What are you doing?" Lydia struggled for the door.

Amelia held her fast. "Just wait a moment. Let your eyes become accustomed to the dark."

"What good that will do?"

"Just a moment."

Someone shoved her to the right.

Joan leaned close and whispered in her ear. "Look closely—you see slivers of light?"

"I do."

"Get closer, look through."

"The drawing room?"

"Exactly. She will take her guests into the drawing room and from here we might see everything," Amelia said.

"There will be no secret-keeping from us." Joan tittered.

"It does not seem right to listen in on a conversation—"

Amelia snorted. "Gah! You are the youngest in your family. Can you tell me you never did such a thing?"

"No one tells the youngest daughter anything," Joan said.

"I expect you were most adept at it."

"Especially when it might get your elder sisters in trouble."

"How would you know anything?" Lydia stomped.

"Oh do not be so self-righteous, dear. It is the way of families everywhere." Joan's face wrinkled into a shadowy sneer. "Tell me it was any different for you."

But it was, surely it was. Papa never answered her questions, and Mama deemed her too silly to understand and too pretty to care. Surely that made it different.

"You see, I am right," Joan said.

"Then it is settled. We will watch for Miss Fitzgilbert's guests to arrive, and meet here and learn what delicious secrets she is trying to hide from us all." Amelia rubbed her hands together.

"Indeed we shall. You as well, Lydia."

"Oh, very well, but we must hurry and get ready for dinner. I … I do not relish missing it."

"Oh, you are right. The old lady is such a cross-patch about such things." Joan opened the door.

Joan was right. Eavesdropping was the way of things at home. There was little enough harm from it. Lydia hurried upstairs and got ready, lest she prove Juliana's pronouncement on her timeliness correct again.

❧Chapter 7

TWO DAYS LATER, Lydia dragged herself to the morning room for breakfast. Juliana had kept her up much of the night suffering a headache so severe she cast up her accounts on no less than three occasions.

Through the wee hours, Lydia fetched water and towels for Mrs. Drummond, ending the night more exhausted than she began. Perhaps, she should have slept on the settee in Mrs. Drummond's office after all.

Some tea and toast might clear the fog in her head.

She reached for the jam pot.

Miss Thornton burst in with a note arrived for Miss Fitzgilbert. She dashed out, ashen and shaking, Miss Thornton on her heels.

Lydia sipped her tea. Perchance, if she petitioned Mrs. Drummond politely, she might be given permission to take a nap.

"Are you going to come with us?" Joan poked her shoulder.

Lydia jumped.

"I told you she was wool gathering." Amelia tossed her head in a superior gesture reminiscent of Miss de Bourgh. "We are going to take a turn about the garden before the weather changes."

"What weather?"

"You mutton head!" Joan flicked her hand. "Just look outside. You can see the clouds. If you want fresh air, best get it now. We may end up shut up in the house for several days."

"Go on without me."

"Suit yourself." Amelia leaned in closer to whisper, "Come find us if you see anyone arrive."

Lydia flashed a shallow smile and ran her hands over her shoulders.

There was a nip in the air. How had she forgotten her shawl?

She wandered upstairs. Mrs. Drummond had warned her against disturbing Juliana. She retrieved her shawl on tiptoes, Juliana none the wiser.

The music room was empty and she found herself inside, playing through a minor scale. Too dull and plodding, a different pattern and rhythm might help.

Yes, that fit the darkening sky and distant thunder.

It sounded a bit like the tune she sang with Widow Randall. She closed her eyes and played several lines. Best she write those down before she forgot. She rose and headed for the little cabinet where the paper was kept.

"Oh, sir! When did you—"

Mr. Amberson towered over her, his eyes crinkled at the corners. A dear little crease knotted his brows though the set of his lips and jaw remained quite serious.

"Not very long ago. I heard scales and had to see who was practicing."

"Was I doing them wrong?"

"Not at all, Miss Bennet. You did them very well." He strode across the room, with steps so impossibly long it seemed he would surely come off balance, and laid his hand on the pianoforte.

His fingers were long and graceful. When he played, really played, not just demonstrated, in the evenings, they flowed over the keyboard like river water over stones, effortless and lively or stormy and turbulent. He spoke volumes through them without ever voicing a word.

"Miss Bennet?"

She jumped. "Pray excuse me."

"What distracted you?"

She stammered and sputtered and looked away. "Your hands, sir."

He held them up and turned them back and forward. "I have not failed to wash them, have I?"

"No, I—I was just noticing them."

Would he be very much displeased?

A tiny dimple appeared in his cheek. "What were you noticing about them, if I may ask?"

"They are … more expressive than many people's faces."

Crimson crept up his neck and along his jaw.

"May I draw them?"

"I would be most honored." He bowed from his shoulders. "I should like to see it when you have finished, though."

"Of course."

Oh, the way he looked at her! His eyes spoke almost as much as his hands.

A shriek from the garden pierced the air. They dashed to the window.

Joan and Amelia stared and pointed at the heather, chattering wildly and ran for the house.

"Do you think?" Lydia sniggered.

"Shall we go and find out?" He gestured toward the door.

Joan and Amelia caught them in the front hall.

"Sir! Sir!" Joan panted.

"There is something in the garden!" Amelia flapped her hands near her face.

"What did you see?" He tapped his chin with his knuckle.

"I am not sure …" Joan looked over her shoulder.

"But it had eyes …"

"And horrible large teeth …"

"And a tail."

"It sounds rather like a rat." He stroked his chin.

How did he manage so grave an expression? Pray let him not look at her lest she lose control and laugh out loud.

"I do not know, but it was big …" Joan held out open hands and stretched them wide.

"Huge."

"Perhaps then, I should look for it. If it proves to be a rat, we might borrow the butcher's dog to deal with it. Have you any talent for spotting rats, Miss Bennet?" His eyebrows climbed just so.

No, she must not laugh now.

"I might be able to help. We had trouble with them when we lived in London."

"You do not want to go out there." Joan reached for Lydia's arm.

She sidled just out of reach.

"Do not be so silly. La! Rats are unpleasant to be sure, but not worth such a fuss." She headed toward the back door.

Only Mr. Amberson followed.

He closed the back door, and she leaned back against it, giggling.

"Do not be so hard on them. Would you be so calm if you thought a giant rat had taken up residence in the heather?"

If he was attempting to look stern, he was failing.

"I was not joking about the rats in London, sir. I remember the beady little eyes very well. We found them, around the garden, in the larders and, occasionally, even in my room at night. They made a fearsome racket. Papa borrowed an ill-tempered terrier to manage the problem."

He licked his lips, and his eyes crinkled. "Very well then, my brave Miss Bennet, lead the way."

She curtsied and pulled her shawl a little tighter over her shoulders.

Gracious, the air had turned chilly.

He took one step for every two of hers. Another gust of damp wind raced through the yard, whipping the heather to a frenzy.

"Oh, look!"

"He is still on duty." He saluted. "Well done, Mr. Birch. Excellent execution of your duties."

"What shall we tell Joan and Amelia?"

He gestured toward the path ahead, and they walked on.

"I could tell them we saw no sign of a rat—which would be utterly true. Or, we might say we saw something and will bring by the butcher's dog as soon as he may be arranged. Equally true, but a mite less forthright. What think you?"

She rubbed her knuckles over her lips. "The second option is certainly more fun, is it not?"

His expression shifted subtly, intensified and darkened. "There is something else on your mind and you are not telling me. I hear a note in your voice."

She inched back. "No, it is nothing."

"Do not argue with a musician over what he hears. I may be all awkwardness and uncertainty over many things, but of my ear, I am entirely sure."

"You sound like my sister, Lizzy She is always certain of what she observes."

And almost never wrong.

How nice it would be to be so clever.

"I do not profess to that level of expertise. My assurance is solely upon my ear."

"You should have confidence in far more than that."

"Ah, now you flatter me. With your eye, you can hardly ignore I have all the grace and figure of a grasshopper." He gestured to the length of his leg with a theatrical flourish.

She snickered.

"And yes, I give you permission to depict me as such. I should be quite amused by it, as Miss Morley was by her duck—which portrayed her quite sweetly."

"She showed you?"

"Indeed she did and proudly, too."

"She asked me to draw another that she has since pinned up above her bed."

"I am pleased you see the difference between toads and ducklings." His eyes sparkled.

Wickham's eyes did that too, but not when he looked at her.

"Joan tried to draw Miss Honeywell as a pudgy little porker. I did not think it a good drawing at all. She wanted me to help her with it, but I thought Miss Honeywell would take offense."

"I imagine you are correct." He cocked his head and lifted an eyebrow. "You are quite adept at changing the subject. I am not as forgetful as one might expect. I still maintain, you seemed troubled."

She clutched the ends of her shawl, breath constricted as though a trap closed around her.

Lizzy made her feel the same way when she observed too much.

"Forgive me for making you uneasy, but it is difficult to see you so uncomfortable. Pray, tell me."

"It is nothing, sir."

"Every time your friends Miss Easton and Miss Colbrane come up in conversation, I hear the same ill-at-ease note rise in your voice."

Oh, he was far too much like Lizzy!

"I do not like it when they are unhappy with me."

"They are unhappy with you often?"

"Oh look! A carriage—do you think that is—"

"They are unhappy with you often?" He stopped mid-step and looked down at her.

It would have made her feel very small, the way Papa did, except for the way his fingertips touched hers, just barely, but enough to promise he was not angry.

How did one keep a secret from such eyes?

"Amelia has lost so much being here, perhaps more than any of us. One cannot blame her fits of pique, I suppose."

"I think your perception generous."

She kicked up a clod of dirt. "She and Joan have been very kind to me."

"Have they? It would seem to me you put up with a great deal to call them friends."

"It is a hard thing to come to a place you do not know, among people who are quite formidable."

"Am I so formidable?"

His eyes were truly astonishing and left her heart fluttering like the heather in the wind.

"No, not so much."

He leaned a little closer. "I should hope that you might consider me among your friends."

"Mr. Amberson!" Mrs. Drummond called from the back door. "Pray, come immediately. I have need of your assistance!"

He nodded curtly and dashed away.

Lydia wandered toward the house. High screechy voices filtered out.

Joan and Amelia? Had Mrs. Drummond discovered their hiding place?

It was a good thing Papa had forbidden his daughters to swoon.

She ran the rest of the way to the house and crept along the wall to the half-open window of Mrs. Drummond's office, stopping half an arm's length from the window.

If she held her breath and stood very still, she might make out the conversation.

"Yes, yes, escort them in here," Mrs. Drummond ordered.

"You need not be so rough!" Amelia screeched.

"Let go!" Joan cried.

"No, no, Mr. Amberson, I require you to stay."

No! He was part of this? He would be so angry with her, if he knew.

His voice faded into dull rumbles, obscuring the individual words.

"Very well, remain just outside the door, but do not leave. I may require you again."

More mumbles and a door closed.

"Explain to me, Miss Easton, what you and Miss Colbrane were doing in the storage room?"

"We were fetching something for Miss Thornton, missus." Amelia probably wore that insincere innocent expression she used to fool Miss Honeywell.

"And what precisely was the item you sought?"

"She wanted a book from a trunk." Joan was certainly trying to imitate Amelia's expression, and failing.

She never quite managed it convincingly.

"Which trunk and which book? You do not recall? Perhaps, Miss Colbrane, you might enlighten me? No? And, of course, you were unaware of how you might be able to see into the drawing room and eavesdrop from there."

"We have not told you the truth, madam," Amelia's voice was very small and almost contrite. "We were only trying to spare Lydia from your displeasure."

No! How could she?

"What has Miss Bennet to do with you being in the closet, spying?"

"It was Lydia's idea, missus. She said we three should meet there to learn of Miss Fitzgilbert's visitors." Amelia was surely blinking her doe-eyes at Mrs. Drummond, looking as innocent as a spotted fawn.

"She made us promise to join her."

"Yet she was not with you."

"She was there, well hidden, near the wall." Amelia said.

"Shall I send Mr. Amberson to fetch her?"

"No, no, surely she has already escaped."

Several loud steps rang out—Mrs. Drummond's.

"I imagine so. She must be a very clever girl."

"Yes, missus; she is always scheming ways to break the rules without you knowing."

"I see. I shall have to speak to her then."

Lydia's knees buckled, and she pressed hard against the wall lest she fall.

"It will be most instructive to learn how she has managed to be in two places at the same time. I found her in the garden whilst you both were in hiding."

"But it was her idea." Joan stomped.

"Then she is exceptionally clever to implicate you whilst remaining safe from all impropriety."

"Indeed, missus. She is wicked clever, far more than anyone knows."

"I am not as simple as you seem to believe."

Something creaked and squealed. Hinges?

"No! Pray, missus, no!"

"It was not our fault!"

"You are well aware of my policy regarding dishonesty."

"But we have not—"

"Another word, Miss Easton, shall double your penalty. You shall be first. I believe you know the procedure."

Lydia dashed away, nearly tripping over her own feet.

How horrid, how absolutely dreadful.

But they had tried to blame everything on her! How could they do that?

Lightening flashed and thunder rumbled on the horizon. The rain would not hold off much longer.

Best get inside.

She dabbed her eyes with her shawl.

The front door swung open and a well-dressed couple emerged. They wore matching expressions of disdain, much like Lady Catherine's when she lectured those beneath her.

What news had they brought Miss Fitzgilbert?

Perhaps, it was best she not know.

Fat wet drops splashed on her face, and she slipped inside.

Distressed voices and cries assailed her. Hinges squeaked, and the voices grew louder. They were coming toward her.

No, she could not see them now.

She raced down the hall and ducked into the closest room. The door softly clicked behind her as she sagged against it.

"What do you want?"

No! How had she ended up in the drawing room?

Miss Fitzgilbert glared at her from the settee, face tear streaked, a handkerchief wadded up in her hands.

"I did not mean to come in here! I am sorry."

"Then why are you here?"

"Joan and Amelia … Mrs. Drummond is angry. I did not want them to—"

Miss Fitzgilbert sniffled. "I suppose this was the nearest place for you to hide."

How did she know about Joan and Amelia? Had she heard them through the walls?

"I did not mean to intrude upon you."

"It is just as well. I am sure everyone will be wild to know what news my visitors have brought."

"I will leave. I am quite sure you do not wish for my company."

"What does it matter, yours, or anyone else's? It changes nothing." Miss Fitzgilbert rose and paced along the fireplace. "Perchance I want to share it with someone, anyone. Keeping it all inside, I might just burst."

A flash of lightening brightened the dim room.

"Should you not tell Mrs. Drummond? Maybe Miss Thornton? You like her very well." Lydia clutched the doorknob as thunder rattled the windows.

"They will only tell me how fortunate I am and I do not want to hear it." She pumped her fists at her sides. "I want someone to understand how miserable I am and feel sorry for me."

"Miss Greenville, then? Miss Long? Juliana?"

"Just go then. You hate me anyway. Why would you want to listen? I expect you would rejoice in my fate."

"I do not hate you. And if your fate is even half as hard as being here, then I surely cannot rejoice in it."

Miss Fitzgilbert sniffled and blotted her nose. "Do you wonder what my brother came to tell me?"

"Everyone does."

"He brought word from my father. He is a peer. By all rights, I am the Lady Annabelle—how fine that sounds. You should address me that way, you know."

"Pray, do not speak of it. Mrs. Drummond would be ever so cross."

What would it be to her to cane another girl today?

"I do not care. It does not matter anyway. My father says I remain unwelcome in his home and may never return there in my current state."

"That is dreadful news."

"My mother still has not recovered from what I have done. She cannot speak my name, much less write to me."

Mama had not written to her either.

"But my brother brings good news, you see. A solution to all my problems. Something that will set everything to rights. Something that will permit my father to admit me once again, that will restore my mother's heart and my respectability." Miss Fitzgilbert pressed her hand to her chest.

"Does it not please you?"

"I am an ungrateful wretch. I know. My brother's wife has already told me so."

"I did not say that."

"Did you not wonder why I am so miserable? Why I would so desire to throw such an opportunity away?"

Thunder rumbled in the distance and a flurry of raindrops pelted the windows.

Would that she would stop talking!

"They have found someone to marry me."

"Married? Is that not a lovely thing?"

"My brother and sister insist it is. But I think it horrid, absolutely horrid. I have worked so hard, repented of my ways. I am proper and trustworthy and respectful, and it does not matter!" She stamped and shook her fists. "None of it matters!"

"But you are to marry. Is that not reward for your improvement?"

"He is so old. Nearly my father's age. A knight and perfectly respectable, to be sure. Sir Anthony, a widower twice over now, having heirs and spares nearly my age. He has finished mourning and wants to return to society with a pretty decoration on his arm and a new hostess in his house." She bowed with a deep flourish.

"You do not like him?"

"I do not even know him. But I know I do not want to marry a man nearly twice my age that I have not even met. I am sure I will never like him, much less love him." She sank onto a nearby ottoman, face in her hands. "I … I wanted to be worthy of love."

But she was so good and everyone admired her, how was it possible—

"So there you have it—my dreadful fate. Make fun, laugh at me, and enjoy it all at my expense."

Lydia stepped closer. "It is a cruel fate, and I cannot laugh at it."

"Truly?"

"What will you do?"

"What I must. I have seen too clearly what awaits me if I refuse. My father will cut me off, and I would have little choice but to seek a position. I do not want to serve some great house as a governess who is expected to tend the children by day and the master by night."

Could that be why Mama had steadfastly refused to hire a governess?

"At least this way, I will be mistress of a home and respectable."

"But never to have love—"

"You understand!" She sprang up like a fox looking to escape the hounds.

"I think many among us would."

"But Mrs. Drummond and the teachers would scold me for my ingratitude if they knew. They will insist I rejoice in my good fortune and be an example for the others. I cannot speak of this, not to another soul." She crossed the room in long, desperate strides and clutched Lydia's hands. "Pray, do not tell—"

"I will not speak of it, I promise."

Miss Fitzgilbert loosened her grip on Lydia's arm. "I am to meet him in a se'nnight's time. He will call upon me here."

"Then what?"

"I do not know. I am so scared. We will need a chaperone for our meeting. Pray, sit with me when he comes?"

"Would not Mrs. Drummond be more appropriate?"

"I should rather have someone who knows how I feel, even if there is nothing I can do about it. Pray, do this for me."

"Perhaps it will not be so bad. Our friend Mrs. Collins married a man she did not really like. She is now very content—and much loved by the parish. "

"Then you will?"

"If Mrs. Drummond permits me."

Miss Fitzgilbert dried her eyes. "I will ask her now."

Lydia stared after her and dragged her hands down her face. Surely Mrs. Drummond would never agree.

She wandered upstairs. Dark storm clouds stole away the light needed to sew, but she might be able to draw, or play pianoforte—anything so she did not have to talk to anyone else.

A hand grabbed her elbow and pulled her inside a room.

She shrieked.

"Stop it you goose cap." Amelia closed the door with her shoulder.

"You could simply have invited me in."

"We don't want to be seen or heard." Joan lay on her stomach across the bed. "We do not relish anyone taking pleasure in our misery."

"We know you will not, our dear friend." Amelia pulled her further in.

Lightening flashed and briefly lit the dim room with its eerie blue-white glow.

How piteous their faces appeared in that light.

Thunder crashed and sheets of rain assailed the window.

"You are so lucky that you were not with us when the old lady found us."

"Did you and Mr. Amberson—" Amelia accented his name so oddly. "Find any rats in the garden?"

"No, we looked all over, but only found some shiny pebbles that might be mistaken for their bright, beady eyes. I think he means to borrow the butcher's dog in any case."

"Naturally, Missus will not pay for a proper rat catcher. Horrid old miser." Amelia threw herself on the bed beside Joan. "Her bloody cane, it feels like fire itself. I swear I thought she might draw blood with it."

"Surely not!"

"I dare say she would have, if Mr. Amberson had not stopped her." Joan propped her chin on her fists.

"He was my rescuer." Amelia batted her eyes. "You see what she did to me." She hiked up her skirts to reveal several deep red and purple wheals across the back of her thighs.

Lydia gulped and clutched the bed post.

"She mistreated us so." Amelia flipped her skirts down.

"And for what? We saw nothing for we were dragged away even before Miss Fitzgilbert's guests were announced."

"If not for Mr. Amberson, I do not know what we would have done. He was so gallant, demanding she stop her brutality and release us. He shepherded us out and—" Amelia knelt on the bed, "—said he thought her quite heartless."

"He promised he would never allow us to face the old lady's cruelty again."

"Is he not a saint?" Amelia slid her feet to the floor. "No wonder you like him so well."

"You think yourself so sly." Joan waggled her eyebrows. "Extra lessons with him, showing him your drawings. We know what you are about."

"He is the old lady's nephew. What better way to garner her favor than to get his?" Joan winked.

"That is ridiculous!"

"There is no shame in admitting the truth. Or do you actually like him?" Amelia leaned in close.

The coy look on her face begged to be slapped off.

"Oh, you do!" Joan covered her mouth and giggled.

"You are jealous of our rescue."

"Stop it!" Lydia stomped toward the door.

"Oh, we have hit a sore point, have we not? You do not like to be teased." Amelia grabbed her elbow.

"You do not need to be that way. We are only playing."

"I do not like it."

"Very well, we shall stop. Do take pity upon us and tell us what you learned of Miss Fitzgilbert's visitors." Amelia pulled her back toward the bed.

"Nothing, I know nothing about them."

"Do not keep secrets from us." Joan pouted. "After all, we have told you everything."

"And, we did not tell Missus about how you were supposed to be with us."

Hardly!

"I do not know anything."

"The maid said you were in the drawing room with her. How could that be?" Joan rose up on her knees.

"I went in by mistake after her guests were gone."

"By mistake? How could you possibly barge in by mistake?" Joan slapped the counterpane.

"Because I am stupid. I heard Mrs. Drummond coming down the hall, and I hid."

"So what did she tell you?" Amelia asked.

"To get out."

"What else?" Joan climbed off the bed and stood with them.

"She was upset she would not be returning to her father's house." Lydia edged back.

Amelia snorted. "And Miss High-and-Mighty made such a fuss over that? She is such a spoiled little chit. Oh, I hate her!"

"She pretended to have such a great secret!" Joan tossed her head. "Now I am truly miserable."

"You are certain there is no bit of sweet gossip to share?" Amelia batted her eyes.

Did she know how ridiculous she looked when she did that?

"The most interesting thing today is that there is no rat in the garden."

Amelia harrumphed. "Perhaps you will bring us some food? I am quite famished."

"Oh, be a dear and do. We missed luncheon you know."

"Or do you not care about us?"

"After all we did for you, not telling Mrs. Drummond you were to have been with us." Joan said.

Yes, they had done her such great favors there.

"I will see if it is possible. Do not blame me if I cannot, though."

"Try very hard for us." Amelia turned her doe-eyes on Lydia.

That was a great deal to ask of her, all things considered.

She slipped out and strode toward the schoolroom.

It was too much. Missing a meal would not kill them.

Chapter 8

A WEEK LATER, Mrs. Drummond called Lydia to her office after they returned from visiting the alms houses. Joan and Amelia gasped and giggled.

Horrid cows! How could they laugh at her plight?

"Yes, madam." Lydia followed her down the hall.

How did anyone maintain an office with nothing on the desk and not an item out of place? Papa's desk at home was always littered with papers of some sort, and Mr. Gardiner's was positively covered with clutter.

"Sit down." Mrs. Drummond gestured toward a chair and sat behind her desk.

"Is there a problem?" Lydia whispered, mouth dry and woolly.

"I would not call it a problem, rather a curiosity."

"I do not understand."

"Nor do I." She drummed her fingers along the

polished desk top. "Miss Fitzgilbert has presented me with a singular request. She tells me she wants you to chaperone her with her caller tomorrow."

"She asked me, but I told her it would be better that you or Miss Thornton did it."

Mrs. Drummond sat back. "You have not persuaded her—"

"I do not know how to chaperone. No one has ever asked me to do such a thing. Far better that I not sit with her. I tried to tell her that, truly, I did."

"She told me you agreed."

"I did, but only because she was so distressed. Pray, do not be angry with me." She scanned the room.

Oh, that must be the squeaky cabinet where she kept her cane!

"Calm down, you silly girl. I did not call you here to punish you."

She released her grip on the chair's arms.

When had she begun to clutch them so hard?

"Now, tell me. Why do you think she asked you? You have never been her particular friend."

"I suppose it is that I came across her when she was very upset. She may have found something I said comforting."

Mrs. Drummond raised her eyebrow and chewed her lower lip. "You grasp the gravity of the situation? I have no doubt she will behave modestly. But it is imperative she not do anything foolish. I well understand her feelings in the matter, or at least I suppose I do."

Lydia squeezed her eyes shut and twitched a tiny nod.

Mrs. Drummond grunted. "She must not do anything foolish."

"I do not think she will."

"Are you equipped to help her if she falters?"

"I know this may be her only chance to escape a life of service."

"Are you trustworthy with such an important task?"

"No one has ever trusted me with anything of value." Lydia stared at her hands. "They were probably right not to."

Mrs. Drummond peered at her with the same sort of look Lizzy wore when trying to make a decision.

"Perhaps they were right at that time, but," she scratched her chin, "I believe you understand what is at stake. Since Miss Fitzgilbert expressed her desire to me most violently, I am prepared to grant her request, assuming you are still willing. Or have you changed your mind?"

"Are you certain it should not be you?"

"If you do not feel you can commit to what is required, I shall do it, but I believe it will be better for her if you will perform the office."

How odd—and nice those words felt. "Yes, madam, I will."

"Very good then. The call is to be at two in the afternoon tomorrow. You will be released from charitable visits for the occasion. You are excused."

Lydia rose and dropped into a curtsy, knees so weak she almost did not rise.

Mrs. Drummond walked her to the door and opened it squarely into Mr. Amberson.

"James … Mr. Amberson, what are you doing here?"

"Have you a moment?" he asked, but gazed at

Lydia.

Mrs. Drummond beckoned him in and shut the door.

What a horrid mess!

She covered her face with her hands and rolled her head against the wall.

Everyone would know when she chaperoned Miss Fitzgilbert and her guest. Joan and Amelia would demand delicious bits of gossip. They would hate her if she said nothing. But what could she say?

Low rumbles filtered through the wall—Mr. Amberson's voice. The words garbled into something indecipherable.

"James, I think it very ill-advised. You fully comprehend the situation?" Mrs. Drummond's voice came through much more clearly.

More rumbling, reminiscent of the piece he had recently played for her, determined, forceful, intentional.

"You realize the implication of such a move—what it may cost you?"

Move? Did he plan to leave the school?

No, no, he could not do that. Who would teach her music? Who would look at her drawings? Who here might understand her? No, it was not fair!

She dashed outside to the garden. Only Mr. Birch could be trusted with her discontent.

The next day after breakfast, Mrs. Drummond directed the students to the kitchen. Cook had baskets prepared for them to bring to the women and children in gaol.

"Where is your basket?" Amelia's voice had that scathing edge she used when someone else tried to take advantage.

"Mrs. Drummond requires I stay behind and help Juliana with her chores," Lydia whispered.

Hopefully no one else would notice.

"How did you become such a favorite? I hate going to the gaol." Joan rifled through her basket.

"Oh, do not be such a fuss." Amelia peeked over Joan's shoulder.

"Well I do. It is so dismal."

"Not as dismal as having to do all the heavy work for Juliana."

"Come along, girls." Miss Thornton ushered them out.

Miss Fitzgilbert entered on her heels. What joy was theirs. The drawing room, with all its fussy corners and delicate garniture, needed to be cleaned.

Cook grunted and pointed at the pantry.

Lydia tucked a pile of dust clothes and flannels under her arm and grabbed the duster and brooms. Cook handed Miss Fitzgilbert the crock of used tea leaves and the dustpan.

Juliana met them in the drawing room. "Mrs. Drummond said the windows need no cleaning today."

"That is something to be thankful for," Miss Fitzgilbert tucked a stray lock behind her ear.

Juliana waddled toward a pair of chairs and took up the nearest one. Lydia dashed to her side and shouldered her away.

"There will be sufficient excitement without another call to the midwife. I will move the furniture."

"She is right. Best you sit at the writing desk and

let us bring you bric-a-brac for dusting." Miss Fitzgilbert pointed to the desk near the window.

"That is not fair to you."

Miss Fitzgilbert gave Juliana a little shove. "I do not need one more thing to agitate my poor nerves. Besides, I hate dusting fiddly things. It makes me sneeze."

Juliana picked up a vase and cleaning rags but graciously submitted. Lydia and Miss Fitzgilbert moved the small furniture to the center of the room and rolled up the hearth rug. They dragged it into the hall.

"I am almost disappointed that the maid will be beating the rug." Miss Fitzgilbert sniggered under her breath.

"You would rather do the chore yourself?"

"Not usually, but today, I think beating something might be very—what is the word Miss Honeywell taught us—cathartic."

"Instead of beating things, would you rather drape the furniture with the dusting clothes or pin up the curtains?" Lydia asked.

"My hands are shaking so! Best leave the pins to you." Miss Fitzgilbert flipped out the folds of a large dusting cloth. "It has been so long since I received a caller. I hardly remember how to conduct myself."

Lydia pinned up the last curtain and sprinkled tea leaves along the sides of the room. "Hurry and cover the last of the furniture so I can begin sweeping. The sooner we finish cleaning, the sooner we can help you dress."

"You must allow Lydia to do your hair as well. She is very good at it," Juliana called over scratchy broom sounds.

"Would you? I shall make a fright of it if I try."

Lydia swept tea leaves and dirt into the dust pan. "If you wish."

Miss Fitzgilbert dragged a chair back into place. "I contemplated just putting a cap on. I am hopeless at doing hair."

Lydia strewed handfuls of damp tea leaves along the center of the room, barely missing the hem of Miss Fitzgilbert's skirt. "It really is not so very difficult. If you merely consider doing your hair like trimming a gown—"

"How easily you say that." Juliana waved her dust cloth at Lydia. "You who can just pick up a pencil and draw any thing you see. I have never known anyone as clever at drawing or painting."

"She is right." Miss Fitzgilbert took the carpet broom from Lydia and swept lightly over the faded carpet. "I cannot wait to see what you are able to do with those watercolors Miss Honeywell gave you."

Lydia picked up several pieces of garniture from Juliana's table and replaced them on the shelves. "I am ever so excited to try them."

"When you do, you must paint something for me. I dare say there is not much room left on your own walls. Mine are so very bare."

Lydia laughed. "Juliana is the one who insists on pinning them all up. Even the dreadful ones."

"There are no dreadful ones. I like them all." Juliana pushed up from her chair and trundled off to replace the last of the bric-a-brac.

"Then you are either a liar or have no eye for beauty—"

"Or she is far too generous to think ill of anyone." Miss Fitzgilbert gathered up the dust cloths from the furniture.

"I am none of those things." Juliana unpinned the nearest curtains and fluffed them as they tumbled to the baseboards. "Rather, I am easy to please."

"Yes, you are a saint. But you still snore." Lydia wrinkled up her nose and laughed.

They returned the cleaning things to the kitchen and headed upstairs.

"How long will you keep your caller a secret?" Juliana asked.

"I would like to become accustomed to the notion of marrying him before facing questions."

"Most will be very happy for you."

"Happy and jealous." Lydia stomped on the squeaky stair. "And there will be some very impertinent remarks, I am sure."

"Joan and Amelia say some very shocking things from time to time." Juliana leaned against the handrail and panted for breath.

"You are far too generous." Miss Fitzgilbert rolled her eyes. "I do not know how you stand them, Lydia. They say horrible things to you."

"I suppose, maybe a little. It does not seem so very bad."

Were they really so objectionable? They had lied to Mrs. Drummond, but only because they were so afraid of her cane. Surely that was understandable.

What they said to her was nothing in comparison to what Papa was apt to say. They never called her names or told her she was stupid.

They really were not so bad.

"And do not go making excuses for them, Juliana. I am entirely unconvinced their remarks might be excused by indigestion or a headache," Miss Fitzgilbert said.

"Oh, but costiveness is responsible for so much ill-humor in young ladies." Lydia peered down her nose the way Papa did when he lectured. "It must be avoided at all costs."

"You do that far too well. You sound like an apothecary trying to sell purges." Miss Fitzgilbert took Juliana's elbow.

"Mr. Lang our old apothecary looked just like a stout little pitcher, pouring out opinions. There is nothing he liked better than a purge, except mayhap a clyster."

They covered their mouths and giggled.

"I do not think Mrs. Drummond would find this a fitting conversation." Juliana looked over her shoulder.

"No, most likely not. Fear not. I will be entirely proper for my caller, but first I must allow my cheek an avenue of escape."

"You are hardly impertinent," Lydia said.

"Yes I am. I have simply grown better at controlling it."

"I am not sure I shall ever learn."

"You do not give yourself enough credit." Juliana patted her arm.

Miss Fitzgilbert nodded vigorously. "You are not half so uppity as I expected you would be when you first arrived."

Lydia flinched. Had she really been so dreadful?

"Oh, I am sorry, that did not come out right at all." Miss Fitzgilbert dropped to the steps and covered her face with her apron. "I am forever saying shocking things. I shall never learn. What a cake I will make of myself to Sir Anthony. Then he will not have me, and my father ..."

Juliana embraced her. "Do not make more of this than there is. We are all friendly and comfortable and speak very freely amongst ourselves. You are always the most proper among us when we are in other company. Dry your eyes now and let us get you upstairs. Lydia must make you beautiful for your suitor."

Chapter 9

HELPING MISS FITZGILBERT proved far more daunting than assisting Jane or Kitty dress. If a young man did not fancy one of her sisters, it was a disappointment. Mama would rail on about it for weeks, but nothing more.

Today, the stakes were so much higher.

Miss Fitzgilbert read them her father's letter. He dictated it to his secretary, not deigning to write the words himself. This was to be her last term at Mrs. Drummond's. Either she marry the suitor he provided, or she find a situation. If the former, she would be admitted to the family circles once again, assuming of course her conduct was beyond reproach. If the latter, she would be dead to them all.

Lydia clutched the hairbrush tightly and tried not to pull Miss Fitzgilbert's hair. Papa said the same thing.

But Mr. Darcy … he promised if Mrs. Drummond declared her improved, he would find a situation for her. But what did improvement look like?

Miss Fitzgilbert? She was everything pretty and proper and dull.

Must she trade imagination for improvement?

"Lydia?" Juliana touched her arm. "Wool gathering again?"

"Just a bit." She tucked another pin into Miss Fitzgilbert's glistening auburn hair. "How do you like it?"

She leaned toward the looking glass and turned to and fro. "I hardly recognize myself. I feel so pretty. I think I can actually face Sir Anthony."

"Then let us help you dress, and you will be certain." Juliana opened the wardrobe and removed a white muslin gown trimmed with the most exquisite lace.

The ethereal fabric flowed like water to the white-worked hem.

"You know, I have only worn this once before. I was surprised I was allowed to keep it when Father sent me away."

"I am glad you did, for it is perfect to meet your knight." Juliana helped her out of her day dress.

"It almost seems too fine for me now." She slipped her arms through the delicate sleeves.

"Not at all," Mrs. Drummond said from the doorway.

When had she arrived?

"It is entirely fitting for the occasion. I would have a few words in private with you now. Lydia, go and put on something pretty as well. You should appear fitting company for Miss Fitzgilbert. Do not be too long at it—Sir Anthony must not be kept waiting."

"I will see she is on time." Juliana hooked her arm in Lydia's and guided her to their room. "Do let me dress you. I know just what you should wear."

Her skin tingled as she peeled off the dark, drab gown and changed it for lovely light sprigged muslin. Light and bright, fit to catch the eye of—

What was she thinking? Sir Anthony must not think her prettier than Miss Fitzgilbert.

She pulled a fichu from the press and tied it over her bodice.

"Perfect." Juliana clapped softly. "Let me fix your cap. It makes me glad to see you so well-looking to-day."

Jane used to say that.

Lydia grabbed Juliana in an awkward embrace and sniffled into her shoulder.

"Do not cry. Your nose will go all red and runny."

They giggled, and the door swung open.

"I am pleased to see you ready. Come downstairs with us now. Juliana, you have been up and about far too much. You must lie down and rest now." Mrs. Drummond pointed to her bed.

Lydia followed Mrs. Drummond out and met Miss Fitzgilbert in the hall.

How pale and frightened she looked—nothing like the confident, commanding head girl who led the line wherever they went.

Lydia took her hand as they walked downstairs. Miss Fitzgilbert clutched her fingers so tightly it hurt.

"Wait in the drawing room, girls. I will show him in myself when he arrives." Mrs. Drummond left them staring at each other.

Miss Fitzgilbert paced along the carpet's floral boarder. "This waiting shall drive me mad."

"Come sit with me at the pianoforte. We can play—" Lydia rummaged through several sheets of music. "—this one together. I am still not very good at it, but you can help me. Or if you do not like that, I can fetch a workbasket from the parlor."

"No, no, music is an excellent diversion, and if he hears, it will show off one of my accomplishments—"

"—and your patience."

Miss Fitzgilbert's jaw dropped. She pressed her cheek to Lydia's and sat at the pianoforte.

Midway through their second repetition, the door swung open and Mrs. Drummond announced, "Sir Anthony, may I present Lady Annabelle and her friend, Miss Bennet."

As if by a fairy's spell, Miss Fitzgilbert transformed into Lady Annabelle.

She curtsied with the perfect posture and flawless grace that Lydia had been unable to attain despite devoted practice.

In Kent's limited circle, she shone as a beauty among the thorns. Mama encouraged her pride and confidence, so Jane's warnings to maintain humility were easy to ignore. Yet, Jane had been right. Compared to Miss Fitzgilbert, she was nothing more than a clumsy little country girl in a vaguely pretty dress.

No wonder the fine gentlemen who visited Rosings never paid her any mind, reserving their attentions for Jane and Lizzy. Only Wickham bothered with her, and then only to toy with as he tried for shy, but elegant, Miss Darcy. He would consider her a tattered bit of muslin next to someone like Lady Annabelle.

Sir Anthony bowed with an elegance to match hers. While certainly no youth, no one would deem him an old man. He could hardly be much above five and thirty.

"I am pleased to make your acquaintance." His tone was smooth and polished, fitting his face perfectly.

He was no dandy, but no doubt he kept his valet well-employed.

"Pray, sit down. I shall send tea." Mrs. Drummond gave Lydia a stern look and left.

Miss Fitzgilbert moved toward the faded couch. "Shall we sit, sir?"

Not a large man, he moved with economy and purpose and sat on the worn wingback nearby. "Was that you playing?"

"Miss Bennet and I were playing together." She held her chin up, but her voice felt as uncertain as Lydia's fingering on their last duet.

"I was told you played well. It was not a misplaced compliment. I am fond of music." His smile felt a little forced, but his tone was genuine enough.

"Thank you, sir. Our music master is an excellent teacher."

Lydia faded back and settled at the dainty writing desk near the window.

"If you like, once you come to Parnam Hall, I will to hire a music master to help you continue your studies." He leaned forward a little, as if to catch her gaze.

A shock of mahogany hair fell across his eye.

"That is very gracious of you, sir, but I would not have you put out on my account." Miss Fitzgilbert gripped her hands tightly and looked away.

Sir Anthony pushed the hair out of his face. "What have you been told of me?"

"You are a knight, twice widowed and newly out of mourning. You have three sons and a daughter, all only slightly younger than I. You wish to reenter society and need a hostess for your homes." Her voice was tight as the highest keys on the pianoforte.

"A drab if factual portrayal, I suppose." He sniffed and glanced around the room. "My first wife died in childbirth with my third son. My daughter is now thirteen and away at seminary. Consumption claimed her mother just after Twelfth Night."

"I am sorry."

Lydia opened the writing desk. Thank heavens they were still there! Fresh paper and a nubby little pencil—something to do as she watched the uncomfortable affair.

"And what have you been told of me, sir?" Miss Fitzgilbert whispered, color fading from her cheeks so rapidly she might disappear altogether.

Lydia nearly dropped the lid of the desk on her fingers. She screwed her eyes shut and held her breath.

Sir Anthony did not look like a cruel man. Neither did Papa, yet that did not stop his sharp tongue.

He rubbed the back of his neck. "You were sent to Mrs. Drummond to curb behavior your father found inappropriate and unmanageable."

She bit her lip and silently acknowledged the truth of it.

He touched her chin and made her look at him.

Oh, the gentleness of his hand and the softness of his eye! Lydia's pencil flew into motion.

"You wonder if I have been privy to all the sordid details of your loss of virtue? Yes, I have."

A cry caught in her throat.

"In far more detail than I will ever repeat." He brushed a stray lock from her forehead. "I expect you also wonder how—not if—I shall hold it against you?"

Miss Fitzgilbert stiffened and turned away, arms rigid and hands balled in her lap.

He cupped her cheek, then stood and paced the length of the room.

Lydia shrank in her seat. Pray let him not notice her!

"A man should expect virtue in a woman, should he not?" He huffed and studied the ceiling roses. "I certainly did, at least at one time, I did."

Miss Fitzgilbert gripped the edge of the sofa.

He barked a bitter-tasting sound that could not rightfully be called a laugh. "Fool that I was, I did, not once, but twice. Do you wish to know what happened?"

"There is no need, sir ..."

"Perhaps not, but at least I shall not ruin your delicacy by telling you."

She hid her face in her shoulder.

Was he more like Papa than he seemed at first glance?

"Not one, but both my wives took lovers and not discreetly. While your disgrace was quietly handled and kept from the scandal sheets, mine was aired far and wide for all to revel in my humiliation."

Miss Fitzgilbert turned to face him full on, such compassion in her eyes, tears sprang to Lydia's. "I am so very sorry. I had no idea."

"I am not surprised." He tossed his head. "Your brother and father are quite keen to marry you off. They would not have you know anything that might encourage you to refuse me."

She stood, her air more that of Miss Fitzgilbert than Lady Annabelle. "Do I not deserve to know the truth about you?"

Lydia nearly dropped her pencil.

Papa would have flown into a rage at so bold a remark.

"They did not tell me you had such a spark." He chuckled, a far gentler sound than before. "I might enjoy a woman with a bit of backbone to her."

"I do not hide it well. Father found it quite disagreeable." She ducked behind the wingback, gripping the back so tightly her fingers turned white.

"I see why he might. Your mother is a meek accommodating soul."

"Who has never voiced disagreement with him or acted contrary to his wishes. She is mild and obedient and pleasant. She has never held an opinion in her life and consults him on all matters, large and small. Is that the kind of wife you seek?"

Did anyone hear the gauntlet land in the middle of the room, bright plate mail clanking on the carpet?

Mrs. Drummond would not approve of this direction of conversation, but only a fool would step between such ready combatants.

Lydia coughed less than daintily.

Miss Fitzgilbert glanced at Lydia and rolled her eyes. "My friend seeks to remind me I should adhere to more proper areas of conversation."

"Good advice to be sure." He swallowed a chuckle and ushered Miss Fitzgilbert back to her seat.

He returned to the wingback. "In answer to your question, I thought I fancied an easy, agreeable temperament in a wife."

"You thought?"

"Yes, and believed I had attained it, only to find my virility questioned in the scandal sheets, gossip planted by those same agreeable women." His face flushed.

Pray, let Mrs. Drummond not ask for the details of this conversation!

She pressed her hands to her scarlet—nearly purple—cheeks. "I cannot imagine."

"I can assure you, those accusations were utterly false." He stalked to the pianoforte. "My reputation has been sorely used. I am not so wealthy that scandals are easily overlooked."

"Which is why you would consider marriage to me, damaged goods, but privately damaged, so as not to add to your public grief. With my excellent dowry and connections, marriage to me may help mend your reputation."

"We are both damaged goods, Lady Annabelle. Though your father and brother may make light of my stains, I do not. Few respectable women would give me a second thought, and I fear the same is true for you. We are equals in many ways."

She stood, all the poise of the lady returning. "Equals? It has been a long time since anyone of worth called me an equal."

Lydia gripped her pencil so hard her fingers hurt.

Had anyone ever considered her an equal?

Sir Anthony turned to Miss Fitzgilbert. "I expect our chances of an amiable match are better than many. Neither of us holds romantic illusions anymore. I believe, though, we share an understanding of being ill-used by others and hope that might inform the way we treat one another."

"That is more than I could have asked for."

"Mrs. Drummond assures me of your character and accomplishments. I do not think her a woman prone to excessive compliments."

A hint of a smile lit her face. "No, she is not."

"I should hope your father and brother's support speaks well of me—at least, well enough."

She twitched her head in a non-committal gesture.

"You believe they would happily see you married to a bounder, if it meant a respectable name and home for you."

"That was the impression they left me with."

His head tipped back and he laughed, full and rich. "You shall be a very different kind of partner in my home. A change for the better, I think. Let me speak on my own behalf then. I am prepared to offer you a generous settlement—"

"You know that is unnecessary. Father will sign anything to be free of—"

"—with sufficient pin money and a jointure that you may be content. I like to entertain often and expect you to be a good hostess to many guests. Travel is another of my pleasures. I expect you to travel with me and fulfill my need for companionship ... in all its forms." His eyes narrowed.

She blushed and closed her eyes, nodding once.

"If you come with child, I will see the babe educated and given the same advantages as my other children."

"What more could a woman ask? You seem quite perfect."

He winced. "Your tongue is rather sharp. I imagine you have been told so?"

"Indeed I have. Whilst I do usually keep it under

good regulation, I find I am apt to slip when my intelligence is insulted."

Lydia coughed again.

"No, I will not retreat. I will not go on pretending we are paragons of virtue. Best we face our flaws before we are linked in name and in misery." She lifted her chin, but it quivered.

Surely this was not the way this conversation should have gone.

His face flushed and he squared his shoulders. "Very well, Miss Fitzgilbert, if you must. I am known as a generous man, but I am also jealous. I do not appreciate other men attending to my wife, nor her accepting their attentions. I am forgetful. That has been mistaken as neglectful, so my wives have complained. I am a vain man and enjoy compliments a bit too much. Apparently, I am not easy to live with."

"In that, I suppose we are equals as well. My sisters accuse me of vanity and being quite impossible. I understand your propensity to jealousy, for I too have a jealous streak. I like attention and am not shy in asking for it."

"So you are imperfect, too."

"Am I still so appealing, knowing my deeper flaws?"

"You think my list is complete? I am surly in the morning; prefer coffee to tea; and like far too many sweets. I dislike feather headdresses on women—they are ladies, not birds—green things on my plate; and improperly starched cravats. "

"And I sir, am apt to speak my mind too easily and hold opinions in contrary to what is popular. I like pretty dresses, balls and parties. I am fonder of chocolate than coffee. I hate to play cards and have all but forgotten how to dance. I have lost my virtue, but I shall not jeopardize my respectability again. I will guard your honor, zealously. In gratitude of the honor you do me, I am prepared to be a pleasing companion to you ... in all its forms."

The tension left his shoulders, and he reached out to her. "Despite my flaws, I hope you might find me a pleasing friend."

She rose and took his hand. "I welcome your friendship."

He brushed her knuckles with his lips. "We are agreed then?"

"Yes sir, it is agreed."

Lydia released a deep breath. How long had she been holding it?

"I shall call regularly that we might come to know one another better whilst the settlement is managed. I expect six, maybe eight weeks, before it is all arranged."

"I welcome the opportunity to know you better." Her eyes glistened, and she pressed her lips into something like a smile.

"From where do you wish to be married?"

"Here, if you and Mrs. Drummond are willing. There is little point trying to be married from my father's house. I fear it would only result in scenes disagreeable to all."

"I expect you are correct. I would prefer to avoid the attention a wedding in town would draw. Assuming Mrs. Drummond is agreeable, I shall make arrangements for you to visit the local dressmaker for a few things. A new dress for the wedding, a pretty, fashionable one would be appropriate. Proper things for the London season can be ordered in town."

"You are very generous, sir."

"Whilst I would have you think that of me, it is not all altruistic on my part. We both have reputations in need of repair. It will help for both of us to look the part."

"I will not embarrass you. I do know how to curb my tongue in company."

"I count on that. Would it be agreeable for me to hire a dance master to refresh your dance steps? I would not have you uncomfortable at a ball."

"The offer is most kind. It will be difficult to be the only one receiving lessons, though."

"Of course, I intended that he would teach all of the girls here."

"With Mrs. Drummond's permission, I think it would be quite agreeable. I would very much like to dance again."

"Then I shall endeavor to make it so."

The door swung open, and Mrs. Drummond bustled in with a tea tray. "Miss Bennet, you are wanted upstairs."

Clearly she was not, but one did not complain about a polite and welcome dismissal.

Lydia gathered up her drawings.

"Excuse me," she approached Sir Anthony. "I thought you might like these to look upon as you become acquainted. I hope it is appropriate." She handed each a drawing of the other.

They pressed shoulders together and looked at both sketches.

"These are remarkable. I shall be very pleased to carry home your likeness." Sir Anthony held it out for Mrs. Drummond to see.

Lydia curtsied and hurried out.

She ducked into the school room and sat near the window, staring at the drawing she did not give away. Her pencil captured their moments of angst as secrets were laid out, far too intimate, too naked for comfort.

How could they have possibly discussed details of Sir Anthony's masculine performance and their expectations of 'companionship'? They had only met moments before.

She wrapped her arms around her waist and rocked. If a gentleman could speak that way to a lady like Miss Fitzgilbert, how might they treat her?

Would a man expect to know everything she had done? Would he judge her the way Papa and Uncle Gardiner had? Was she now second-hand goods only fit for a man tainted by scandal himself?

Lydia pressed her temples and screwed her eyes shut, but that did not make answers come more easily. A scream welled up in her chest, but she must not allow it out. Yet, if she did not, the pressure would surely kill her.

Trembling hands fumbled for the easel and affixed her drawing—two anguished profiles facing one another. She pulled out the water colors Miss Honeywell had recently begun to teach her to use. Her brush strokes evoked a thunderstorm, echoing the faces even as it obscured them.

How much better for the turmoil in her heart to take form on paper. There she might examine it, consider it, control it.

Her final stroke off-balanced the easel and sent it clattering to the ground. She fell to her chair, face in hands, weeping.

"Miss Bennet?" Mr. Amberson's voice came from the doorway. His long steps approached.

She looked up into his deeply lined face and struggled to choke back a fresh sob.

"What happened to your easel? Are you hurt?" He scanned the room as if that would provide answers.

How could words express what her paint might barely contain? She shook her head and pointed to the easel on the floor.

He righted it and stared at the painting. Edging closer, he peered at the figures and drew in a ragged breath. Tears welled in his eyes. He dragged his sleeve across them.

She gasped.

He understood! He understood!

The realization tore through her, rousing fresh sobs, and she crumpled to the floor.

Warmth surrounded her and pulled her into a strong angular shoulder that smelled of shaving oil, rosin and wood smoke. She pressed into the safety of his arms.

"Sir Anthony, he was so direct about her disgrace. If she is tarnished, then I am ruined …"

He held her more tightly and cradled her head under his chin.

"I am worth nothing. My own father will not have me! No one will ever have me! What hope have I?"

He crooned a soothing sound and held her to his shoulder with one hand. With the other he fumbled in his pocket and pressed a crumpled handkerchief into her hand.

"Our world is a very unforgiving place, Miss Bennet." He hunkered, tailor style, beside her. "Intolerant and often very cruel."

She sniffed and pressed the soft silk to her face.

It smelled like him.

"It takes very little to be ruined, and there are many ways in which to be stained. For some, all it requires is to be different from what is typical, something I know well. Those of us who perform for the pleasure of others are welcome enough to entertain, but the very things which make us pleasing also make us suspect. We must satisfy ourselves with only the fringes of polite society. I have seen it many times."

"Why?"

"I suppose, though I do not rightly know, that art invokes such passion it cannot be deemed entirely safe or proper, nor can its practitioners. Anything or anyone that reminds polite society of anything uncomfortable risks being called undesirable."

She scrubbed the freshet of tears trailing down her face. "Then everything they said was true. I am—"

"I do not think you are ruined. You have been tried and are learning from those trials. It is the way one acquires depth and honesty in their work."

"What matter is depth and honesty when no one will even look at you?"

"Who do you need to look at you? Those fops and dandies on the street? Those proud and judgmental matrons whose goodness is defined in their distance from your sin?"

She pulled back and huddled into a tight knot, face in her hands.

Long, sinewy fingers urged her to look up.

"We are all sinners, Miss Bennet. The only differences are who knows about it and how harshly others judge it. But, I believe, at the end of days, no one can claim innocence."

"Then why is there so much condemnation?"

"Condemnation is far easier than compassion,

though I cannot pretend to understand why. You are not the only unfortunate to have known the sting of a fall. I came to my Aunt's establishment in hopes that my own transgressions would fade in society's memory. I am not proud of many things I have said and done. Do you hate me now, knowing I am far from untainted?"

She brushed an unruly lock from his forehead. He leaned into her fingertips, and she traced the creases beside his eyes.

"I could not ever hate you."

His lips curled into his funny lopsided smile. "I am pleased to hear it. I should loathe you thinking ill of me."

He cared for her good opinion?

His cheeks bunched up and he chuckled. "Perhaps it will amuse you to know, Aunt Drummond made certain I was well-repentant before she permitted me a place here."

"So she is as formidable toward you as she is to the rest of us?"

"More so I think."

Lydia laughed with him until more tears flowed.

"A bit ridiculous is it not?" He blotted his eyes with the edges of his coat. "So you see, my dear, Miss Bennet. We are equals." He caught a stray tear from her cheek with his thumb.

"Mr. Amberson? Miss Bennet?" Mrs. Drummond's sharp voice split the air. Her footsteps beat a tattoo on the floorboards until she towered over them. "I would see you in my office immediately, James."

He flashed his eyebrows at Lydia and clambered to his feet.

"Miss Bennet." He helped her up, bowed and left.

Lydia snuffled and dabbed her eyes, hands quivering again.

"Why were you on the floor?"

"I was clumsy and knocked the easel over. Mr. Amberson helped me right it."

"That does not explain why you were on the floor just now." Mrs. Drummond crossed her arms over her chest and tapped her foot, just like Mama did when she suspected prevarication.

"It is just too much to bear, madam, the things Sir Anthony said to her! He sees her as disgraced." She wrapped her arms around her waist, but it offered little comfort.

Mrs. Drummond's eyes widened and her eyebrow arched.

"She is the best among us, and if she is so low—" Lydia bit her knuckle.

It would not do to weep again.

"You have had a painful revelation. Still, Miss Fitzgilbert has been offered a rare and precious opportunity to redeem herself, one that very few receive. It may not fulfill romantic fantasies, but now is not the time for fantasies. We must do all that we can to help her move forward. She has requested you be her chaperone and companion throughout her courtship."

"Me? Why?"

How could she face Sir Anthony again, knowing what he thought of Miss Fitzgilbert … and her?

"I do not know. You have shown yourself enough improved that I am inclined to give my permission. I expect you to keep her confidences and guard her best interests. This is a position of trust and not to be taken lightly. You must help her if she falters. She does not fathom that I might be sympathetic to her feelings. While I am, her feelings are secondary to the reality of her situation. Can I rely upon you?"

Lydia studied her feet and the dusty floor. "I will help her."

❧ Chapter 10

THAT EVENING, AT THE end of dinner, Mrs. Drummond stood and addressed her students. "I have a very exciting announcement."

Amelia leaned toward Joan and Lydia. "She has found rich suitors to marry us all."

Joan giggled.

Was it possible they knew of Miss Fitzgilbert's caller?

"An anonymous benefactor," Mrs. Drummond stared straight at Lydia, "has determined you all should be able to dance."

Gasps and excited titters filled the room.

Why was Mrs. Drummond staring at her so?

"A dance master has been arranged to instruct all of you, beginning later this week. Following your lessons with Miss Thornton, you shall report to the music room where Mr. Chadwick shall tutor you, with the assistance of Mr. Amberson on the pianoforte. Keep in mind, this is a privilege, one that may be revoked if I am given reason. The music room will have to be cleaned each week prior to your lessons. The duty will be rotated among all of you. You are all dismissed." Mrs. Drummond rose and led the teachers out.

"Did you hear—a dance master!" Joan squealed.

Amelia hugged herself. "I am wild for dancing! It has been ever so long. I am shocked missus would permit us to dance, even if someone else pays the bill."

"I wonder who it is paying," Joan whispered as they walked in to the parlor. "She was looking right at you when she said it. I wonder why."

"You know how cross she is. Perchance she was scowling at the soup I dripped on my dress." Lydia plucked at the splotchy bodice.

Hopefully the broth would not leave permanent stains.

Amelia sidled close. "I think you know a great deal more than you are telling us."

"Yes, you were here when we were all out. You must have seen or heard something."

Lydia backed away. "I did not go near her office at all."

"Perhaps that was not necessary. Word might have come to you." Amelia poked her shoulder.

They filed into the parlor. Joan grabbed her elbow and dragged her to an empty corner. She tried to pull away, but Amelia blocked her path.

"Why would anything come to me?" Lydia peeked around Amelia and sidestepped, only to be cut off again.

"We were sent for the post yesterday."

"There was a letter for the missus that bore the Darcy crest." Amelia waggled her shoulders and smirked.

"How would you know the Darcy crest?"

Why would Mr. Darcy write to Mrs. Drummond?

Her heart drummed against her ribs so hard it hurt.

What would Mrs. Drummond tell him?

"I think he ordered the dance lessons," Amelia whispered.

"Why would he do that?"

From the corner of her eye she saw Mr. Amberson sit at the pianoforte.

"Why does any woman need to be able to dance?" Joan sing-songed.

"We think he wants to marry you off so he won't have to maintain you any longer."

"If so, at least it is to a man who likes to dance."

Lydia retreated and dodged to her left, but Joan blocked her way.

Botheration!

"What if he is a dance master who does not wish to be humiliated by a cloddish wife?" Joan leaned in to her face and sniggered.

"Who will beat you if you get the steps wrong?" Amelia rubbed the back of her skirts.

"Just stop it! You are horrid." Lydia shoved Joan away.

"You cannot take a joke can you?" Joan brushed her sleeve.

"I am in no mood." Lydia stalked away.

Ruth and Juliana beckoned her over.

"They have been in high dudgeon all day," Ruth

muttered. "Would you believe they were jealous you got to stay behind to help with chores?"

"I would rather polish andirons than go anywhere with them." Lydia sat between them at the small card table.

"They hate visiting the gaol." Juliana glanced over her shoulder. "I hate it too. You cannot blame their ill-humor."

"You are far too generous," Ruth said. "I can certainly blame them. They have been awful to me all day. They were supposed to help me carry the big basket."

Lydia shuffled the cards, more to keep her hands busy than in hopes of playing.

"Joan helped a very little, but Amelia disappeared shortly after we left and did not reappear until we had nearly made it back. She complained about how her back and shoulders hurt from carrying all the load herself."

Lydia fumbled the cards and restarted the shuffle. "Sounds exactly like her. Does Mrs. Drummond know?"

"I had thought to tell her, but she has been so very preoccupied today." Ruth glanced toward Mrs. Drummond.

"Did Miss Honeywell and Miss Thornton not notice her missing?" Lydia asked.

"Miss Honeywell asked after her. Joan said she had gone on an errand for Miss Thornton. But I was with Miss Thornton all day, and I know she never spoke to Amelia."

"And Miss Honeywell probably never thought to ask Miss Thornton about it?" Lydia rapped the deck on the table.

"I guess not."

"Oh, listen, Mr. Amberson is going to play for us." Juliana pointed. "I have never heard anyone who plays like him."

Lydia turned to face the pianoforte. He drew a deep breath and half closed his eyes, the way he always did when he was about to play something he composed. Music of his own arrangement was a special treat.

The notes started softly at first, a kitten peeking around a corner, jumping at dust motes in a sunbeam.

Lydia rose and drifted toward the pianoforte. She had to watch his hands.

They flowed and danced across the keys, tension building. The veins and small bones stood out as his key strokes grew stronger, darker. The playful kitten turned into a stalking cat, instilling fear into its prey.

His wrists and arms corded, strength surging with each note.

Her heart matched the tempo of the music, catching in her throat and stealing her breath. She clutched the side of the pianoforte, lest her knees give way.

That melody, though she had never heard it, she knew it. It was the keening of her heart, the song of the painting she had shown him, played out for everyone to hear.

How could he?

She cast about the room.

Some were talking among themselves; some played cards. Miss Long read. A few listened, but none, not even the teachers truly heard what he was playing.

His eyes opened and caught her gaze.

He was playing for her and her alone.

Her vision blurred.

He could not leave the school now. Pray let him not!

Three days later, anticipation of the dance master's visit ruined Miss Thornton's geography lesson. Whispering and wool-gathering rendered her students exceptionally stupid. She finally surrendered to the futility, and set them to copying the map of Europe hanging on the wall.

Copying maps was a dreadful dull exercise. But it was far better than hearing Miss Thornton drone.

Lydia trimmed a sheet of foolscap in half and smoothed it across the desk. Where to begin? A compass rose perhaps? That at least could be made interesting.

Amelia shoved a wrinkled piece of paper at her.

I know your secret.

Lydia shoved it back.

How could Amelia have found out about Sir Anthony? How long before she told everyone?

The maid saw you with him while we were all at the gaol.

Lydia's face turned cold, and she nearly dropped her pencil.

Mr. Amberson?

Amelia smiled her special thin sneer.

You are trying to seduce him.

Lydia snatched the note and crumpled it into a tiny ball. Amelia tried to grab it away, but Lydia dropped it into her bodice. It lodged just under her stays.

Miss Thornton leveled a narrow-eyed gaze at them. Amelia huffed and returned to her map.

Lydia's heart thumped against the scratchy paper.

She had not behaved badly towards him. Even if she did like him a great deal.

A very great deal.

She dragged the back of her hand across her eyes. Surely, Mr. Amberson would ensure Mrs. Drummond knew the truth.

Young ladies were not supposed to like their tutors, though. Mama and Jane both warned her against it.

No tutor had been like Mr. Amberson.

Did he even like her?

Mrs. Drummond strode into the school room. "The dance master has arrived. Put away your lessons and assemble in the music room."

The room erupted in excited chatter and titters.

Lydia hurried away from Amelia and joined Miss Fitzgilbert, Miss Greenville and Ruth near the front.

"Are you well?" Miss Fitzgilbert looked over Lydia's head toward Amelia.

"I wager Joan and Amelia are being horrid again," Miss Greenville muttered.

"Amelia is so full of herself. She got another letter from her 'dear friend Frances'." Ruth looked down her nose, the way Amelia often did.

"It is a wonder she has not read it to us all—twice," Miss Fitzgilbert mumbled as they filed into the corridor.

"Why bother reading it to us when she makes it all up in any case?" Miss Greenville tossed her head. "She might as well be reading from a novel."

Made up?

"No one is so cakey as to think that nonsense she reads us is true."

Mr. Amberson and another man waited near the pianoforte.

"Mr. Chadwick, may I present your students." Mrs. Drummond introduced each of the girls.

Mr. Chadwick was a tiny black beetle of a man with a shiny bald pate and beady black eyes. His belly bulged just a little, but he had well-formed legs encased in very tight black breeches. Next to Mr. Amberson's unruly shock of dark hair and comfortable trousers, he seemed very hard and tight and pinchy.

"How many of you have received prior instruction in dance?' Mr. Chadwick looked directly at Miss Fitzgilbert.

Did he have to be so very obvious?

"Excellent, excellent. Stand up with a partner, and I shall see how you perform."

"Stand up with me." Miss Fitzgilbert grabbed her arm.

Mr. Chadwick directed them to take the place at the top of the set.

"I will take the gentlemen's side." Lydia moved to the left hand line.

"Quickly now, take hands four from the top." Mr. Chadwick seized his walking stick and struck it on the floor twice.

Lydia joined hands with her partner and the next couple.

Mr. Chadwick rapped the floor again. "Attention, now. Drop hands and set to your partner."

Lydia skip-stepped to her right and left, matching steps with Miss Fitzgilbert.

"Set to your corner."

She repeated the exercise with Miss Greenville, the feeling of the footwork slowly returning.

How long had it been since she danced?

"Turn your partner by the right hand."

Lydia took Miss Fitzgilbert's right hand, and they danced a full turn back to their places.

"Turn your neighbor by the left."

Miss Long extended her right hand toward Lydia. Mr. Chadwick thumped her left calf with his stick.

She yelped.

"Left, Miss Tall, left."

"Miss Long," she squeaked and snatched her right hand back.

"Long, tall—it is quite all the same. Learn right from left!" He smacked her left leg again.

"Yes, sir." Miss Long stretched out her left hand.

Lydia took it, and they danced the turn.

"Join hands and circle left, one time around."

They turned in their circle, narrowly avoiding collision with the next group in the set.

"No! No! No!" Mr. Chadwick's cane punctuated each word as he stomped toward the second group of four.

"You—" he pointed at Juliana. "You are waddling, not dancing."

"Yes, sir." Juliana looked at the floor.

"Dance is light, bright and sparkling, not plump and ponderous." He waved his stick at Mr. Amberson. "Play some bars."

The music began and Mr. Chadwick counted aloud. "One —two—three—four. One—two—three—four. Turn with me, Miss Waddles."

He offered Juliana his right hand and dragged her

through a turn. Juliana barely kept up.

"Now take hands and circle left … keep the count. You must return to your place by the last count. No! No, too slow!" He rapped his stick in time to the music. "Faster now. Light and bright. No fat ducks, beautiful swans. Faster! One, two, three—"

Juliana clutched her belly and screamed.

Mr. Amberson stopped playing.

"Look!" Lydia's eyes fixed on at a small pool of liquid near Juliana's feet.

Her arms and legs went stiff and she fell into Lydia, who eased her to the floor. Her eyes rolled back in her head, and she convulsed.

"James, bring the midwife." Mrs. Drummond dropped to her knees beside them.

Lydia pointed at Miss Fitzgilbert. "You and Ruth hold her, keep her from hurting herself. Miss Long, Miss Greenville fetch towels, as many as you can. Tell the cook to ready water for tea should the midwife have need."

Juliana went limp.

"She's dead! She's dead!" The voice sounded a bit like Amelia's.

Lydia leaned down over Juliana's face. "She breathes! She lives! Juliana, Juliana!"

She moaned and stirred but did not awaken.

"I have seen this in my mother's last confinement. We must get her to bed." Lydia said.

Mrs. Drummond's brows rose high "How singular that you should have been exposed to such an indelicate—"

"Mama had singular notions regarding all things concerning confinements, travails and lyings-in."

Mrs. Drummond nodded. "Mr. Chadwick, assist us."

"Give them room," Miss Thornton ordered, pushing several gawkers out of the way.

They carried Juliana to her room. Girls trailed along behind them, like lambs following their ewe.

"Miss Thornton, gather everyone downstairs. Send word to the parsonage that you will be bringing the girls to tea."

Would Mrs. Drummond send everyone away if she anticipated a good outcome? Lydia's stomach knotted.

"Yes, madam." Miss Thornton ushered the girls down the hall.

They laid Juliana on her bed just in time for her to convulse again.

Lydia grabbed Juliana's arm and held her secure until the seizure stopped. She ran for the dresser and plucked a nightdress from the drawer.

Mrs. Drummond unfastened Juliana's dress. "Release her stays and help me get her into the nightdress."

The stay laces broke in Lydia's hand. "Do not worry. I shall replace them for you."

While they changed her, the maid rushed in and pulled the curtains shut. Lydia blinked in the sudden darkness.

Why must a room be so dark and warm and closed up for a birth?

The maid started a large fire. Ruth followed a moment later, laden with towels and sheets.

"Put them on the other bed and join the others downstairs," Mrs. Drummond ordered.

Ruth dropped her burden and fled.

Miss Fitzgilbert arrived with a pitcher of water and still steaming kettle. She placed the kettle over the fire and set the pitcher on the washstand. "May I help?"

"No, Sir Anthony might deem that inappropriate. I refuse risk that. Go downstairs. You too, Lydia."

"No ..." Juliana groaned and clutched Lydia's hand. "Pray, do not leave me ..."

Lydia stroked hair back from Juliana's forehead. "No, no, I will stay. I sat with my mother through three lyings-in. There is no reason to keep me from here."

Miss Fitzgilbert kissed Juliana's cheek. "Everything is going to be all right."

Juliana groaned and clutched her belly. Blood-tinged water stained her nightdress and the bed clothes. Her head fell back and another seizure shook her.

Mrs. Drummond covered the bed with toweling. "Are you certain you wish to stay?"

This could not be worse than Mama's last lying-in, could it?

Mrs. Harrow burst in, a large bag in hand. She brushed past Lydia and checked Juliana over, muttering under her breath.

"Her waters broke with the first fit. The fits continue ..." Mrs. Drummond whispered.

"Her labor is progressing very fast." Mrs. Harrow trundled to the wash basin and washed her hands. "Whatever happens, it will not take long."

Juliana tossed her head against the pillow and breathed hard.

"The pains are close together now." Mrs. Harrow clucked her tongue.

"My mother's last birth was like this." Lydia swallowed hard and looked from Juliana to Mrs. Harrow and Mrs. Drummond.

"How did she fare?" Mrs. Harrow dried her hands on a clean towel.

"She lived, but has not had another confinement since."

"And the baby?"

Lydia shook her head and squeezed her eyes shut.

It had been a boy. Papa did not suffer the loss easily.

"We shall pray that Juliana may enjoy the same safe delivery." Mrs. Harrow sat beside Juliana and took her hand.

Juliana's eyes peeked open. "Hurts."

"You are fortunate, it is progressing quickly. Very soon it will be time for you to push." Mrs. Harrow stroked her forehead.

Juliana's eyes closed again, and she sagged against the pillows.

"It is the fits, they have left her exhausted. Here, girl, brew some tea with these." She passed Lydia a packet of herbs.

Lydia took the herbs and hurried to the kettle. Behind her Mrs. Harrow and Mrs. Drummond whispered. If she paid attention, she might be able to hear—

No, she did not want to hear it. Judging by their faces, their conversation was grim.

She added the herbs to the hot water and watched dark tendrils float through the water, swirling and dancing together.

What was in this brew? Would Papa approve? Did he even know about such things?

"I can see the head!" Mrs. Harrow cried.

"Come help me." Mrs. Drummond moved to the head of the bed.

Lydia hurried to the other side.

"Move her to the foot of the bed. We will help her to sit up. It will make the babe come easier."

Mrs. Harrow and Mrs. Drummond slid Juliana so that her legs hung off the end of the bed. Lydia helped Mrs. Drummond lift Juliana's shoulders.

"I can sit behind her and hold her against me," Lydia said.

"Do that." Mrs. Harrow prepared towels at the foot of the bed.

Lydia climbed on the bed, and Mrs. Drummond lowered Juliana's limp form against her.

How heavy she was, her skin cool and clammy with sweat. She moaned and stirred restlessly.

"I am right here. The babe will be here soon," Lydia whispered in her ear.

Even if it were not true, it was best that Juliana believe that for now. If she gave up, things would only be worse.

"So soon?"

"Yes, it will be an easy birth." Lydia wrapped her arms snuggly just above Juliana's belly.

"Push girl, push."

Juliana stiffened, and her head fell hard against Lydia's shoulder. Convulsions wracked her body. Lydia struggled to hold her in place until she finally went limp.

"She has no strength to push," Mrs. Drummond said.

"At the next contraction, get above her belly, and push for her."

Mrs. Drummond clambered up on the bed.

Lydia scooted aside as far as possible. "Shall I get down? There is no room."

"No, you need to hold her up. I will manage." Mrs. Drummond maneuvered around Lydia and placed her hands on Juliana's belly.

Lydia felt the contraction begin as Juliana cried out.

"That's it. Help her push now, until I tell you to stop. The head is coming now, keep on … now stop."

"Hold on, you are doing well," Lydia whispered.

Juliana probably could not hear her, but still, it felt right to say something encouraging.

"Push again!"

Mrs. Drummond's face turned red, and she panted with the effort.

"Keep on, the baby comes … now stop. One or two more."

Lydia wiped Juliana's brow with the corner of her apron. "The baby is almost here. Just a little more. Do not give up. Just a little more."

Juliana's eyes fluttered open. "He is born?"

"Not yet—very, very soon. Help us now—"

"Push!"

Juliana's eyes screwed shut, and she hunched up, her face flushed bright. Mrs. Drummond continued to push on her belly.

Mrs. Harrow yelped at a wet, slippery sound. Mrs. Drummond rushed to the foot of the bed.

"Is it a boy? Can I see him?" Juliana whispered, eyes barely open.

"I will get the baby." Lydia gulped and tiptoed to the midwife.

The room was far too quiet; quiet like it had been

with Mama's last two births.

A tiny boy, covered in blood and fluid, lay barely moving on a blanket. Mrs. Harrow rubbed him briskly. He gulped in a little breath, but he did not cry. She rubbed and coaxed and cajoled for several more minutes, but his breaths remained slow and shallow.

Mrs. Harrow shook her head and frowned.

Lydia took the tiny infant and carried him to Juliana. "See, it is a boy. Just as you hoped."

Juliana took him and cuddled him to her chest. "He is so tiny, but he is such a good boy. See, he does not even cry. Such a very good boy …"

The baby's eyes fluttered open, and he gazed at his mother.

"His eyes are blue, just like his father's." She stroked the tiny cheek, and his eyes closed again. "Such a very good boy."

Her eyelids fell, and she breathed slow and deep, asleep.

Lydia stared until her vision blurred, locking the image in her mind. She dragged her sleeve over her cheeks and gently took the still infant from Juliana's arms.

"Her bleeding has stopped. That is a very good sign." Mrs. Harrow muttered, pushing up to her feet.

Mrs. Drummond took the baby from Lydia's arms. "It is good she got to hold him. She may not remember though, when she wakes. You will have to tell her."

How distant the whole scene felt, like seeing through a window from afar.

"She is going to sleep for some time now. Go and refresh yourself, we will tend to her. I will call you when you can help her once more."

Lydia curtsied on weak knees and stumbled out.

She staggered down the hall to the schoolroom, and fell into the desk by the window. A sheet of paper and a pencil found their way into her hands.

Long grey shadows, extensions of her soul, painted the schoolroom. If only she might stay here forever and never see, or feel, or think again.

How would she ever close her eyes and not see Juliana and her baby, their one moment together? If she could just capture it on paper, then, only then, might it cease to haunt her. The rough bite of the pencil on the paper consumed her senses.

Two, peaceful, sleeping faces took shape.

She would do more than tell Juliana about her son. Juliana would see him.

Chapter 11

"THAT IS REMARKABLE."

Lydia jumped and nearly dropped her pencil. "Mrs. Drummond!"

"Calm down child. I only came to check on you." She laid a hand on Lydia's shoulder. "This has been a difficult day."

"I did not know what else to do."

Mrs. Drummond examined the drawing more closely.

The words tangled in her throat. How did one put into words the thoughts and feelings colliding and vying for space within her chest? It was all too much!

"I want to give it to Juliana. So she does not forget."

Mrs. Drummond lifted her glasses and wiped her eyes. "I have an old frame I think would do very well for it. Might I send it off to be properly framed?"

Lydia's jaw dropped and her eyes grew very wide. "It is a very generous offer, madam. This is just a rough sketch. I can do a much finer one to be framed."

"This one though, captures the moment in a visceral way you are unlikely to replicate. Juliana should be able to feel the moment, not just see it. Perhaps you might be willing to render one for me, though."

"I would be happy to do another for you. I did not know you enjoyed art."

"I suppose I sound a bit like Mr. Amberson, do I not?" She laughed and pulled a stool near. "He has taught me to see things a little of the way he does, but he is apt to go on in ways that utterly baffle me."

"He has taught me a great deal. I am very grateful to him."

"He has not known a pupil like you before."

"I am not half the musician Miss Fitzgilbert and Miss Greenville are."

"But they do not speak the language of art the way that you do." Mrs. Drummond steepled her hands and tapped them to her lips.

"I did not understand it myself until he explained it."

Had he any idea of what he had done for her? Perhaps she should tell him, but how?

"I have never seen a student take to it as you, craving it like the very air she breathes."

Mrs. Drummond understood!

"I do not know what I would do without it now. It makes me feel so … I do not know how to explain. I am not lost anymore … and I like that. I like who I am now. I am not a stupid, silly, shatter-brained creature here. I have something I can do well, and even friends to share it with. It is all so different."

Mrs. Drummond chewed her knuckle. "I do not think you are the same girl who came to me some months ago."

Mrs. Drummond had just complimented her? What a very, very strange day indeed.

"Mrs. Harrow and I are grateful for your help with Juliana."

"I am glad you permitted it."

Mrs. Drummond stared at her in the most peculiar, uncomfortable way.

Lydia rolled her pencil between her palms.

"I have made a decision, Miss Bennet. Give me your cap."

"My cap? I do not understand."

Mrs. Drummond gently slipped the mobcap off. "Today, you have earned the privilege. Ordinarily I would do this with greater fanfare, over dinner, but I am not sure that would be appropriate today."

Cool air rushed over the top of her head.

She had become so accustomed to the mobcap. How odd—and a little frightening—to be without it.

"Are you certain? I did so little."

"That confirms to me exactly why it is the right time." Mrs. Drummond rose. "I trust you will not disappoint me."

Several hours later, a commotion at the front door drew Lydia from the school room. The front hall filled with girls, teachers and the Weatherbys. The housekeeper led the Weatherbys to Mrs. Drummond's office. The girls milled about near the stairs.

Lydia lingered at the top of the stairs as they whispered among themselves. Company, well, certain company, would be far more welcome than the echo in her mind.

Miss Fitzgilbert saw her and swept up the stairs. "What news of Juliana?"

"She lives, but the baby …" Lydia shrugged and swallowed hard. "The midwife is with her still and fears her recovery may be a long and difficult one."

"You are so very brave. Was it very awful?" She touched Lydia's arm.

Lydia bit her lip and studied the scuffed stairs. "It is not so terrible when you have attended one before."

"But the blood …"

"That is not very pleasant, but … it was his face …" Her throat closed and chest pinched so tight she could hardly breathe.

She clutched Miss Fitzgilbert's hand and pulled her into the school room.

A second drawing, one for Mrs. Drummond lay on the desk by the window, lit by the final rays of afternoon sun.

She pointed to it.

Miss Fitzgilbert picked it up, tears flowing down her cheeks. "I have never seen a baby so tiny. They both look … so peaceful." She returned it to the desk and embraced Lydia.

They wept into each other's shoulders. Handkerchiefs proved insufficient and aprons were finally employed to blot their cheeks.

At least she could breathe again, the crushing weight eased.

What was it Mary used to say about a burden

shared?

"Where is your cap?" Miss Fitzgilbert asked.

"Mrs. Drummond took it." Lydia touched her hair. "It feels very strange to be without it."

"I remember when she took mine. I felt almost naked without it." Miss Fitzgilbert sniffled. "Shall I call you Miss Bennet now?"

"No, I think I would look over my shoulder for one of my sisters if you did."

Miss Fitzgilbert giggled. "Then will you call me Annabelle? I should very much like to have a friend who would call me so even for the short time I have left here."

"Annabelle."

How warm and fuzzy and friendly to speak a particular friend's name.

"Would you share my room while Juliana recovers?"

"I had not considered … I thought I would tend her."

"You must also have a place to rest yourself, though."

"Are you sure? I thought having a room alone a privilege."

"With the wedding coming in just six weeks, I find myself very much in want of company."

"I suppose sharing with you would make it easier for me to do your hair when Sir Anthony calls. If Mrs. Drummond approves, I should like it very much."

Annabelle squeezed her hand. "I am sure she will. We ought to go back downstairs though. I am not the only one hungry for news."

But there would be so many questions.

She squeezed her eyes shut against the images of blood and babies who did not cry.

They made it only halfway down the stairs before Miss Thornton stopped them. Below, Miss Honeywell quieted the girls into an audience of demanding, anxious eyes.

What did one say when there were so many staring?

"Does Juliana live?" Miss Thornton asked.

"Yes."

Miss Thornton followed with several more questions, all brief and comfortably answered. Though curious expressions remained, she did not persist in her interrogation.

Blessed, merciful woman!

Mrs. Drummond appeared at the back of the group. "Pray, your attention, girls. Cook has a cold meal for us in the dining room. Come now. The vicar and his wife shall be joining us."

Lydia parted company with Annabelle and took her usual seat with Joan and Amelia. The dinner ritual should have felt comforting, but Juliana's absence filled the room with emptiness bigger than her vacant chair.

Plates of cold meat, cheese, bread and jam, pickles and a platter of meat pasties graced the table. Mama would deem it a shameful meal to serve guests, but anything more would have felt an insult to Juliana's suffering.

The Weatherbys did not seem taken aback. He set to properly serving his wife and Mrs. Drummond from the nearest platters, mindless of the simplicity of the food. Mrs. Weatherby, with the round, rosy cheeks and perpetual pleasant expression, commented on the pleasantness of the cheese and flavor of the jam, a perfect, gracious guest.

"I am surprised you would continue to associate with the likes of us," Amelia shoved a plate of cheese toward Lydia.

Joan tugged the lace of her mob cap. "I suppose we should be calling you Miss Bennet now."

"I would not answer to it if you did." Lydia rolled her eyes.

"You say that now, but I am sure you will enjoy lording over us soon enough," Amelia muttered. "What you did do to get missus to—"

"Girls," Mrs. Drummond rose and straightened her fichu.

The hum of whispered conversations and shuffling bodies ceased.

"This has been a very difficult day, and I know you have many questions. I will speak privately to any of you who wish. In the meantime, we must care for Juliana as she recovers."

"How long will her recovery be?" Annabelle asked.

"We cannot know. Mrs. Harrow is concerned she is already showing signs of child-bed fever."

A collective gasp filled the room. Even Mrs. Weatherby's features lost a little of their bloom.

"We are not without hope. It is possible to recover from even that affliction."

"My mother did, after her last confinement," Lydia said, more to herself than anyone else. "I should like to sit with her if I may."

The corner of Mrs. Drummond's lips lifted just a mite. "Thank you, both for your encouragement and your willingness to offer your assistance."

Amelia snorted softly. "So that is how you did it."

"You anticipated my next remarks, Miss Bennet," Mrs. Drummond emphasized her name. "Juliana will require much support in the coming days. Any of you who wish to offer aid will be quite welcome. Miss Thornton, Miss Honeywell and I will, of course, be active in attending her."

"I should like to help," Annabelle glanced at Miss Long.

"And I too." Miss Long nodded vigorously.

Amelia leaned forward, elbows on the table. "I will sit with her, too."

"And me," Joan said.

Miss Greenville scowled from across the table. She glanced at Ruth and Stephanie beside her. They both swallowed hard and twitched their heads in agreement. "The three of us would be pleased to assist as well."

"Excellent. With so many, not all of you will be needed to sit in the sickroom. Ruth, I am well aware of your squeamishness. I appreciate your willingness but, I would have you take charge of the extra washing. That chore is very much a part of her care. Joan and Amelia may join you in the task."

"Thank you, Mrs. Drummond." The color returned to Ruth's face.

It had been a brave thing for her to volunteer, considering she was apt to swoon at the blood from a needle-pricked finger.

Amelia grumbled under her breath. "Had I known we were to slave at execution day, I would never have said anything."

"What is that, Amelia?" Mrs. Drummond cleared her throat. "Do you object to your assignment?"

"I had no idea housework would be involved."

"Is that to say you are unwilling?"

"I … I …"

"I am certain Ruth does not need grudging assistance. You may be excused from the task. Joan, I suppose the same sentiment applies to you?"

Joan looked from Amelia to Mrs. Drummond, shifting uneasily in her seat. "Ah, no, I am willing to help."

"Very well. Assignments will be explained tomorrow morning." Mrs. Drummond returned to her dinner.

Amelia elbowed Lydia. "You could have warned me she was looking for laundresses."

"Why would I know?"

"You are her new favorite."

"I am no such thing."

"I expect you think you will share our room and order us about." Joan sniffed.

"No, I do not."

"You are right about that," Amelia said.

"I know you do not want my company, so I shall not impose on you." Lydia took a pasty from the platter and handed it to Joan.

Joan served herself and passed the platter on. "We never said that. Do not be that way. Of course, you will stay with us. It will be great fun."

"No, you have complained so many times that your room is not large enough for two, much less three. Miss Fitzgilbert has a room to herself. I shall share with her."

"Let her be," Amelia sneered. "Miss Bennet is far too good for us now."

Joan shrugged and attended to her dinner.

Lydia struggled to chew and swallow, her throat

tight and dry. Perhaps she should …

Annabelle smiled at her from across the table.

No, Annabelle was much better company, even if her room was small.

Mrs. Drummond dismissed them to the parlor. Lydia lingered behind the group. Mr. Amberson had not attended dinner. His absence meant little hope of music to lighten their spirits. Games hardly seemed appealing.

Was this what Lizzy felt when forced to keep company in Lady Catherine's drawing room? Who knew keeping company could be so very taxing?

Lydia leaned against the banister, allowing the others pass by. Ruth and Stephanie brought out cards and suggested a game of commerce. Annabelle and Miss Long both stopped and encouraged her to join them, but she declined. Watching through the parlor door was sufficient for now.

"Do you not wish to play with the others?" a soft voice behind her asked.

Mrs. Weatherby stood in the shadow of the staircase. She was not smiling, not with her mouth. But everything else about her seemed to radiate warmth.

"Thank you, no." Lydia shrugged and avoided eye contact.

"I have never been much of a card player, especially when other things weigh upon me." She stood very close to Lydia. "Mrs. Drummond told us of your bravery this afternoon. She also said you had sat with your mother at such a time. It must have been difficult."

Why would Mrs. Drummond tell her that?

"I never thought much about the matter."

"Perhaps you should."

"Why? What does dwelling on such things achieve? Why linger upon the sad and difficult?"

If she dwelt upon them, the melancholy would overwhelm everything, perhaps even her will to live. Best look only at today and the ones to come; the ones she could impact; the ones that had not already been tainted.

"A fair question, child. I believe during those times, we are allowed a glimpse at ourselves. Those are the moments when our true character is exposed. That is worth examining."

"I am not certain that is something I wish to look at. I have been told my character is at least very silly, if not very bad."

"Mrs. Drummond showed her faith in you very clearly this afternoon." Mrs. Weatherby cocked her head and lifted an eyebrow.

Lydia touched her hair. "I do not know what to make of it."

"You do not need me to tell you. The signs are all around you. You just need to look at them and believe in what you are seeing."

Would she not stop talking in questions and riddles?

"Ah, Mrs. Weatherby," the vicar strolled in, Mrs. Drummond at his side. "It is time for us to take our leave. Soon the night will be too dark for us to walk home."

"It would not do to overstay our welcome." Mrs. Weatherby flashed a knowing glance at Lydia and took his arm.

Mrs. Drummond saw them out.

At last! Her nerves were raw enough without Mrs. Weatherby's helpful company.

Lydia settled back against the banister as the game in the parlor continued. Ruth and Lucy appear to be in possession of very good hands. Odd, in all this time here, she had very little cause to talk to Lucy, who hung back in the shadows and said little. How could such a mousy thing have got herself into enough trouble to be sent away?

"You should join the rest of the girls."

Lydia jumped.

How had Mrs. Drummond snuck up on her?

"You really ought to have a little amusement to-day."

"Pray, madam, no ..." Lydia glanced from Mrs. Drummond to the parlor and back again.

"Are you well, child?" She pressed her hand to Lydia's forehead.

Mama had often done the same thing when she thought Lydia's behavior odd.

Why did mothers always think one ill when they did not understand one's feelings?

"I am well enough, but too weary for games to-night."

Mrs. Drummond nodded and pressed her eyes with forefinger and thumb. "We all have reason to be weary tonight. Why not go to bed?"

"I cannot sleep now. May I sit with Juliana? I would rather stare at her than at the ceiling wishing for sleep. Perhaps you should sleep, though."

Mrs. Drummond rubbed her temples. "Tell Mrs. Harrow I sent you. She will tell you what to do. I will take your place in a few hours."

Lydia curtsied and climbed the stairs. She turned down the hallway and paused, safe from observation. Leaning against the wall, she let her head fall back against the faded blue paint. The darkness of the hall enveloped her, spoke to her of another dark corridor.

At home, they never spoke of Little Thomas's illness. Nothing had alleviated her little brother's sufferings and in just a few days, he was lost. Since then, Papa flew into rage at any mention of his only son. Mama wore a ring with Thomas's hair on her small finger. It had been on her finger so long, she could no longer remove it.

Perhaps, Juliana's fate would be better.

The corridor still smelled vaguely of blood. Would that stench ever leave her?

Lydia peeked into Juliana's room. Hot and stuffy, a low fire glowed in the fireplace, casting an eerie orange-red light over everything it touched.

Nothing looked pleasing touched by that hue.

She slipped inside. Mrs. Harrow slumped like a half-used sack of flour in a chair near Juliana's bedside.

"Mrs. Drummond sent me."

Mrs. Harrow pushed up from the chair as though she weighed twice as much as she had when she sat down. She shuffled to Lydia and beckoned her into the hall.

"What may I do for her?"

"She sleeps, but I do not expect it to last long. She is in the grip of fever. If she has a cold fit, abate its violence with warm diluting drinks. I have a kettle near the fire with wine and whey should she need it. There are bricks heating on the hearth if they are needed to warm her. Use the tongs and wrap them in the towels near the hearth before you place them near her."

"I will not allow her to get burnt."

"Keep the basin near her in case she vomits. In the water jar you will find a saline draught with a touch of laudanum. Give her a tumbler of that if she purges."

Lydia nodded.

"If she becomes too hot, or her belly pains her, there is a pail of vinegar water beside the chair. Soak cloths in that and place them on her belly and limbs. Do not let them dry out. Can you do all this?"

"Yes, madam, I will."

"Very well, I will be just down the hall should you need me." Mrs. Harrow shambled away.

A low moan filtered through the door. Lydia slipped inside.

Juliana's forehead glistened with beads of sweat. Lydia wrung cooling cloths and draped them over her face and neck until she began to shiver.

The cold fit seemed like it would never pass. Warm bricks and drinks finally settled her and her fever abated.

The reprieve should be relished whilst it lasted.

Lydia dipped her handkerchief in the vinegar water and scoured the sweat from her face and neck. Dirty stains streaked across its length. It smelled more of sweat than vinegar now. She threw it into the corner pile of used linens and stretched.

Why must a sickroom be kept so hot and stuffy?

Exhausted, beyond exhausted. How else to describe tiredness that leached the strength from one's bones? Perhaps one day she would draw it, but who would want to see such a thing?

The door edged open and Mrs. Drummond slipped in. Cool air rushed in behind her. She looked better for a few hours' sleep, but deep creases still shadowed her face. A weariness beyond the mere physical washed over her being, dull, grey and worn.

"You have got her to sleep?" Mrs. Drummond touched Juliana's forehead with the back of her hand.

"Only just, and with the help of Mrs. Harrow's saline and laudanum draught."

"I do not much like the use of laudanum in this house. Do not allow it to be known there is any within these walls."

"Someone here?"

"Yes, and it would not do to bring them into temptation."

Who? She rubbed her eyes. Lucy was the only one whose story did she not know.

Ames might have survived drinking too much laudanum, but Lydia was no Lizzy, and her father was not here to advise treatment. She would guard her tongue especially carefully around Lucy.

Mrs. Drummond straightened Juliana's blanket. "Go rest. You may use the settee in my office."

"Annabelle, that is Miss Fitzgilbert, asked me to stay with her."

Mrs. Drummond rubbed her eyes with thumb and forefinger. "I approve."

"Thank you." Lydia tiptoed to the door, but paused before opening it. "I cannot sleep now, not after being so stifled in this heat. May I sit in the garden, on the bench near the door? I promise to be very quiet and go nowhere else. I … I need some fresh air."

Mrs. Drummond sighed. "You realize—"

"I know it very improper. I am sorry. Perhaps I might just open a window, then?"

"I understand the need for fresh air. The garden is walled and gated, and the moon is full. Stay to the bench near the door and do not stay out long."

Lydia curtsied. "Thank you, madam. Shall I come back afterwards?"

"No, Miss Honeywell will sit with her next." She patted Juliana's hand.

"Juliana is so strong, more than any one of us realizes."

"Yes, she is."

Lydia slipped out the door and shut it softly behind her.

Moonlight through the hall window washed the corridor in cold, otherworldly light. Unladylike snores filtering through closed doors might have been the muffled roars of some unnamed creature of darkness.

She rubbed away sharp prickles dancing up her arms. Silly, foolish girl. She must not allow ridiculous fears to take hold. There were far too many real, tangible things to fear.

She sat on the creaky top step.

In Papa's house she had kept those fears at bay with gaiety and fun and flirtations. Without those well-placed defenses, what would—what could—hold them back?

Would she ever feel safe again?

Lydia rose. Darkness enveloped the stairway and the short hall to the back door. A tiny sliver of moonlight poured in beside the back door.

Who had left it open?

She slipped outside and latched the door behind her.

How cool and wonderful the night air! Smooth and silky, caressing her sweat-ravaged limbs with a soothing silver balm. Night creatures chirruped and twittered, far less frightening than the sounds within.

What? Was that a groan and a shadow near the house—

"Mr. Amberson?"

"Miss Bennet?" He jumped to his feet.

His lanky limbs cast exaggerated shadows along the garden path. How very much taller than usual he seemed.

"You should not be out."

"Mrs. Drummond gave me permission."

"Does she not think it improper?"

"What are you doing out here?"

Though deep shadows covered his face, tell-tale swollen eyes and glistening cheeks stood out in the moonlight. She brushed his cheek with fingertips.

What did it take to make a man cry? The only tears Papa had ever shed were for little Thomas.

"My heart is heavy and my soul, grieved, and only the night can contain it." He grasped her wrist and pressed her palm to his cheek. Eyes closed, he leaned into her hand. The lines around his eyes softened.

"Do you wish to speak of it?"

"I should not unburden myself upon you, but I fear if I try to contain it, I might shatter with the ef-fort."

He took her hand and led her to the bench. She perched upon it, but he hunkered tailor-style on the ground before her.

"Tell me what troubles you."

He scrubbed his face with his hands. "You will think ill of me for knowing."

"I cannot imagine what you could tell me that would make me think ill of you."

"You have great faith in me."

"Perhaps. Or perhaps I am far more difficult to shock than a proper young lady ought to be." Her chuckles had a raw edge.

"I helped bury him today. The midwife christened him, wrapped him in a sheet and gave him to me. I took him to the vicar, and we buried him in the churchyard near some climbing roses. No marker, no mourners." He raked his hair into an unruly mass. "They say the loss of a baby or even a child is a negligible loss. A father, a husband, that is a life worth mourning."

"You do not agree?"

"Is it wrong to mourn instead for the life that was never lived? The potential lost to us forever?"

"I suppose you are correct. But consider, the babe spent the whole of his life staring into the eyes of one who loved him more deeply than you and I might even understand. Surely, there must be something of great beauty in such a life."

He grabbed her hands and pressed his forehead to them, great, heaving sobs wracking his bony shoulders.

"I pray my son might have lived the life you described."

"Your son?" Her cheeks flushed cold and her fingers numbed.

She tried to pull them away, but he held her fast.

"My son, Miss Bennet." He stared into her eyes, so ragged, so exposed. She forced herself not to turn away.

Silence, punctuated with gasping breaths, filled the

air between them, heavy and uncertain. Perhaps she should return to the house.

"Do you not wonder why a man of my talent is a teacher at a school for sullied girls? There is good reason, I assure you. You will find my sins are no different to your own."

He released her hands and she slipped an arms' length back.

"My skill gave me favor among those above me. I was a favorite among society. Though the proper mamas and papas frowned upon their daughters keeping company with a musician, flaunting their restrictions proved exhilarating."

Lydia pressed her fist to her mouth.

"In time, one of them fell with child. I will never forget the moment she told me."

"What did you do?"

"I am not proud of my first inclinations. I spoke harshly to her, but in truth, it was myself I was angry at. She gave her virtue easily enough, but it was I who cajoled it from her."

"What did you do?"

"I offered her marriage, but her father wanted a titled man for her. I thought some of my connections might be able to secure me a knighthood. He embraced the notion. So I left to London to make what efforts I could to that end." He pushed to his feet and walked into a distant shaft of moonlight.

She followed a few steps behind.

"While I was gone, he sent her to distant relations. She went willingly as I understand. He never intended to accept my offer, and my failure to secure the knighthood sealed my fate."

"Do you know what became of her?"

"I tried to find her, but my efforts led me to be run out of town by the magistrate."

What lengths had he gone to?

"I learned, through clandestine communication with her abigail, that she bore my son. He survived only three days. I pray he was loved even half so well as you describe. What grieves me most is that I may have had a child in the world and never known. Many a father has helped his natural child, has he not? To have that chance taken from me—I find it difficult to forgive." He scoured his face with his hands.

A cloud drifted across the moon, shrouding them in momentary darkness.

"Fool that I am, it was only six months ago, after learning of her wedding to a baronet, that I relinquished all hope of her. Her abigail assured me she did not repine my loss. She had little use of a simple musician when offered a titled man instead." He turned away and strode several steps into the night.

She tiptoed into the darkness and laid her hand on his arm. "I know what it is to be forsaken by the one who you hoped loved you."

He whirled and caught her shoulders, his eyes flashing and wild. "You are a rare treasure, Miss Bennet. I have met no one else who sees the world as I hear it. So sensitive, so perceptive." His hand strayed to a loose curl by her ear. He wound it around his fingers and gently pulled it through. "It seems my aunt has finally begun to appreciate you even as I do. I have restrained myself for both our sakes, but tonight, grief has made me reckless. I cannot bear the thought of losing you before we have even begun."

"Begun?"

"Begun, Miss Bennet." He caressed her cheek. "Or

have I misunderstood the look in your eye and the tremor in your voice? For many weeks now, I have considered you as more than my student and hoped, even dreamed that you might feel the same."

"Sir, I ..."

"Then I have been mistaken." He released her shoulders and turned aside.

"Wait, no."

He stopped.

"I have been most pleased with your company, sir."

"Only pleased?" He stepped closer.

"I must not, I cannot, I should not consider anything more. I am here for improvement."

That was the right answer, was it not?

"My aunt believes you have improved." He ran her curl through his fingers again.

"Would she approve? Or my ... my brother Darcy approve?"

"Do you approve?" He leaned close, into a moonbeam that bathed his profile in a silver-blue glow. "Just a word from you, and I shall never speak of this again."

"I approve, but what of them?"

"I do not care. Only your opinion matters." His palm cupped her cheek, running his calloused thumb along the crest of her cheek. He smoothed her eyebrow, and she closed her eyes. A feathery touch glided over her eyelid, and he tipped her face up.

Warm, soft lips met hers, igniting an effusion of warmth that spread from her heart, filling her chest and all the way to her fingertips. Softly, gently, reverently, giving, not taking, offering her every opportunity to pull away. His longing rang as passionate and intense as his music without the raw edge of hunger and lust present that Wickham had offered.

She leaned into his kiss, though she should not. This, just this and only this, she could not deny him.

He pulled away and whispered. "I must leave you, lest temptations visit this garden, and I prove myself unworthy." He caressed her cheek and faded into the darkness.

Emptiness swirled about her, cold and sharp.

She turned back toward the house.

Something moved in one of the windows above. Perhaps there were rats in the garden after all.

Chapter 12

WHEN SLEEP FINALLY CAME, it embraced her like a lost love. Foggy memories intruded, tempted her away: someone helping her to Annabelle's room, trays of broth, gruel, and sweet wine with water. They swirled in the back of her mind, elusive and dreamlike until slumber claimed her again.

Rays of warm brightness streamed onto her face, demanding, pleading. Lydia blinked and rubbed sandy eyes.

How long had she slept?

She hurried to dress. How and when had she undressed?

An empty, soundless corridor greeted her. The house should not be silent this time of day.

She darted down the hall and pressed her ear to the cool wood of Juliana's door. More gut-wrenching silence.

The door inched open and Mrs. Drummond waved her in. Juliana snored softly beside her!

Lydia's vision wavered at the edges and her knees turned soft.

"We were beginning to worry for your health." Mrs. Drummond caught her before she stumbled.

"How long have I been sleeping?"

"A day and a night now, but you seem all the better for it."

"How is Juliana?"

"The fever continues, but she has suffered no more fits. She takes a bit of broth from time to time, though mostly she sleeps. It is far too soon to tell, but we are hopeful." Mrs. Drummond smiled a tense, tired smile.

Miss Thornton peeked in. "Shall I sit with her now? Miss Honeywell is preparing the girls to visit the workhouse."

"Very good. I shall speak to her before they leave. Come, Miss Bennet. You should break your fast with some proper food."

Lydia's stomach rumbled as she followed Mrs. Drummond out.

"Have your breakfast, but do not to go out with the rest of the girls. Miss Fitzgilbert is expecting a call from Sir Anthony this morning and requires you as chaperone."

"I am hardly fit to be seen, madam. I do not wish to embarrass her."

Mrs. Drummond tucked a stray curl behind Lydia's ear. "I know you are exhausted, but we are very much at the mercy of his leisure. We cannot refuse him."

"I understand, madam."

Poor Annabelle! How was she faring?

Mrs. Drummond pursed her lips and sighed. "You should be presentable for Miss Fitzgilbert's sake. Go back to your room and prepare. I shall have a tray sent to your room."

"To my room? But—"

"Yes, I am well aware of my own rules, Miss Bennet. Sometimes exceptions must be made." She chuckled and continued downstairs.

Lydia trudged to Annabelle's room. Several of her gowns hung in the closet. Her hair brush lay on the dressing table, and the dresser contained still more of her things. Someone must have brought them whilst she slept.

Annabelle shouldered the door open, tea tray in her hands. She deposited the tray on the narrow table near the window.

"Selfish creature that I am, I am so glad you are to chaperone Sir Anthony's visit today. I know it is a great deal to ask, when you are only barely back to rights yourself. Here, let me help you dress."

Lydia slipped off her dressing gown and pulled the dress Annabelle handed her over her head.

"You missed quite a to-do yesterday. Sit down and let me do your hair. It looks so very pretty without your cap." Annabelle picked up Lydia's hairbrush.

"What happened yesterday?"

"You can imagine, the whole house is quite at sixes and sevens over Juliana. Half the girls are afraid any sound at all could force a turn for the worse. The rest are babbling like brooks, as though too much quiet might invite the specter of death." Annabelle unwound Lydia's hair and brushed it smooth. "Then there is Amelia."

Lydia's stomach knotted.

"I envy you, away from her blithering and complaining. If she is not declaring that she is not a maid, she is decrying Mrs. Drummond's favoritism."

"What does she consider favoritism?"

"Only her favorites enjoy the privilege of sitting with Juliana." Annabelle snorted. "Poor dear, if she is not bleeding, she is casting up her accounts or succumbing to loose bowels. If I did not love her so well, I would not sit with her and deal with her mess. But Amelia does not seem to grasp that side of the privilege. She is truly dreadful."

"I can imagine. Do many share her opinions?"

"Just the same ones who are always apt to attend her."

Lydia scuffed her foot along the floorboards. How easily she might have been part of that group.

Annabelle swept up her hair into a tidy knot and tucked in several pins. "You look lovely. Given a little more time, I could have fashioned you some curls, but that will wait for another day. Pray, eat something."

Lydia dabbed jam on a slice of toast. "You have not changed your mind about liking Sir Anthony well enough, have you?"

"No—yes—no—I mean, I am determined that I shall like him. It is my best choice is it not?" Annabelle wrung her hands in her lap. "He went to see my father about the settlement, and I have no idea what to expect."

"You said your father wishes—"

"My father wishes me settled on any terms, no matter how meager. I doubt he would argue with whatever Sir Anthony proposes."

"You will be very pleased, I am sure." Lydia brushed crumbs from her fingers.

"How can you say that? My father will care only that I will not be a burden on him should I be widowed. Only a small jointure is required to accomplish that end. I suppose it is entirely selfish, but I would like some kind of pin money in the settlement."

Lydia grabbed her hand. "Sir Anthony is a generous man. He will offer an agreeable settlement for you."

"He did say that. You are right. That is precisely what he said." Annabelle set the brush on the dressing table and paced the length of the room. "This is why I need you with me. I am ever so addlepated! I need someone sensible to help me through."

"Sensible? I am flattered, but no one has ever considered me sensible."

"Well, perhaps not with numbers, but when it comes to sensibilities, you are very sensible indeed."

"Listen to what you are saying! Here, have some tea and a bit of toast. It will settle your stomach and your nerves." She rose and pushed the chair at Annabelle.

Annabelle perched on the chair and accepted a cup. She sipped and nibbled and peered out the window. Halfway through her toast, she sprang up.

"Oh, look, look! There is his carriage! We must to the drawing room!"

They arrived downstairs just in time to hear Sir Anthony's sharp rap at the door. Three breaths later, Mrs. Drummond showed him into the drawing room.

"Miss Bennet, Lady Annabelle." He bowed.

If the creases in his cravat became any sharper, they would surely slit his throat.

Lydia curtsied and removed herself to the dainty writing desk beside the window and withdrew pencil and paper. With a little bit of fortune, they would both forget her presence.

"My visit with your father proved most successful." He lifted his chin and straightened his shoulder, a bit like a peacock about to display.

From his pocket he withdrew several crisply folded sheets.

Sir Anthony and Annabelle's father must have agreed to a marriage settlement.

Lady Annabelle would be married in just a few short weeks. She would be respectable and out amongst society again, hosting parties, attending dinners and balls.

Oh, to keep company in society again! Would she ever be respectable enough for that? Only marriage might render her so.

Marriage.

What had Mr. Amberson meant in the moonlight?

That kiss … oh, his kiss! So unexpected … so completely improper … so entirely wonderful. Wickham had never kissed her that way: gently, tenderly, respectfully.

Was it possible to be so improper and yet respectful at the same time? It made no sense, but it certainly seemed so.

How many of her drawings had been inspired by his music? Half, maybe more? Not including the one of his hands, and that secret portrait of him which would never see the light of day. To look at her sketch book, it would seem Mr. Amberson consumed her idle thoughts.

She never thought so much about Wickham. Only

about how jealous her sisters would be, and how Mama would think her so clever for finding a husband.

Mr. Amberson had become such a part of her daily existence. He was so very, very dear. How would it be not to see him every day, to make music with him, and talk about their art?

A prickly flush crept up her jaw.

Was it possible he felt the same?

"Do you find the terms agreeable?" Sir Anthony asked.

Annabelle pressed her hand to her chest. "Indeed sir, I am most grateful. You described yourself as generous, and you did not exaggerate."

Sir Anthony's smile was nothing less than smug. Could it be Annabelle's approval pleased him?

At least his actions warranted it.

He tucked the papers back into his coat pocket. "He also agreed to the date we established."

Annabelle swallowed. "Just five weeks or so from now?"

"Indeed, and I have a surprise for you: an appointment this morning with the best modiste in Summerseat. Have you given thought to who you wish to stand up with you when you wed?"

"I would like it very much if Miss Bennet could stand with me."

Lydia jumped.

"Then bring her with you, and she shall have a new gown as well."

Lydia rose, hands trembling. "That is most kind of you sir, but I am sure I cannot accept."

Sir Anthony's brows knit and his face became stern, a little like Papa's.

The hair on the back of her neck prickled.

"I insist. If we are to make a proper entrance into society, it must begin at the wedding. It is essential that both of you look the part. My offer is a generous one, but I fully expect a benefit from dressing you both properly. Mrs. Drummond will agree." He crossed his arms.

The tiny twinkle in his eye belied his gruff tone, something Papa's eyes never did.

Annabelle glanced at Lydia. "I cannot argue with your reasoning. It may, though, take me a little time to begin thinking of life in those terms once again."

"I will have the society pages from London sent to you that you may familiarize yourself with the fashionable set."

"What ironic material to be studying during my final days with Mrs. Drummond."

"I shall inform her of my wishes lest she interfere."

"I expect it will require your explanation." Annabelle bit heir lower lip and rolled her eyes.

"I left instructions with the dressmaker and a liberal allowance for both gowns. I will inform Mrs. Drummond of your appointment."

"You have not already designed the gowns yourself?"

"Are you calling me overbearing?"

"I said nothing of the sort. I simply asked, have you already designed the gowns?"

"No, I did express my preferences, but I leave gowns to the purview of those who will be wearing them." Sir Anthony chuckled.

"You find me amusing, sir?"

"I do, Lady. Your spirit is refreshing and just as

your father warned me it would be."

Annabelle's eyes narrowed. "What did he say of me? That I am headstrong and unmanageable and in need of very firm supervision?"

"I respect you too much to repeat his exact words. Just as you respect me too much to disregard my desires in this matter."

Their gazes locked; neither one giving ground. He reached toward her and she met him halfway. He clasped her fingers.

"You are quite correct. And I do appreciate your generosity."

"We shall make a good go of this, you and I. This will be an agreeable situation." He raised her fingers to his lips.

"I value your faith in me, sir."

"I shall speak to Mrs. Drummond and leave you to the modiste. I will call again in a few days." He bowed and withdrew.

Annabelle stared after him.

Lydia hurried to her side. "So, the settlement?"

"I am astonished. It is far more than I deserve. By all appearances, he means to treat me as though I were not … as I am." She sank back onto the couch.

"I am very happy for you." Lydia clasped her hands.

"I am so happy you will stand with me."

"Are you sure?"

"Absolutely. Who has stood with me through all this? And you are to have a new gown, too!"

"I am all astonishment. Even understanding his reasoning, it still seems very generous."

The door swung open, and Mrs. Drummond swept in.

"Hurry, get your wraps and bonnets and be off to the dressmaker immediately. It would not do to keep her waiting." Mrs. Drummond's brows drew together and her eyes narrowed. "Remember, these gowns are not to please yourselves, but to please him. Since he has already spoken to the modiste, listen to her and take her advice. You will, of course, not speak of this to the others."

"Madam," Annabelle said softly, "may the rest of the girls attend the wedding?"

"If it pleases Sir Anthony, I am of no mind to deny him. He has already suggested we have the wedding breakfast here and has offered a very liberal sum to pay for it. Now go. Mr. Amberson is taking the post in today. He will see you to the dressmaker." Her eyes lingered on Lydia.

Why did she stare so?

They dashed upstairs for their wraps. Her red cloak stared back at her from the shadows of the closet. The nip in the air made it an appropriate choice. But they were walking with Mr. Amberson. She reached for her dark blue pelisse.

Mr. Amberson waited for them near the front door, his long fingers around a thick stack of letters. "Miss Bennet, Miss Fitzgilbert," he bowed, "shall we be off?"

He opened the door and ushered them out into the bright afternoon sun.

Lydia strode past with a sideways glance, but he did not return her gaze. While he had never ogled her as Wickham had, he had never failed to look at her.

Did he despise her now?

He closed the door behind them and followed. His long strides crunched through the dry leaves and pebbles, regular as counted measures. He had never been prone to excessive conversation, but this silence sliced with a cold, sharp edge.

Oh, how he must hate her.

Annabelle glanced at her and her eyebrows rose. She looked over her shoulder and tipped her head.

Lydia turned aside.

Annabelle stumbled.

"Are you injured?" Mr. Amberson caught her elbow.

She clutched her ankle. "Thank you, sir. I think I am well, but my half-boots have come untied. I feel like such a cake. You go on whilst I tie them. I shall catch up in just a moment." She waved them on.

Did she have to be so obvious? Kitty had used the same ploy often enough. It had seemed so clever then, but surely Mr. Amberson would only disparage her all the more for it.

"If you are certain." He walked on.

Lydia stared at Annabelle, but she did not seem to notice. She rushed to catch up to him.

One, two, three, four steps. The gravel-crunch stopped as the road turned dusty with soft dirt.

He cleared his throat. "Miss Bennet?"

"Yes." Her voice was little more than a squeak.

"I wish to know … that is to say … might I ask…" He ran his finger around the inside of his stock, spoiling the folds of his cravat.

"My father hated it when I dithered about a point."

"I see, then … then I shall come out directly … as I should. Yes, yes I should."

No wonder Papa despised it!

"I … I received some new music recently."

"Music?" She stopped mid-step and stared at him.

"Yes, quite. It is a very fine piece, one of my favorites actually." He dabbed sweat from his brow with his crumpled handkerchief. "I like it very well, you see. And it is … it is a duet."

"A duet?"

"Precisely. And I wondered if … if you might … if it would be agreeable that I might teach it to you, in our lessons. If you wish to continue them. My aunt … she intimated perhaps a drawing master might be more appropriate to your accomplishments."

She gasped and her knees softened.

He caught her forearms. "Miss Bennet!"

"No, no, I am well. It is just …" she gulped air like a tench out of water. "Lessons, yes … I am not nearly accomplished enough in pianoforte. I should very much like to continue lessons. If you are still willing to be my teacher."

"You do not wish to study under a different master?"

"I have barely learned to play duets. That is a very necessary accomplishment?"

He mopped his upper lip. "Yes, Miss Bennet. I believe so."

"In what way do you agree with my friend?" Annabelle looped her arm in Lydia's and slipped between them.

"That all of you should continue to practice performing after dinner. It is a most entertaining way to pass the evening." He fingered the pile of letters under his arm, a crimson flush creeping up his jaw.

She pouted. "And I thought I might have missed an interesting conversation."

"I fear my conversation has rarely been considered

interesting."

"Might I ask a favor, sir? Sir Anthony sent me a piece of music, but I am a little uncertain of the fingering of certain passages. I should very much appreciate your help with it."

"I would be happy to address it in your next lesson. And Miss Bennet," he reached into his pocket and handed her a tightly folded paper. "Pray, review this score for our next lesson."

She took the music and tucked it in her reticule.

Pray let him not notice how her hands shook!

They stopped beside a lovely shop window.

"The dressmaker's shop. I shall leave you now." He bowed and held the door for them.

The distinctive smell of a dressmaker's shop greeted them: the faintly coriander scent of Indian silks, the green, sheep-y aroma of wool, beeswax, a touch of expensive perfume and fresh flowers.

Butterfly tingles fluttered against her ribs. How she loved the dressmaker's!

She had spent many a pleasant hour with Mama at the modiste, helping her choose fabric and trims. Even though her own gowns were handed down from her elder sisters, it had been jolly fun to look through the fashion plates and imagine new gowns.

"Miss Fitzgilbert?" A stern looking matron in a striped dress approached.

How stunning!

Her gown was deceptively simple, without ribbon or lace. Instead, the stripes were cut to form patterns and the eye swept around the skirt, pausing at diamond pattern poufs on the ruffles' peaks.

What a brilliant design.

"Yes, madam." Annabelle curtsied. "—and my

friend, Miss Bennet."

Lydia bobbed. "What you have done with the stripes on your bodice is utterly striking. You have used them to create—"

"An illusion of shape and size, tasteful, yet drawing the eye to a woman's assets. You have a very fine eye, Miss Bennet. I see you will be a great help to your friend. Based on the gentleman's suggestions, I have some drawings for you to consider." She led them to a high table and gestured to a pair of stools. Several fashion plates interspersed with hand sketches—not very good ones—lay spread before them.

Lydia scanned the images. Sir Anthony did have an admirable eye for fashion. Still, the sleeves on the first would not flatter Annabelle's broad shoulders. The skirt on the second was far too embellished and would not accentuate her graceful, elegant walk. But the third …

"This one," Lydia tapped the third fashion plate. "—in a pale silk, perhaps with a net over-dress, like in the last drawing, embroidered with roses, or perhaps that lace there."

"That lace is very expensive, beyond the budget I have been given."

Annabelle glared at them both. "I have not even viewed all the drawings, yet. Permit me to do so before you go about designing the particulars of my gown."

Mama used to mutter the same sort of nonsense, but eventually learned just to trust to Lydia's recommendations.

"Go ahead and do, but you will agree with me once you have."

"Your friend has made excellent suggestions." The

modiste glanced at the lace.

Probably developing an argument to convince Sir Anthony of the necessity of it.

"Whilst you wait upon my considerations, do begin on Miss Bennet's gown."

"Of course. Come." The modiste beckoned Lydia to another table, also laid with drawings. They were lovely, though not nearly so fine or fashionable as the ones shown to Annabelle.

"This one." Lydia slid a drawing closer. "It is very much like the gown you are wearing."

The modiste fingered the edge of her sleeve. "I am surprised you noticed."

"Few could have turned such a plain gown into something so extraordinary."

"I have a growing reputation for quality gowns, different to what anyone else provides."

"Have you a paper and pencil?"

"Just a moment." She disappeared and reappeared a moment later.

Lydia quickly sketched out a figure, blending the modiste's stripes with elements of four of the drawings before her. "This, in muslin, with a subtle stripe on the top, made like yours, but the bottom like that one."

The modiste hovered over her shoulder and tapped the drawing. "Yes, yes I see. With ruching to make the stripes cascade down the sleeve."

"Exactly." Lydia laid down her pencil.

"I have exactly the fabric." She hurried off to the back room and returned with a frothy bundle of white-on-white wide stripe muslin.

"Exactly what I was thinking of!"

Her eyes narrowed. "It is outside your budget."

Lydia turned her drawing over and pulled it close. "I suppose I shall make it myself."

"But such a gown requires great skill."

"I am sure I could sort it out. Although the modiste who created such a garment would receive a great deal of attention."

The modiste grumbled. "I did acquire the fabric for a cancelled order. It was partially paid for. The remaining balance is close enough to your budget. I am willing to accept it."

"And you will enjoy trying your hand at my design and suggesting it to other customers?"

The modiste cleared her throat.

"I think it fair payment, my design for the difference in the fabric."

She took the drawing. "Very well, I will call my girl out to take your measure."

After she was measured, Lydia returned to Annabelle, still poring over images.

"Oh, I cannot decide. I do not understand how you could put your ideas together so quickly." She planted her elbows on the table and pressed her forehead to her hands.

Lydia sighed and retrieved a blank sheet of paper from the other table. She roughed out another sketch. "Here, this is your gown."

Annabelle opened her eyes and gaped. "It is beautiful."

"That is what I described to you before."

"I am not nearly so adept at picturing things as you. This is just perfect."

"Yes, yes, it is very good." The modiste stroked her lips with her knuckles.

"You may have this design as well, if it will purchase that lace." Lydia pointed to the lace draping over a nearby shelf.

The modiste chewed her lip.

Lydia covered the drawing with her hand.

"Do proper drawings for both these dresses and paint them, and I will see she has the lace."

"Agreed."

"You cannot!"

"Yes, I can. They are my designs and my drawings. I may do anything I like with them. All you need worry about is pleasing Sir Anthony with your clever economy."

"The deal has been made. I will bring fabrics for you to see." The modiste slipped the sketch out from under Lydia's hand.

"Whilst you select fabric, allow me to dash across the street to the haberdasher's. I need to get some stay laces for Juliana."

Annabelle bit her lip and blinked bright eyes. "You should not go alone."

"I will be a quarter of an hour and no more. I will be back before you make a decision." She patted Annabelle's shoulder and hurried out.

Gracious heavens, had she really just traded her art for something of value?

She wandered across the street, barely dodging two passing carriages and peered into the haberdasher's window. Those ribbons, plaited perhaps, would do very nicely for Annabelle's hair. And there were the laces, on the shelf just beyond.

"Oh, Beverly!"

That voice!

She looked around, but no one was there.

"Oh!"

Lydia sidled along the wall and peeked down the narrow alleyway between the buildings.

Amelia slumped against the stone wall, head thrown back, eyes closed. A dandy pressed his face to her ample bosom, nearly scooped out of her bodice. Her skirt was rucked up, one of his hands well under it, his hips pressed to hers. Was the fall of his trouser unfastened?

"What the bloody hell are you looking at?" He snarled, glaring at Lydia with lust-hazed eyes.

Amelia's eyes flew open. She jumped away from him, fluffing her skirts and tucking her bodice. "Oh, Lydia?"

"What are you doing here, and who is he?"

"This is Beverly, and what I am doing here is none of your business." Amelia marched to her. "If you make it your business, I shall tell everyone what I saw of you and Mr. Amberson—alone, in the garden, in the middle of the night. I cannot imagine you want Mrs. Drummond to know of your behavior right under her roof."

"I … I had her permission to be outside."

"Perhaps you did, but she did not give you permission to kiss her nephew."

"It was nothing!"

"Are you so certain? I dare say she will send you away, and perhaps even Mr. Amberson. Are you willing to risk that? Not to mention, I know everything about Miss High-and-Mighty's wedding plans. What do you think would happen if her precious knight received a little note detailing her assignations with—oh I do not know … perhaps, Beverly's brother."

"She has done no such thing!"

"But will he believe that? As I understand, he has a

particular sensitivity to such accusations, or so the scandal sheets would suggest."

"You would not!"

"It seems we each have something the other wants. You shall hold your peace, help me elope and in return I shall say nothing to Mrs. Drummond or Sir Anthony to jeopardize either of your loves."

Lydia stared dumbly.

"We are agreed then. Go off now, and leave Beverly and I be."

Lydia turned and shuffled away, squeezing her eyes shut.

How could she keep such a secret, much less help in such a scheme? But if she did not, what price was to be paid?

Best get back to Annabelle.

Lydia slipped into the modiste's shop. She pressed her back against the door and gulped a desperate breath.

"Did you find the stay laces?" Annabelle asked, not looking up from the table laden with fabric and trim samples.

"What? No, I did not like their wares."

Pray do not let her ask further!

"No matter, it is an excellent excuse to visit the other. I have settled on this fabric. What do you think?" The white silk pooled in her hand and flowed back to the table like a stream held in time.

"It is the one I described to you. Did you forget? You would save a great deal of time if you would just listen to me like Mama did. She was very pleased to leave all her choices to me."

Annabelle huffed and muttered something under her breath.

The modiste jotted down a few more notes. "Very good, I should expect a fortnight or so for a fitting. You will have my drawings for me, yes?"

The hopeful lilt to her voice raised the hairs on the back of Lydia's neck.

"I shall have one prepared for the fitting, the other when the gowns are complete."

The modiste looked at the ceiling, probably working out how much the drawings were worth to her.

"Very well. I will send a girl when the gowns are ready for fitting." She helped them with their wraps and showed them out.

Annabelle clutched her arm, words tumbling out like lambs turned out in a field. "You are so clever. I would never have thought of bartering with the modiste. That lace is so beautiful, but you did not need to get it for me. You should have got something for yourself."

"Did you not see? The dreamiest striped silk for my gown."

"You must let me trim a bonnet to match your gown, then. I have one that I have been meaning to pull apart. The shape will suit your face so much better than mine. Please? Working on it will help me pass the time and not fret so."

A movement in the corner of her eye caught her attention. Lydia glanced over her shoulder.

"What? No!" Annabelle dashed toward a young woman walking rapidly in the opposite direction.

Why did Amelia have to appear just now?

Lydia ran towards them.

Annabelle caught up to Amelia. "What are you doing walking alone in town?"

Amelia rolled her eyes and held up two spools.

"Miss Honeywell sent me to purchase thread to teach the little girls to sew today. Joan was to accompany me, but she nicked off to the confectioner just across the way." She pointed to a bright red door at the far end of the street.

A pair of young dandies lingered there, one very familiar.

"You allowed her to go by herself with those two fops loitering near?" Annabelle stomped like an irate pony, raising a little cloud of dust.

"You know how headstrong she can be. I told her not to go near those young men."

"I rather thought you fancied one of them." Annabelle folded her arms across her chest. "Did I not see you talking to him once?"

Amelia flicked her hand. "La, I suppose I did talk to him once or twice. But fancy him—hardly."

"We cannot leave Joan alone any longer. Come, we must fetch her." Annabelle tossed her head and marched across the street.

Lydia hesitated.

Amelia glared a warning and dashed after Annabelle.

Lydia caught up with them just before they reached the confectioners.

"Wait here with Lydia whilst I fetch Joan." Annabelle strode forward, offering the fops at the door a cut direct as she swept between them.

They sniggered as she passed, vulgar gestures flying between them. Wickham had used those gestures too, when offended by ladies above his station.

"She is so puffed up and proud. I should send her knight a friendly note about her. That would take her down a peg or two. You should not have let her see me." She poked Lydia's chest with a sharp finger.

"Perhaps you should have been more mindful."

"Perhaps you should recall what is at stake."

The confectioner's door flung open, forcing the fops to jump out of the way.

Annabelle bustled out, dragging Joan by the elbow. "You know better than to go off by yourself! Not to mention you abandoned Amelia."

Joan swatted at Annabelle's hand, protesting in half-formed words and noises.

Amelia sidled up to them. "What kind of a friend are you, jeopardizing my reputation for your love of sweets?"

Lydia slipped back and tugged her bonnet forward. The deep poke brim might hide her cheeks better that way.

Had she not done the selfsame thing when she left Annabelle at the dressmakers? Should Annabelle not be furious with her too?

"We will walk with you back to the workhouse." Annabelle turned Joan and Amelia in the right direction and gave them a little shove.

"Why were you not at the workhouse?" Amelia's eyes narrowed.

"You can stop that line of thought right now. We were on an errand as directed by my father with Mrs. Drummond's full knowledge and approbation."

Annabelle would be a very effective mistress of the house with that voice.

Amelia snorted and Joan snuck a sidelong glance at her. They would surely have words tonight. But it would end as it always did. Joan lacked the stamina and the wit to stand up to Amelia.

Miss Honeywell met them at the workhouse door.

"We have lost nearly the whole day waiting on you." She waved Lydia and Annabelle on.

"I fear I am in no mood for more shopping today. Do you mind if we look for bonnets another day?" Annabelle straightened her spencer.

"I think it just as well we return to Mrs. Drummond."

She looped her arm in Lydia's. "I am glad we do not have to continue in their company. They are quite horrid. I probably should not say it so freely, but there it is."

If only she knew how horrid Amelia could be.

Annabelle carried the whole of the conversation on the way back; muttering about Amelia; gushing over gowns; and prattling about the letter she must write to her mother who now deigned to correspond with her.

Thanks to Lizzy's patient example, Lydia knew how to nod and make sounds of interest enough to maintain the conversation. She performed the task so well she did not have to utter a single word all the way back.

Chapter 13

AT THE HOUSE, Annabelle rushed off to find Mrs. Drummond. No doubt a full report of the trip, including Joan's transgressions would be summarily delivered. Surely Mrs. Drummond would understand the true nature of the situation and act to keep them all safe.

Would Annabelle tell her of Lydia's transgression as well? Probably not intentionally, but Annabelle was a bit overzealous as head girl. Mrs. Drummond might well discern and she would not be pleased. At best a stern discussion would be in the offing. At worst …

She cringed.

Lydia trudged upstairs to the music room. Practice would pass the time and numb the dread threatening from so many directions.

She sat at the pianoforte. Her hands trembled so hard she nearly failed to extract the tightly folded music from her reticule. She drew a deep breath over ten counts and released it over as many again. Once more, and the shaking eased enough to coax the paper flat.

Had he written this score himself? His hand was even, regular, and very neat. But these black notes danced across the page in an uneven march; too close together in some spots; too far spread in others; many smudged in haste.

He never smudged.

Only great vexation of spirit might explain this score. If only he had written her some kind of note!

But that would be most improper. Music, just music; that was safe to pass between pupil and teacher.

She smoothed the creases over her lap and arranged it on the music stand.

The score was no simple piece. What could he mean, giving her something she probably could not even play?

It began slow and steady, proper and even formal. A conventional, if complex melody. The time signature changed.

Ouch.

She winced at the chord and tried the fingering again. That could not have been correct. So discordant and uneven. While her playing was certainly imperfect, it was not so bad as this.

But no, that was what he wrote.

What could have pushed him to pen these mournful, lonely strains?

She swallowed hard, tracing the tortured notes with her fingertip.

The next movement changed key and character. The smudged, crowded notes rendered a melancholy melody: regret, tinged with an edge of sorrow and hope.

How did one describe it? Repentant, perhaps?

The final movement changed keys yet again, rich with longing and laced with optimism and desire, but incomplete. It needed a second part to complete it.

She turned the music over, but the back was blank. Part of the music was missing.

Would she ever get to hear it? Somehow she had to.

"That was beautiful." A wan voice whispered from the doorway. Gaunt and ashen, Juliana clutched the side of the door frame.

Lydia dashed to the doorway, barely in time to catch her as her knees gave way.

"You should not be out of bed!"

"I could not help it, the music was so beautiful. I had to hear it more clearly."

"You are still feverish."

"I feel ever so much better. It hardly hurts, and the room only spins a little when I stand." She tried to pull herself upright, but could not stand unassisted for more than a moment.

Lydia pulled Juliana's arm over her shoulder.

"I am more pleased than I can say, but we must get you back to bed. It is not safe for you to exert yourself too much."

Juliana allowed Lydia to return her to her room. Lydia tucked her into bed and ran for Mrs. Drummond.

She burst into Mrs. Drummond's office without knocking. "She is awake! She came to me in the music room and the fever has nearly broken!"

Mrs. Drummond and Annabelle sprang to their

feet.

"I pray this is good news. Go fetch Mrs. Harrow." Mrs. Drummond rushed past them. Her staccato footfalls rang through the hall and up the stairs.

Hours later, Mrs. Harrow pronounced Juliana improved enough to keep company with the other girls. But she must not exert herself.

That evening, the girls gathered upstairs in the music room after supper. They made a merry time of it, singing and playing pianoforte. Miss Long and Miss Greenville arranged a game of charades that quickly dissolved into hilarity. Even Miss Thornton and Miss Honeywell joined in.

Mr. Amberson, though, kept away.

Afterwards, Lydia and Annabelle helped Juliana back to her room. Face flushed and sporting a light sheen of sweat, she perched gingerly on the bed, panting.

The room looked and smelled very much like a sickroom. Perhaps she and Annabelle would clean it next Sunday morning. At the very least, they could air it out properly.

"You look entirely worn out." Lydia fluffed the bed pillows. "We should leave, and let you rest. You cannot exert yourself too much, yet."

Juliana sniffled and shook her head. "I am a dreadful selfish creature. I know, but I do not want to be alone. I feel as if I have been alone since … since it all happened."

"You have not been alone at all. We have taken turns sitting with you." Annabelle draped an arm over Juliana's shuddering shoulder.

"I … I think I understand." Lydia wrapped her arms around her waist.

"By all means tell me then, for I am utterly confused."

Lydia crouched beside the bed and looked up into Juliana's face. "It is him, is it not?"

"Lydia!" Annabelle hissed.

"No, not him, the baby."

Juliana nodded, tears glistening on her cheeks. "Mrs. Harrow and Mrs. Drummond will not speak of him at all. They merely say I should thank God for His mercies that spared my life. But …"

"There is a hollowness you want to fill with some memory of him. You need something to remind you that it was real. But you cannot because no one will let you." Lydia rocked slowly on her heels.

"Yes. How do you know so well?"

"That is how it was for my mother after her losses. Papa did not permit us to speak of any of them, or of little Thomas either. We were to go on as if nothing at all had happened; as if they had never been; as if our suffering had never been. I am convinced our grief lingered far longer than needed because of it."

"I wish I could have held him, seen him—is it wrong to want that much?" Juliana hid her face in her hands and wept.

Annabelle embraced her.

Lydia found a handkerchief in the dressing table and tucked it into Juliana's hand. She slipped out and gathered several sheets of paper and her sketchbook.

"Here, look." Lydia held out a drawing of Juliana and her son.

Juliana lifted her face from her hands.

"I put him in your arms right after he was born. He looked at you and knew you were his mother. You told him how dear he was and what a good boy he was. You fell asleep with him in your arms."

"I did?"

"Yes, and then Mrs. Harrow christened him."

Juliana gulped back a funny little squeak. "What name?"

"You once told me you liked the name Michael."

"I did … I do ... that was his father's name." Juliana rocked against the pillows.

Annabelle touched the edge of the paper reverently. "I did not get to see him, but I feel as though I was there; so very beautiful."

"Is this … May I …" Juliana fingered the corner of the drawing.

"Mrs. Drummond asked to have this one. But the first one, the one I drew that day, she sent it to be framed for you. I am sure though, she would not mind if you kept this one until the other is finished."

Juliana pressed her fist to her mouth.

"Mr. Amberson and Mr. Weatherby buried him properly in the church yard, near a climbing rose. He will show you where when you are stronger."

"I love roses." Juliana handed the drawing to Annabelle and fell upon Lydia's neck weeping.

A few tears were good for the soul to be sure. But that point came and passed and the wracking sobs continued.

Annabelle rubbed her back. "You must calm yourself or you will make yourself ill."

"I know." Juliana gulped and dragged the handkerchief across her cheeks.

"There must be something we can talk about to cheer you up." Lydia bit her lip and looked about the room.

"Oh, I know, I have the most amazing secret.

Have you a drawing of us?"

"I do, in my sketch book, several in fact." Lydia placed her sketchbook in Juliana's lap. "If you stop weeping you will be able to look at them."

Juliana gulped in several shuddering breaths. "I … I shall try."

Annabelle pressed her finger to her lips. "You must not breathe a word of this to anyone. Everything is now settled. I am to be married."

"So soon? You have barely just met him. Surely you jest."

"No, it is entirely true."

"And you like him well enough to marry him?"

"I think so."

"And he likes you?"

"Most definitely. Let me show you." Lydia flipped her sketch book open. "Here, the day they met in the parlor."

"It is a brilliant likeness." Annabelle cocked her head and studied the image.

"Of you both." Juliana traced his profile. "I can tell, he thinks you are very pretty. The look in his eye is clear."

Annabelle pressed her hands to her cheeks. "Oh, I had not thought … he has never said … but I mean, are you certain?"

"Of course I am. See his expression."

"But is that truly how he looked at me, or is that the way you hoped he would?" Annabelle raised an eyebrow at Lydia.

"I suppose, at first, it was the way I wanted him to regard you."

"There you see—"

"But then later, even today, that was the way he

stared at you."

"So, I was right." Juliana leaned back against her pillows, pulling the sketchbook with her. "You really do sketch the most expressive faces. It makes me feel as though I am there with them, and they are talking to me." She flipped to another page. "Whose hands … oh, Lydia!"

"Let me see." Annabelle crowded in close.

She turned away.

"I can almost see his fingers moving! He is playing that very somber piece he wrote. I recognize that bit of a phrase there." Annabelle pointed at the tiny piece of music near the top of the drawing.

"There is a bit of a shawl along the edge of the keyboard. Is this the night Miss Long caught her shawl on the pianoforte and knocked over the card table? Oh, he was quite cross that night." Juliana giggled.

"Gracious, I remember that! Oh, let us see another."

Lydia reached for the book. "No, those are just silly little bits of fluff."

How could they read so much into them?

"I hardly think so." Annabelle flipped open another page. "Oh, oh, here is my dress, the one for my wedding. Lydia designed it you know. When did you draw in the modiste and her shop? I do not remember seeing that before."

"The dress looks just like what you would wear. Oh, but look—that is the modiste, is it not? She was not very pleased, was she?"

Annabelle chuckled. "She was—"

"No, no, let me puzzle it out. I am sure it is all here …" Juliana traced the gown with her finger. "Let me see, there are dress sketches here and a length of some fabric here. The sketches look nothing like the gown, but the fabric matches the bodice. There is a clock, but I cannot see the time, so I do not think that important—"

"But it did ring the funniest little chime. I never heard one like it before." Annabelle leaned in a little closer.

"So I must guess either the modiste was unhappy you did not choose one of her designs or you bargained a very good price for the dress fabric. Am I right?"

"It was both." Annabelle giggled. "She really was put out by it all. How do you put all that into your sketch? It is a bit like looking at one of Rowlandson's images with all the little stories he hides there."

"Miss Honeywell would caution you against so many compliments lest they go to my head." Lydia closed the sketch book.

"Well I say great talent deserves praise." Annabelle rose. "But it is late and Juliana should sleep. Let us help you get ready for bed."

"And I shall put this here, near your bed, so you may look upon him whenever you wish." Lydia set the picture of mother and baby on the bedside table.

Juliana's fever returned with the force of a scorned lover, clinging and tormenting for another se'nnight complete before surrendering its hold. Annabelle and Lydia kept vigil at her bedside.

After the fever passed, Mrs. Harrow insisted Juliana keep to her room a full five days more. During that time, Lydia and Annabelle were granted permission to move into Juliana's room. The room was crowded to be sure, but the camaraderie was well worth the inconvenience.

The conversations Lydia shared with Kitty under cover of nightfall never went beyond ribbons and young men. But in their shared room, weightier topics reigned.

Annabelle and Juliana expressed their troubles readily enough. Though they pressed her, Lydia found little to say.

Giving voice to things so fragile, so uncertain, seemed an invitation to disaster.

After a full week free of fever, Mrs. Harrow declared Juliana might make her first journey out of the house to be churched.

Dressing for holy services that day rivaled the excitement of preparing for an assembly.

"Your stays, are they comfortable?" Annabelle adjusted Juliana's laces.

Juliana smoothed her hands down the front of her dress. "It has been so long since I have worn them, it feels quite odd. But everything feels rather odd right now." "Thank you for replacing my old laces."

"We ought to make you some new stays." Lydia looked over her shoulder into the looking glass.

It was still peculiar seeing herself without a cap.

"If we work together, I suppose we can finish before—"

The door flew open and Mrs. Drummond bustled in. "Girls, all of you, come downstairs directly. Sir Anthony has arrived, unexpected, and he wishes to see you."

Annabelle blanched. Juliana and Lydia each took

one of her arms. They walked together down the stairs, and Mrs. Drummond led them into the drawing room.

"Sir Anthony." Annabelle curtsied, shaking so hard she nearly did not make it back up.

"Sir, may I present Miss Morley?"

Juliana dipped in an equally unsteady curtsey. Lydia bobbed with her, keeping a firm grasp on her elbow.

Sir Anthony removed his hat and bowed. "Good morning, ladies."

His suit fit him like he was born in it—a testament to his tailor and valet. Obviously he was particular, but with excellent taste.

"To what do we owe the pleasure of your company, sir?" Annabelle's thin tone did not match the question.

"Do you not recognize the date?" His look suggested she should. "Three weeks from our wedding—the vicar shall begin to read our banns today."

Annabelle gasped. "The banns?"

"Yes, it is time for that. I suppose it is a fitting way for the girls to learn of your betrothal." Mrs. Drummond stroked her chin. "Will you join us for dinner afterwards? The Weatherbys are planning to be with us."

"Lady Annabelle, would you like me to dine with you?" He cocked his head as if uncertain of her answer.

"How do you feel about impertinent questions? There will be quite a number demanded of you if you sup with us."

"I have a great deal of experience with impertinent questions. I would be pleased to accept your invitation."

"Does it please you to walk to church with us as well?" Mrs. Drummond asked.

"No. Though I should like to sit with you for services this morning, I would avoid creating a spectacle when we enter. I thought it best to arrive before the church is full. My carriage is at our disposal. I have room for four quite comfortably. Perhaps your ... convalescent friend might also drive with us."

"That is most gracious of you, thank you. May she ride with us, madam?"

"Your offer is most kind sir, but have you considered the reflection her company might have upon you both?"

Juliana studied the floorboards.

Of course, Mrs. Drummond was correct. But, how beastly unfair!

"I am aware, madam. But if my bride is agreeable, then I see no issue. It is not as though we will remain long in Summerseat in any case."

How difficult it would be when Annabelle left. At least Juliana would be nearby at Mrs. Harrow's.

"Very well, you may go. Fetch your wraps; I will have a word with Sir Anthony."

Mrs. Drummond had that look on her face. They made haste from the drawing room.

"I do not think she is accustomed to someone making decisions without consulting her." Annabelle tittered.

"He is a bit high-handed." Lydia glanced back at the drawing room door.

Would Mrs. Drummond have the temerity to scold him or would his power to determine Annabelle's future constrain her?

"But generous, just as you said. Few gentlemen would have included me. No, no, do not be all prickly about it." Juliana laid her hand on Annabelle's arm. "I am resolved not to pretend things are other than they are. I will be grateful for whatever kindness I find."

Annabelle drew her upper lip over her teeth. "He is kind. You are right. I must be grateful that after all he has endured he is not simply bitter."

Juliana kissed her cheek. "Remember that when he seems overbearing, and you stand a very good chance at being satisfied in your new life."

Sir Anthony's carriage was as plush and well-sprung as Mr. Darcy's. Did he and Lizzy take the carriage when they went to church, or did they walk?

Mary's last letter said that Lizzy was happy in Derbyshire and was settling into her new role as mistress of Pemberley. Perhaps she should write to Lizzy, but their parting had been so bitter. So many things she regretted saying. At the very least, Lizzy deserved an apology.

They arrived at the little parish church before the rest of the parishioners. Sir Anthony guided them to their usual pews.

"Are you sure you wish to sit here?" Annabelle asked. "We do not have to sit with the rest of the school if—"

"I am not going to begin a habit of being embarrassed by you—or your connections. If it helps, consider that I expect no less from you. Sit down. I will join you in a few moments, but I need a word with the vicar, first." He bowed and left.

"I do not know what to make of him. He is such an odd mix." Annabelle took a seat and smoothed her skirts.

"A little like coffee made too strong then sweetened." Lydia said.

"You shall be the cream that mellows him and makes him palatable." Juliana sat beside Annabelle and patted the spot beside her.

Lydia took her place and settled in to observe people as they arrived.

As Sir Anthony returned and sat beside Annabelle, the whispers began. The startled glances they attracted would find their way into her sketch book soon. He distracted them with a summary of his latest correspondence with Annabelle's father.

Was she aware her brother had recently purchased a new hunter? Her mother was much in anticipation of the coming London season, and her sister would soon come out. A grand ball was being planned, and they might be able to attend.

The whispers grew louder at Mrs. Drummond's arrival. Ignoring them, she greeted the vicar and made her way in. Mr. Amberson, Miss Honeywell and Miss Thornton followed close behind.

Miss Greenville, Miss Long and Ruth gasped and covered their mouths as they entered. Mrs. Drummond had obviously not warned them.

The murmurs rose to a deafening roar.

Juliana snuck her hand into Annabelle's and squeezed.

Lydia caught her gaze and mouthed: *Ignore them.*

Mr. Amberson filed into the pew and stopped beside Lydia. He asked permission with his eyes before he sat down.

At least the thunder of her heart now drowned out the mutterings around her.

His warmth reached out to her, touching but not touching. From the corner of her eyes she studied his mien.

So somber, worried, but with maybe just a touch of hope.

She moved her hands to mimic a keyboard and played a silent opening measure.

He sucked in a sharp breath and blinked hard. His cheek twitched, drawing his lips up just a fraction. His fingers danced across an invisible keyboard playing the first measure of the missing part.

Mr. Weatherby opened the service. "I publish the Banns of Marriage between Sir Anthony Sheridan of Parnam and Lady Annabelle Fitzgilbert of Summerseat. If any of you know cause, or just impediment, why these two persons should not be joined together in Holy Matrimony, ye are to declare it. This is the first time of asking."

The low whispers erupted into full scale talk.

Sir Anthony nudged his hat to cover his hand as he grasped Annabelle's tightly. She clung to him.

One more image for Lydia's sketchbook.

As soon as Mr. Weatherby closed the service, well-wishers—or more rightly curiosity seekers and gossips—converged on the newly announced couple. Lydia and Juliana closed ranks around Annabelle. Sir Anthony stood slightly ahead of her, answering questions and receiving good wishes. Annabelle nodded and curtsied as required.

They lingered until the crowd thinned enough to permit escape. Sir Anthony announced something about being expected for dinner and blazed a trail back to his carriage. They piled inside, and he pulled the door shut behind them. Never had the clank of a carriage steps being lifted been so soothing.

He threw his head back and mopped his forehead with his handkerchief. "Good God, I did not anticipate that. These vultures are every bit as voracious as those in London."

"They were quite animated." Annabelle's face was white as the muslin of her gown.

"Had I any idea it would be like that I would have obtained a license instead. It was not my intention to put you through—" He waved toward the church.

Annabelle huddled in the seat. "I am sorry, sir. I fear my reputation …"

"Mine is every bit as colorful and possibly more familiar to that rabble. I am as much to blame as you." He corrected his posture and straightened his lapels. "I have come to a conclusion and a decision."

Lydia leaned into Annabelle's shoulder.

"I have far more experience dealing with these gawkers and magpies than you. I know I can endure them. It is clear you do not enjoy the same thick skin. I fear you will not be able to manage what will be required of you."

Annabelle stammered word-like sounds but they were choked by stifled tears.

He raised his open hand.

"I should have said: I cannot expect you to manage it *alone*. You require a companion to support you as you take your place beside me. I can find one for you or you may select one of your friends to accompany you." He looked from Lydia to Juliana. "A very fair allowance and a comfortable situation will of course be assured."

"Sir!"

He pinched the bridge of his nose. "I cannot have you so drained by the harpies that you cannot properly perform your duties."

The carriage rolled to a stop at the school.

"Wait here whilst I speak with the school mistress. I will not have another inquisition over dinner." He pushed the door open and jumped down before the coachman could lower the steps.

"That was quite a scene." Lydia chewed her lip. "At the church I mean …"

"For all his highhandedness, he is a good man. You are very blessed." Juliana squeezed Annabelle's shoulder. "He is entirely right, you know. You will fare far better with someone familiar by your side."

"I know this should make me very happy, but how am I to make such a dreadful choice?" She wrapped her arms around her waist, cheeks glistening.

Lydia and Juliana traded glances.

"You must take—"

"Lydia."

"Juliana. No, listen and do not argue—"

"I have arrangements with Mrs. Harrow. You have no such fixed plans."

"It will be months at least before you are strong enough to begin even normal chores. Simply dusting this morning was almost too much for you. Or have you already forgotten?"

"That was simply a matter—"

Lydia glowered, aping Mama's sternest expression. "That was a sure sign that your convalescence is only just begun. How long will it be before you can be of use to Mrs. Harrow?"

"Not very long I am sure, perhaps a fortnight or so." Juliana gazed at the floorboards.

"It will be months before you regain your strength." Lydia leaned across Annabelle's lap and clutched Juliana's hand. "I am not trying to be cruel. Indeed, I am not. I fear the money that would have paid for your apprenticeship will instead be spent upon your upkeep as you recover. Then what will you do?"

"But you—"

"My brother, Darcy, promised two years here and to find me a situation after, if he had Mrs. Drummond's assurance I had improved. I will make sure she can give him such a report. I despise the thought of losing you both, but I cannot be so selfish as to deny you the chance of a comfortable future." She swallowed hard but the lump in the throat remained stubbornly in place.

Annabelle looked from one to the other, eyes brimming.

"You must ask Juliana, for if you ask me, I shall refuse. I shall not be moved." Lydia folded her arms over her chest and set her jaw.

Juliana and Annabelle fell on her neck, sobbing and murmuring unintelligibly.

How would she ever do without them both?

Sir Anthony returned and handed them out of the carriage. Only his eyes bore evidence of his discomposure. Every other facet of his being appeared entirely correct and presentable. Had he and Mrs. Drummond exchanged words?

He took Annabelle's hand in the crook of his arm and escorted her inside. Juliana trailed a few paces behind.

Lydia hung back. A burn, like a hornet's sting, scorched her chest. She took a step closer to the door.

No, the emptiness threatened to overwhelm. If she entered the house she might just shatter with the effort to contain it.

She skirted the front door and slipped into the garden behind the house. Shaded and private, solace might reside there.

Was that why Lizzy was forever walking in Kent?

She passed the clump of heather where Mr. Birch kept watch. He was a little more visible since the stalks withered with winter's approach. None had claimed to have found him and Joan completely avoided the garden, still fearing large rats. Only Mr. Amberson shared her secret.

Mr. Amberson.

Was she a fool to give up a chance to live in society for the opportunity to study with him a little longer?

It was not as if she were a fine musician or ever would be. She was good enough to make quite a pleasing show in drawing rooms and enjoy the compliments from it. But she had not the true gift of music, not like he did.

She sank to the ground and wrapped her arms around her knees.

Staying here was not about lessons, nor about Darcy's promises regarding her future. There was only one reason to ignore such an opportunity.

"Miss Bennet?"

She started and looked up into weary, worn eyes. "Yes, Mrs. Drummond."

"You have been missed at dinner. Are you unwell?"

"I had not expected services to be so …"

"I found it unsurprising. If only Mr. Weatherby or Sir Anthony had spoken to me first, a great deal of unpleasantness might have been avoided. They seem to forget I have a fair amount of experience with these things." Mrs. Drummond looked over her shoulder.

"Are the other girls—"

"All in uproar? Indeed, and it will take some doing for it all to settle down. You must harden yourself for a few days of very intense curiosity."

She pressed her forehead to her knees.

Harden? She would have to become stone itself to endure the barrage. Perhaps she could just make her home out here for the duration.

"Did they tell you of Sir Anthony's offer?"

"No."

The word usually did not have three syllables.

"He determined Annabelle needs a companion. He told her she could select one of us to join her. I expect he will approach you soon with terms for Juliana's situation."

Did it hurt when her eyes bulged like that?

"Juliana? She chose—"

"I insisted. Juliana's health is too fragile. What better place for her when her father withdraws his support?"

It was not untrue. One dare not lie to Mrs. Drummond.

Mrs. Drummond stared, agog.

"I shall miss them a very great deal."

"You should return to the house now. This intelligence will soon be common knowledge. If you stay away, someone will infer you are resentful of Miss Fitzgilbert's choice."

Rumors of animosity would do nothing to ease her suffering. A brave face for the parlor was not too much to ask.

Lydia rose and shook out her skirts. A few dry heather stalks clung to them. She picked them off and tossed them at Mr. Birch.

.

Chapter 14

THE COMPANY WAS ALREADY assembled in the parlor.
Lydia followed in Mrs. Drummond's shadow.

Amelia sidled up to her. "How kind of you to join
us. You were missed at dinner."

Had she been lying in wait? No one else seemed to
notice her entrance.

"We were all so pleased to hear you will stand as
bride's maid for dear Miss Fitzgilbert." Amelia looked
over her shoulder towards Annabelle standing beside
Sir Anthony. "I suppose you expect to be made head
girl in her place."

"I am in no hurry for her to leave."

"How very good you have become. What a clever
actress! I think perhaps even Mrs. Drummond is
fooled."

Oh, that look! Would that she could do what was
necessary to remove it from her face!

"Do not interfere with them."

"Or what shall you do? I know. You will help me. I have my own escape planned. I count on your assistance." Amelia flounced away.

The rest of the company gathered around Sir Anthony and Annabelle. She looked almost comfortable beside him.

They were quite attractive together. That should soothe his vanity quite nicely.

"Will you play, sir? I should like to see what my coin to the dance master has bought me." Sir Anthony gestured toward Mr. Amberson.

"Have you a particular dance in mind?" Mr. Amberson moved to the pianoforte.

"Something lively and fun. Perhaps 'Hunt the Squirrel' or 'Lord Byron's'Maggot'?"

"Shall I play both? The hunt first?"

"Capital plan." Sir Anthony took Annabelle's hand and led her to the top of the room.

Juliana blanched. "I shall sit out, I think."

A chill snaked down her spine. Juliana's near dead weight in her arms still haunted her dreams.

Surely Sir Anthony did not realize what had happened during their first lesson.

"We may watch the dancers together." Mrs. Weatherby took Juliana's arm and gestured toward the worn couch. "And have a bit of a chat."

"Come, come, do not be shy about it. Hunt the Squirrel requires six couples at least. Miss Bennet, will you not assist?" Sir Anthony waved his hands like a music conductor.

Miss Greenville stood nearby. Lydia extended her hand and they took their place as second couple. She urged others into place and soon two sets of three couples waited for Mr. Amberson's opening notes.

Perhaps without Mr. Chadwick's sharp tongue and smart cane it would be a less trying activity.

Mr. Amberson's lively, happy music buoyed her spirits. She lost herself in the fun of pursuing her partner through the forest of the other dancers.

Miss Greenville stumbled over a pucker in the carpet and caught herself against Ruth who squealed at the shock. The whole set laughed as they hurried to get back to place in time for the next couple to begin their chase.

Odd, how this was even more pleasing without the demands of a full-on flirtation during dance steps.

Applause followed the final notes.

"Take hands four for Lord Byron's Maggot." Mr. Amberson called.

"We need new partners first." Amelia shoved Joan aside.

She hurried away from Amelia and clutched Ruth's arm.

Did she look just a little relieved at the distance?

Amelia sashayed to Annabelle. "You cannot keep the most desirable partner in the room to yourself." She tried to edge between Annabelle and Sir Anthony.

He did not give way.

"I believe the choice is the gentleman's, not yours, Amelia." The shift to Lady Annabelle was always amusing to observe.

Did Lizzy become Mrs. Darcy the same way?

"Lady Annabelle is quite correct." Sir Anthony stared down his nose. "I will dance with my betrothed."

Amelia sidled a little closer to him and batted her eyes.

"If I were to choose to take another partner, it would not be a rude, self-promoting little chit who does not understand her own rank and place in society."

A gasp tore through the room.

Amelia turned no less than three shades of crimson, ending in a remarkable puce.

Even Papa had never attained that color in the height of dudgeon. How would one obtain that shade in watercolors?

She tossed her head. "Perhaps you should be more aware of who you so easily insult."

"Perhaps you should apply yourself to your teacher's lessons in etiquette." Sir Anthony turned his shoulder to her.

Amelia stormed out.

Mrs. Drummond and Mrs. Weatherby hurried after her, determined old ewes chasing down a wayward lamb.

A sheepdog might bark and nip, but one did not stand in the way of a leading ewe.

"Join your partner and take hands four, our musician awaits." Sir Anthony clapped sharply.

The room jumped into motion. Lydia faded back to the couch, with Juliana.

"How do you feel about living under the roof of such a man?" Lydia whispered.

"It is not as though she did not deserve his rebuke."

"Still, being called out like that in front of so many is … quite horrible."

Juliana leaned her head on Lydia's shoulder. "I am sorry someone did that to you."

How did she know?

The music closed to many happy cries and clapping hands.

"We must have refreshments before another dance." Sir Anthony declared.

Miss Honeywell and Miss Thornton agreed and hurried out.

"Lydia you must play for us whilst we wait." Annabelle caught her gaze and tipped her head toward the pianoforte.

Mr. Amberson offered her his seat.

How had her feet carried her to his side before she knew she had taken a single step?

"Have you a piece of music in mind?" His voice was soft and sonorous, caressing the deepest part of her soul.

Had anyone else heard?

None but Annabelle and Juliana even looked their way.

"I do." She sat down.

"Shall I fetch music for you?"

"No, I have committed the piece to my heart."

His Adam's apple bobbed and he licked his lower lip, eyes wide and warm. She made room on the bench, and he sat beside her.

A hush rippled through the room, barely notable over the rush of blood in her ears.

How did one play a duet without practice, without ever having heard the other part?

He placed his fingers on the keyboard and waited for her to follow. Long, powerful fingers danced over the keys, weaving a melody familiar, though she had never heard it.

A tap of his elbow on hers and she joined in her part, a line that seemed both melody and harmony as it wove around and through his. The lines merged together, overlapping into a single unified sound so tight they could not be pulled apart. Everything else faded; her consciousness focused upon the resounding joy of their joint efforts.

Was this what a bird felt when it took flight? No wonder they loathed to come down.

Another tap to her elbow, and he began a repeat of the soaring chorus. She followed, but her fingers took a mind of their own, improvising around his melody, weaving something entirely new, in keeping with what he had written, but wholly her own.

He responded with another improvisation, harmony to her melody, content to follow where she led. No, not content, it was jubilant, accenting her contribution and blending it seamlessly into the whole.

He took the lead once again, and she followed into the final closing bars. As the closing notes faded away, gripping, aching silence oppressed the room.

Did he feel the emptiness?

Glistening trails ran down his cheeks and sweat beaded his forehead.

Yes, he did.

The room erupted in applause and delighted calls.

He took her hand, raised it to his lips and kissed it, so reverently, so gently she was not sure he had touched her at all.

From the doorway, Mrs. Drummond watched, her face etched into an expression Lydia might draw, but could not name.

Sir Anthony called for more dancing. Mr. Amberson obliged with two merry jigs. For Annabelle's sake, Lydia went through the motions of the dance. Thankfully her feet knew the steps; her mind could never have kept up.

At last, their guests departed. Annabelle hurried to their room, Lydia and Juliana close behind.

Annabelle pressed her head against the worn oak door. "I hardly know what to make of any of this."

"That duet you played," Juliana sat on the end of the bed, "I have never heard anything like it."

"Did he write it?"

Lydia wandered to the window and pulled the curtain through her fingers. "Yes, although at the end … when we played it through the second time, it was just improvised."

"You improvise very well," Juliana said.

"Is it not time you tell us about him?" Annabelle dragged Lydia to the bed and sat down.

Lydia grabbed a pillow and clutched it to her chest. "There is nothing to be told."

"Of course there is. We saw—"

Juliana placed a hand on her shoulder. "She doesn't know what to say. Here—" She handed Lydia her sketchbook. "Draw your duet."

She pushed it away. "I cannot."

That would be worse than dancing naked in the parlor.

Annabelle pushed the sketchbook at Lydia. "It is only fair. You know all our secrets"

Lydia struggled to open to an empty page. But, the pencil settled into her hand, an extension of her heart and soul. Soft lines formed two profiles blending into one and dissolving into a staff of notes taken from their duet.

"You are in love with him," Juliana whispered. "I think you have been for a very long time."

Lydia pushed the sketchbook aside. "He kissed

me. In the garden."

Annabelle gasped, wide-eyed.

"I went out; I could not sleep. He was there, grieving your loss. We have barely spoken since. Not until tonight at the piano."

"What kind of a declaration is that?" Annabelle rolled her eyes.

Lydia shrugged. "We neither use words well."

Annabelle grasped Lydia's shoulders. "Someone surely needs to and soon. You are so well formed for one another."

"I hardly know what I think myself. Besides, I am far more concerned with Amelia and her temper right now."

"She should be the least of your worries. What more trouble can she possibly cause, particularly after Mrs. Drummond has dealt with her?"

What trouble indeed?

Sunbeams through the curtains teased Lydia awake before Annabelle and Juliana stirred. Lydia dressed quietly and slipped into the hall. Best let them sleep whilst she started their chores. As pleasing as their companionship was, a few solitary moments for contemplation were welcome, too.

She gathered cleaning supplies from the kitchen. The odd, stale scent of the thrice-used tea leaves tickled her nose. The earthy fragrance echoed back to Mama's garden.

Perhaps in the spring, Mrs. Drummond would allow her to revive the forgotten corner of the garden. It would be nice to have a patch of her own to tend once more.

The spring ... what would it bring? She would be as alone as she was when she first arrived. No, that was silly melancholy. Miss Greenville, Miss Long, Stephanie and Ruth, they were all friendly with her. There would be new students, too.

And Mr. Amberson would still be teaching.

She pinned up the curtains and spread dusting sheets over the furniture.

Was Annabelle right? Were they so well- formed for one another?

Did he believe so?

When they played together—oh, those last choruses were like a single soul shared by two minds. The tears on his cheek spoke everything—or did they?

Perhaps Annabelle was right, though. Were there not words that needed to be spoken too?

"Miss Bennet." Mrs. Drummond bustled in, a soggy note in her hand. "This came from the modiste. I expect it is in regards to the wedding dresses, but her girl dropped it in a puddle. I cannot make it out. Can you?"

She extended the sodden missive. It dripped on the not-yet-clean floor.

Lydia held it up in a sunbeam. The ink had not been dry long enough to darken properly. The faint lines faded to obscurity amidst the water and muddy patches. It made for an interesting effect, though. She might intentionally decorate a paper that way sometime.

"I am sorry, madam, I cannot make it out either."

Mrs. Drummond huffed and took the note back, her face wrinkled to match the paper.

"Shall I go to the modiste, once the parlor is clean,

and ask what she wanted?"

"Best go now. You have done your share. Go quickly. The modiste has a bit of a temper. I do not wish her to suggest to Sir Anthony anything that smacks of ingratitude. Take this with you." She pressed the disheveled message at Lydia, "Make sure she is well aware of where the fault lay in this affair."

"I will leave directly." Lydia curtsied and hurried out.

The scullery maid met her at the door, ordered to accompany her into town. Papa would not have cared if she walked alone.

The girl was quite a chatterbox, talking from the moment they left until they reached the modiste. Her brothers, were employed as under-gardeners at a nearby estate, but might soon be promoted. One meant to quit at the next quarter day and go to work for another.

The maid herself would do no such thing. Mrs. Drummond's was an enviable place to work. After all, there were no men about who believed she was there for playing at rantum-scantum as well as for mopping and scrubbing. It was a tense time when Mr. Amberson came to be sure. He might have been like the sons of the nearby estate. But he kept his breeches buttoned and his hands to himself. That was her idea of a gentleman.

Mr. Amberson was indeed gentlemanly in all his ways, but those reasons had never crossed her mind. Lydia swallowed hard. A life in service was only a step above one as a public woman. A very small one when masters thought a girl's wages as good as a whore's socket-money.

They slipped into the modiste's shop. Lydia handed her the illegible missive, and offered Mrs. Drummond's explanation. The modiste rang her girl a fine peal over the sodden note and bade Lydia return with Annabelle for a fitting that afternoon.

The maid began her chatter anew as they left the shop.

"Wait, hush. Is that—" Lydia pointed across the street.

Amelia sauntered down the lane on the arm of her Mr. Beverly.

"It is, Miss. She oughten not be doing that. The missus ought to know." The maid headed toward Amelia, but Lydia pulled her back.

"Wait, let us follow her and see what she is about."

They ducked into an alley way, and Lydia held her finger to her lips.

Amelia glanced their way once, but she shrugged and continued on with her beau.

They followed the couple to a fashionable street, lined with houses quite as nice as Uncle Gardiner's. Amelia withdrew something from her reticule and pressed it into Beverly's hand. She shooed him, and he marched to a freshly-painted red door. He rapped the knocker three times and waited.

Great heavens, Sir Anthony's man answered!

Lydia grabbed the maid's arm. "Go to Mrs. Drummond. Tell her exactly what we have seen."

"Will you not accompany me?"

"No, I must do … something … lest this all go entirely arsey-varsey."

The maid scurried away.

Beverly entered the town house while Amelia paced the street, half a dozen houses away.

Perhaps she should confront Amelia, but what

would that accomplish? Beverly was already with Sir Anthony.

The door swung open. Beverly sauntered out and rejoined Amelia. He tipped his hat and winked. She took his arm, and they left the way they came.

Once they turned the corner, Lydia dashed for Sir Anthony's door. She pounded the knocker, the frantic rhythm matching her heart.

His man opened the door.

"Pray, sir, I must see Sir Anthony. It is a matter most urgent, concerning the letter just delivered to him."

"Wait here." He pointed to a hall chair.

She sat and clutched her hands in her lap, though her heels drummed frantically beneath her chair.

A young lady did not call upon a man, unless it was a matter of business. Was not Annabelle's marriage a business matter? Many would say it was. Surely that was sufficient to excuse her appearance here.

Still, the vestibule remained inhospitable with no paintings and only a very plain paper on the walls. The hall chairs and small cabinet between them were also very plain—his taste or the landlord's? Neither seemed to welcome her presence.

"Come now, Sir Anthony will see you."

She jumped up and followed him down a short hall. He ushered her into a narrow office, lined with book cases and dominated by a large mahogany desk. Sir Anthony looked up, his face a cacophony of angst.

"The young lady, sir."

"Miss Bennet." Lydia stammered.

"I am well aware of your identity." Sir Anthony did not rise, instead shoving a creased paper toward her. "I presume you are familiar with the contents of this letter?"

"No, sir I am not. I saw it pass from Amelia's hand to Mr. Beverly's, the young man who delivered it. Whatever it says is a falsehood carefully constructed to create a great deal of misunderstanding." She leaned forward a little, trying to read the missive, but the angle made it nearly impossible.

"And how do you know this?"

"I have lived with her for many months now. You saw her performance last night. Truth and forthrightness are not her strong suits."

He rose and turned his back to her. Three sharp strides took him to the window seat. Bracing his foot on the seat, he leaned on his knee and hung his head.

"Gossip has nearly ruined my life, Miss Bennet. I take these things very seriously. Even you coming here is a dangerous lapse in judgment."

"Annabelle is my very dear friend. I would not see her future shattered by a vindictive, unfeeling girl like Amelia."

"What have you to gain in this? You expect to be Lady Annabelle's companion, I suppose?"

"She is my friend. I count her gain as my own. And no, I do not expect to be her companion. She has asked Juliana."

"I imagine you want me to intercede on your behalf? To tell her to take you instead as payment for this service you render?" He looked over his shoulder at her.

Wickham had offered her the same expression of derision when Darcy refused his demands.

"No. Juliana is far better suited to be her companion."

"Why? Accompanying Lady Annabelle would be

to your advantage." He brought his foot down with a thud.

"It does not signify. I am not here for my own sake, but for hers."

"Then tell me, do you know what she is about?"

"I do not fathom your meaning."

"Can you vouchsafe for her actions, her whereabouts?"

"I am with her almost constantly. We have shared a room since Juliana took ill. When she is not with me, she is with Juliana or Mrs. Drummond."

"Then explain this!" He stalked to the desk and towered beside her, pointing to a spot in the letter.

In the garden, under cover of night I witnessed a tryst between Mr. Amberson, our music teacher, and one of our students—a figure very familiar to us both. The kiss I witnessed I will not soon forget.

Lydia clutched the edge of the desk, the room wavering about her. She sucked in a deep breath as though it were her last.

"It says nowhere this is Annabelle."

"The implication is clear!" His fist bounced off the desk.

She flinched. "No, it is not. It … it could have been any of the girls."

"I cannot rest with such uncertainty! After all I have been through, I cannot take a chance." He clutched his temples and groaned.

Lydia backed away and whispered, "It was not her."

"That is not enough. I must know who."

"It was not her."

"Why should I trust you? Tell me who."

His hot breath burned the back of her neck, like a predator bearing down. She dodged away, putting a chair between them.

"It was me. I was in the garden ... with him. We did not mean to be there, but were both grieving Juliana's misfortunes and became far too unguarded. Annabelle was upstairs asleep. Mr. Amberson is her music teacher and nothing more."

He glared at her, eyes narrow. "And he will verify your story?"

Lydia screwed her eyes shut and nodded.

"I shall not be satisfied until I hear it from him." He stormed to the doorway. "Ready the coach. I would go in a quarter-hour."

Sir Anthony dismissed her before the coachman had the carriage ready.

He was right. Riding alone with him would be a breach of propriety. But insisting she retreat through the kitchen doors and keep to the mews stung. She was not his servant to command. And not offering to send a maid with her—that was insulting. Mrs. Drummond would surely call him on his lack of consideration.

She kept her head down and walked as quickly as she could. If only running might not have drawn more attention! Several months ago, this journey would not have bothered her, but now, it felt very uncomfortable and exposed.

What would he tell Mrs. Drummond? Would he cast Annabelle off?

Pray, let that not be!

Sir Anthony's carriage stood before Mrs. Drummond's. What was he telling her? She tiptoed inside, greeted by an eerie hush.

The scullery maid found her. She was wanted and should wait outside Mrs. Drummond's office.

Cotton wool filled her mouth and her chest constricted so hard she could barely breathe. Surely this would not go well.

Strident, muted voices poured through the walls, difficult to make out over the roaring blood in her ears. She leaned against the wall and sank to the floor.

"I demand satisfaction—did you or did you not have secret meetings with this … this man?"

"I have told you, she did not." Even muddled through the door, Mr. Amberson's low, serious tones soothed her.

"As have I." Oh the expression Annabelle must be wearing! "Twice over to be precise. I well understand your jealous nature and from whence it comes, but sir—"

"You were seen in the garden with a young lady, who was it?"

A fist, surely belonging to Sir Anthony, thumped the desk.

"It was entirely my fault. There is no need to impugn her reputation because of my weakness."

How did Mr. Amberson remain so very calm? Perhaps it was all his practice with difficult music students.

"You leave me no recourse but to seriously reconsider my intentions toward Lady Annabelle."

"You would force me to choose which young lady's future—"

"If Lady Annabelle has done nothing wrong, then exonerate her. Allow the other girl to bear the burden of her wrongs."

"What you ask is ungentlemanly."

"I insist."

Lydia sprang to her feet and burst in.

"Tell him, Mr. Amberson. I have already confessed it to him. He simply needs corroboration to believe my witness." She turned to Mrs. Drummond. "I should not have been in the garden that night; should not have stayed when I saw him there."

Mrs. Drummond sank into her chair, clutching the edge of the desk.

"James, is this true?"

Mr. Amberson stepped slightly in front of Lydia. "It is my fault, not hers. Miss Bennet had your permission to be there. She and Miss Fitzgilbert are entirely innocent."

Sir Anthony heaved a great sigh and sagged back into his chair.

"Are you satisfied?" Mrs. Drummond said very, very softly.

She would have been far less frightening had she shouted.

"Yes," he swallowed hard. "I am. I will have her."

Annabelle stood. Her hands quivered at her sides.

"How very nice for you, sir. Perhaps, though, I will not have you, or had you considered that? Your performance has been utterly unseemly and your steadfast refusal to believe my word is unacceptable. I want nothing to do with you." She tossed her head and marched out.

Jaws dropped.

Annabelle was regal in her fury.

Sir Anthony gripped the arms of his chair, frozen. "You must speak to her, madam."

Mrs. Drummond's jaw clenched, leaving her voice high and tight. "I shall remind her of her circumstances, sir. You might also wish to speak to her yourself … in a day or so when tempers have cooled."

He rose and adjusted his cravat. "This is not at all what I expected, madam."

"Nor what I anticipated, sir. Be sure I will be dealing with Miss Easton for her part in this unfortunate affair. However, it would behoove us all to consider how our actions have contributed to this situation."

"Excuse me? Do you imply—"

"I imply nothing. I have said exactly what I intended to say."

"Indeed, madam." He bowed and strode out.

"Close the door, Miss Bennet."

Mrs. Drummond paced behind her desk, keeping in it between her and them.

Mr. Amberson hovered close to Lydia.

Mrs. Drummond clutched her temples and squeezed her eyes shut. "James, I cannot believe what you have done. You assured me that this sort of behavior was behind you."

He pulled himself straighter. "It is of little value, I know, but this is not the same thing, not at all."

"I am … I am aware of that, but it changes nothing. You have violated my trust in you and the trust my students' guardians have placed in me. Girls do not come here to be imposed upon by my teachers."

Lydia craned her neck to look up at him. The lines and shadows of his face spoke more deeply than any words might.

"He did not impose upon me, madam."

"Whilst you might see it that way I doubt anyone else, including Mr. Darcy would interpret it thus. This is a very grave failure on my part."

"You are not at fault, Aunt."

"Everything that takes place here is my responsibility. Had I realized how serious things had become, I would have put an end to this altogether."

"You knew?" Lydia gasped.

"Miss Bennet, I am acutely aware of everything under my roof. I have been mindful of your attachment to one another. It was wrong of me not to stop it."

Mr. Amberson cleared his throat. "And yet you did not."

"I can see there is a unique … bond you share. I thought you would be able to manage it within the bounds of propriety. I see I was wrong." She stalked to the corner and turned to face them. "I have no choice. James, you must leave immediately. I shall give you your wages for this quarter, but you must be gone tonight."

"I understand." He bowed from his shoulders.

"But, but—"

"She is right, Miss Bennet. It is for the best." He took her hand and kissed it. "Adieu."

She clutched his hand, but he pulled away and slipped out.

She stared at the void left in his wake, numbness blanketing her.

"Will you send me away too?"

"I suppose I could lay the blame upon you and be done with it all. But it would not be right. I must own this lapse. I am disappointed in you to be sure, but I gave you permission to be in the garden. I must write to Mr. Darcy and apprise him of what has happened." She dragged her hand down her face. "Go now, and make no attempt to interfere with James's departure."

"Are you not going to punish me?"

Lydia glanced at the cabinet containing the cane.

It was not as though she would feel that, nor anything else right now.

"No, I do not see it would do either of us any good."

"I am sorry, madam. I did not mean for any of this to happen."

"It is not entirely your fault. Go now. I have a great deal to manage." Mrs. Drummond sank to her chair, slumping like a forgotten sack of flour.

Lydia tiptoed out.

Halfway down the hall, Juliana caught her arm.

"Thank heavens you are here. I have no idea what to do and something must be done!" She hauled Lydia toward the parlor.

"Pray, not now. I cannot possibly deal with anyone else's matters."

She tried to pull away, but Juliana clung steadfastly.

"They are shouting at each other and will not stop. He threw Miss Thornton out when she tried to stop him. Everyone is cowering upstairs. But he just might listen to you."

Juliana shouldered open the parlor door and propelled her inside.

Annabelle eyes blazed as she glared across the carpeted expanse.

Sir Anthony held his ground near the fireplace, brandishing his walking stick like a sword. "I will not have—"

"You are in no position to go about declaring what you will and will not have."

"I will not be spoken to with such a tone." He rapped his walking stick against the floor.

"Then do not offer that tone to me. It would be

wise to recall, a man is apt to receive what he gives."

"Perhaps you should take your own advice."

"You think yourself the only generous one in this partnership? You are sorely mistaken. Perhaps you are too self-absorbed to notice. Despite your wealth and title, few women are willing to associate with you. Fewer still are keen to consider a connection to you. You may be offering me your material goods, but I have offered you myself. I expect, nay, demand you respect that offering."

"To whom else—"

Lydia marched to the center of the room, hands raised. "Stop! Both of you! Stop!"

They stormed toward her.

"Do not get involved, I do not need—"

"How dare you!"

"Stop." She grabbed Annabelle's hand. "Listen to yourselves. You are, both of you, better than this. I saw you face that mob at church together, side by side. You were excellent together. Are you truly willing to allow someone like Amelia to ruin your chance for happiness?"

"But the letter," he sputtered.

Lydia leaned in close and glared. "Truly, what did you expect from her when you treated her so abominably."

"You heard her for yourself. The girl was wholly out of line."

"Yes, she was, yet you dealt with her equally badly." Lydia stalked two steps away, and then stomped back. "You think she has no feelings, but I assure you, she does. She felt your words as deeply as Lady Annabelle might have. Do you do this often, lash out and then react in surprise when others retaliate?"

He snorted and tossed his head. "She deserved to be set down."

"Perhaps you deserved your wives'—"

Sir Anthony grabbed Lydia's shoulders and shook her.

She broke away, retreating several steps. "No one deserves to be mistreated. You have as good a chance at an amicable match as any I have seen. Better than many, truth be told. If you cool your tempers and confront what Amelia did the way you managed the curiosity-seekers, you might be surprised at the results. Remember your common ground and what you stand to gain as allies. Juliana, go and fetch a cooling drink from the kitchen."

She darted out.

Annabelle edged toward him. "I do not blame you for being angry over Amelia's letter. Let your anger be toward her alone."

"Annabelle has done nothing," Lydia said. "You know it was I."

"Yes, yes. That has been made clear." He wandered toward the windows, clutching his forehead, or maybe hiding his face. "I still do not appreciate your insinuation regarding my behavior."

"Lydia is right. If this is how you treat those who displease you, then you do provoke retaliation. I have no desire to be publicly humiliated if I should do something to offend you. I cannot live with that … and I will not."

"You think me a cad."

"I do not know what to think right now." Annabelle turned her back and studied the bookcase.

He paced several circuits around the room, his steps transforming from irate and purposeful to slow and reflective. On his fourth circuit, he paused beside her. "Miss Bennet, would you leave us? There are some things I would say privately."

His angry scowl was gone, and his soft voice without its earlier sharp edge. She squeezed Annabelle's hand and slipped out.

Juliana met her in the hall with a tray.

"Leave that beside the door. They need to talk without interruption."

"I knew you would know what to do. I am sure it will all be better now the shouting is over."

"Let us hope so."

Chapter 15

HOURS LATER, LYDIA, Juliana and Annabelle clois-
tered themselves in their room.

"What choice did he have but to confess? What
else could he have done?" Lydia said softly, head in
her hands.

Juliana and Annabelle sat close on either side, arms
around her shoulders.

"It was still utterly cruel that she sent him away,"
Annabelle said.

"Mrs. Drummond had no alternative either. How
could she permit him to stay? I am fortunate that she
did not dismiss me as well."

"What is she doing about Amelia?" Annabelle
frowned and shook her head sharply.

"I am not sure I care."

"Perhaps it would be best if you go as Annabelle's
companion."

Lydia squeezed Juliana's hand. "It is sweet of you to offer. Pray forgive me, I certainly do not wish to be part of his household."

"I am not sure I do either." Annabelle slumped against the wall.

"Are you still going to marry?" Juliana asked.

"Mr. Weatherby has begun reading the banns. There is little choice. However, the date for the wedding is no longer fixed."

"What have you done?" Lydia craned her neck to stare at Annabelle.

"I told him I thought him a bully. I am afraid to live with such a man. I went on to suggest his outbursts could cause any sensible woman to flee for comfort. He stormed out of the house after that. To his credit, he returned an hour later, with a bunch of crocuses and an apology, heartfelt from the look on his face."

"You are not the only one to whom he owes an apology," Juliana muttered.

"He is aware of that."

"You did not accept his apology?"

"I told him an apology with or without flowers was insufficient. If he was truly repentant, he would offer restitution to all he had wronged by his outburst. He needs to make an honest effort to make right the pain he has caused."

"What do you want him to do?"

Annabelle shrugged. "It is for him to determine and to act upon. Once he has, we will set a date for the wedding."

"He agreed?"

"It was a quite a conversation, but I am as stubborn as he and, in the end, he agreed."

"What if he does not?"

"Then we do not marry, and I am free of what would certainly have been a disastrous situation. If he carries out my request, we have established the future nature of our relationship. We will both be the better for it. Either way I have won. I would rather be a companion or governess than live with that sort of temper."

"Do not throw away this chance because of me," Lydia whispered.

"I am loyal to you, my friend, but be assured this is for me. I am grateful to have seen this before the wedding whilst I still have options and choices."

"What will Mrs. Drummond say?" Juliana asked.

Annabelle tossed her head. "I truly do not care what she thinks of it right now. I am the one who must live with him, not her."

The door squeaked as it swung open, and Miss Thornton peeked in. "You are all wanted in the parlor. Mrs. Drummond wishes to address everyone."

Juliana grabbed Lydia's hand and gripped it tight.

Dear girl always seemed to know when to do that.

Annabelle, Juliana, and Lydia slipped into the parlor, already full of anxious girls. Miss Thornton followed them in and shut the door.

Mrs. Drummond sat in front of the fireplace in a chair especially placed there for her. Usually, the force of her presence made it easy to forget her tiny frame, but tonight, the wide wingback dwarfed her. Lines and shadows etched her features, reinforced by the silent tension filling the room.

Lydia hugged the edge of the room and stopped behind the couch. In front of her, Miss Long, Miss Greenville and Stephanie wrung hands and tapped feet.

Mrs. Drummond's eyes seemed focused somewhere over their heads. "No doubt there are many stories circulating. Let me begin by saying I have a share in the blame for everything that has taken place."

Joan stood. Her eyes were puffy and face pale. "Pray, madam, it was not your fault. If Amelia's father could not stop her, then you are in excellent company."

"I appreciate your sentiment but what happens here is all my responsibility. I will be writing to all of your guardians and informing them that one of our girls was able to escape my supervision and become involved with a local boy."

A ripple of whispers flowed across the room.

"She has been placed as a servant in Mrs. Harrow's house. Her affairs are her own now, and she will not return to the school under any circumstances. Do not attempt to contact her or accept any familiar behavior from her as she is in service now. She has chosen her station, leave her to it."

"A servant?" Annabelle whispered.

"You are satisfied?" Lydia kept her eyes on Mrs. Drummond.

"Horrified. I thought at most she might be caned."

Mrs. Drummond cleared her throat and licked her lips. "Further, our music master has been dismissed."

"No!" Several voices rang out making it hard to tell from whence the protests came.

Several girls aimed objections at Mrs. Drummond, but Miss Long and Miss Greenville looked at Lydia with such sympathy, she nearly lost her composure.

"I appreciate your sentiments, but any breech of

decorum for a teacher here is grounds for dismissal." She drew a deep breath and raised an open hand.

Annabelle and Juliana pressed in close at Lydia's sides.

"I apologize to all of you for what has taken place. It is possible some of your guardians may choose to withdraw you from my care for these lapses. New rules of accountability will be in place soon to prevent future incidents."

Gasps and more whispers surged from one side of the room to the other and back again.

Mrs. Drummond rose, looking frail under the weight of the day. "Finally, Miss Fitzgilbert's wedding. In light of what has transpired, it will be postponed several weeks. When she leaves us, Miss Morley shall attend her as her companion. I anticipate several new students will join us after that." Her voice broke. "I only hope that I might tend them better than I have you these last few months."

Annabelle stepped around the couch to face Mrs. Drummond. "I am grateful for everything you have done for me, madam. I will not soon forget the lessons you have taught me. You received me when my own mother put me out, and I will always be grateful."

She threw her arms around Mrs. Drummond. Juliana and several others joined her.

Another image for Lydia's sketchbook.

Over the next se'nnight, a heavy grey mantle settled over the house. Hushed voices and soft footsteps prevailed. None practiced piano nor sang. The teachers did not make note of these lapses, though. Perchance they too felt the aching emptiness of Mr. Amberson's departure.

He had never been a brash, forceful presence among them. He had never raised his voice unlike other music masters she had known, and rarely scolded. His passion for his art and his drive to share it had changed each of his students, and the teachers he worked with.

Now he was gone and nothing could fill the void.

Lydia sat at the desk in the schoolroom's window, fighting with a blank page. She wanted to draw Mrs. Drummond, embraced by her students, but her pencil refused to cooperate. The harder she tried, the more stubborn it became.

She tossed it aside. Perhaps she ought to go downstairs and sew.

Her feet refused to move. How many garments for the workhouse children had she fashioned in the last few days? Enough to leave her fingers and mind numb.

If she did not create something fresh soon, she would surely burst!

She glanced over her shoulder toward the music room. No, that was not possible. Even the thought of it threatened to strangle the breath from her.

She wrestled the easel into place and set up the watercolors. It mattered not what she painted, so long as brush met paper.

Dark shapes coalesced into alarmingly familiar features. Mr. Amberson's eyes, just his eyes, at the moment he said 'adieu', stared back at her from the easel.

The brush slipped from her fingers, clattering lifeless on the floor. She sank into her chair, face in her hands. Wrenching sobs welled in her chest, forcing shallow gasps for air.

She had not wept since he left.

The tears were always there, just beneath the surface. If she gave in to them, something of him would trail away with them. So she held her breath and wrapped her arms around her chest. If she could not be with him, then she must cling to what remained of him.

"Lydia?" Annabelle stood in the door way. "Are you well?'

"I … I am. I just dropped my brush."

Annabelle's gaze locked on the paper. "Oh, Lydia." She dabbed her eyes with her apron. "I hate to call you away right now. But a carriage approaches, and I am certain you will be wanted downstairs."

"Is it Sir Anthony?"

"Just come." Annabelle grabbed her by the arm and urged her to the stairs.

Halfway down, the door knocker rapped three times, filling the vestibule with sharp, ominous echoes.

Three more steps and Mrs. Drummond came into view, standing near the front door. She glanced back at them, nodding as she opened the door.

A tall figure, swathed in a fine, familiar great coat stepped in.

"Mr. Darcy, I presume."

He nodded gravely and stepped aside. "Mrs. Darcy, may I present Mrs. Drummond?"

Lizzy—no, it was Mrs. Darcy, garbed as finely as her husband, walked in.

Mrs. Drummond curtsied.

Lydia's knees buckled. Annabelle caught her elbow. Between her and the stalwart banister, Lydia just managed to remain upright.

"Mr. Darcy, Mrs. Darcy." She stammered and struggled through a disgracefully ungainly curtsey.

They both looked up, as though they noticed her on the stairs for the first time. Mr. Darcy's eyes widened slightly and he pulled his head back just a bit. Did he not recognize her?

"Lyddie?" Lizzy rushed to her side, jaw gaping.

"I … I had no idea of your coming."

"Our trip was a bit ... spontaneous." Lizzy stared at her, studying, analyzing, dissecting.

Lizzy looked so different to the last time Lydia had seen her. She carried herself with a different air—not arrogance or entitlement, but what was it? Peace? Confidence? Perhaps a bit of both.

Whatever it was, she had blossomed in Mr. Darcy's care. What would Papa and Mama think to see her now?

Lizzy's gaze weighed heavy on her. Some things would never change.

Lydia turned her face aside.

"We are very pleased to welcome you here." Mrs. Drummond's eyebrow rose.

That meant Lydia should echo the sentiment, but if she uttered such a falsehood, Lizzy would call her out on it in a mere heartbeat. Surely not a propitious way to begin their reunion.

"Is there a place where my sister and I might talk whilst you speak with Mr. Darcy?" Lizzy looped her arm in Lydia's.

"Show them to the parlor, Miss Fitzgilbert."

Annabelle curtsied and ushered them into the parlor and shut the door.

Lydia paced along the edge of the fireplace. "Would you care to sit Liz ... Mrs. Darcy? Shall I send for tea? Have you had a long journey today? Is there anything which might be done for your comfort?"

Lizzy stopped in the center of the room, staring as though she hardly knew her. "Lydia?"

"I ... I ... Oh Lizzy, I am so sorry." Her feet moved without permission, and she rushed to Lizzy.

Warm arms embraced her. A torrent of wracking sobs surged forth, punctuated by babbling confessions, promises of change, and pleas of repentance. All words she never planned to say, but seemed right and fitting in the moment.

Somehow they made it to the sofa. The restful posture served to free untapped reserves of tears that poured out as she clung to Lizzy's shoulder.

Lizzy held her and stroked her hair, murmuring soothing sounds. The flow of tears faded to a trickle. Lydia gulped in several deep, searing breaths.

"Pray, do not send me away from here. I know ... I know I did not do right. But I ... I have improved ever so much. I think I have ... I know I have. Pray, let me stay. Do not send me back to Papa."

Lizzy caught Lydia's chin with a gentle touch and lifted it until their eyes met. "You do not wish to go home?"

"No!" Lydia sniffled and blinked hard, but the burning blurriness refused to dissipate. "I ... I do not like the person I was there. I do not ... pray do not make me go back."

Lizzy produced a handkerchief from her reticule and pressed it into Lydia's hand.

Fine soft muslin, smelling of lavender and Lizzy.

Lizzy rocked slightly, biting her upper lip. She did that when she was thinking, especially when she was surprised by something.

It did not happen often.

"I will not send you back to Papa."

Lydia gasped into the handkerchief.

"If you see Papa's house as I now do, I cannot send you back."

Lydia hid her face in the handkerchief. More tears would be unseemly, but by what other means might such profound relief be expressed? She held her breath and stiffened her spine until the impending paroxysm subsided.

Later she would draw—something.

The door eased open and Annabelle slipped in, arms laden.

"Forgive me for intruding and for being so forward as to introduce myself. I am Lady Annabelle Fitzgilbert. Your sister is my dearest friend."

Lizzy's brows rose high on her forehead. Under other circumstances, the expression would have been comical.

She would draw that, too.

"You are the daughter of—"

"Pray madam, that is not why I came in. My connections are not significant right now." Annabelle slid a footstool toward Lizzy and carefully placed her burden on it.

Her sketchbook, watercolors and Juliana's framed picture!

"You must have many questions about Lydia's time here. You may not realize, but when Lydia feels deeply, she speaks most eloquently in her drawings. I brought these so she might more easily share her story." She opened the sketchbook to the first page.

"Lydia draws?" Lizzy chewed her upper lip.

"Indeed, madam, very well. And though she hardly considers it the case, her pianoforte performance is quite accomplished, too. I shall leave you, though. I am sure you have much to discuss." She curtsied and left.

Annabelle was right. The images told everything she might want Lizzy to know—and everything Lydia would rather she not. Others might miss the outpouring of her soul into her sketches, but Lizzy? She was the one person who would see them for what they were.

Lizzy fingered the edge of the sketchbook. She knew it too.

"May I?"

To be so exposed—Lydia sniffled and screwed her eyes shut. This might be her only means of staying here, with Mrs. Drummond.

"Go ahead. They are only silly, little sketches. Miss Honeywell taught drawing and watercolors to all of us."

Lizzy pointed to the first, primitive sketch of Mr. Birch. "There must be a tale here, would you tell me?" She sat, head cocked, eyes bright and ready to listen.

Lizzy had always been a good listener.

How much should she tell? But then, what point in concealment. Lizzy would eventually know everything.

"It is a picture of a ... a character I made up, a sailor, Mr. Birch."

How long ago it all seemed.

With Lizzy's patient encouragement, she told the full story of Mr. Birch's inception and Mr. Amberson's role in it.

Lizzy flipped pages, and Lydia continued her narration. As the drawings became more intense, Lydia spoke less and Lizzy asked less. By the final pages they sat in silence, tears flowing.

Lizzy set aside the sketchbook and forced Lydia to look her in eyes. "Lyddie, I had no idea you would become …" She gestured to the sketchbook. "I am very, very proud of you.

"Proud of me?"

No one had ever said such a thing.

"Yes, and Mr. Darcy will be as well. You have so honored the gift he gave you. I expect that is what Mrs. Drummond is telling him now."

"I do not imagine so. I fear I have disappointed her greatly."

Lizzy brushed back loose hairs clinging to Lydia's tear-streaked cheeks. "I never thought to hear myself say this, but, I think you may be too hard on yourself."

A giggle escaped before Lydia could contain it. "You are right. I never thought to hear that from you."

Lizzy snickered and something snapped. They both fell into peals of laughter.

None of this was truly funny, but after all the tears, how else to spend the overflowing emotion?

The door peeked open and Juliana slipped in. "Excuse me, madam, but Mr. Darcy wishes you to join him in Mrs. Drummond's office."

"Wait here for me, Lyddie." Lizzy rose and followed Juliana out.

Lydia fell against the back of the couch and stared at the ceiling. Dust had gathered in the moldings there.

Best remember that next she tidied the drawing room.

What brought the Darcys here? Was it a good thing or one more pending disaster?

Was it possible Lizzy was proud of her?

She was not apt to lie, so it must be true. But was it enough?

Juliana appeared at the doorway, and Lydia waved her in.

"Is that your sister? You look very like her." Juliana sat beside her. "She is quite pretty, but a bit intimidating, I think."

"Mr. Darcy must be affecting her."

"He is very intimidating too, so tall and somber."

"Yes, he can be frightening, especially when he is cross." Lydia sniffled. "I used to think him altogether horrid. But he sent me here when Papa cast me out. I did not recognize his kindness to me then. I am ever so grateful to him, now."

"I owe him a great deal as well then. I do not imagine I would have lived without you."

"You are most generous, but I am quite sure I did not do so much as that."

Juliana leaned her head on Lydia's shoulder. "Did she say why they came? Sir Anthony arrived a few minutes ago. He is with Annabelle in the parlor. I am sure he has something to do with this."

"If Sir Anthony had a hand in this, I do not know what to think. He has already made such a cake of things. I cannot decide whether his help is worth having."

"I am certain he means very well."

"That is hardly reassuring. You think everyone means well. You sound like my sister Jane."

Juliana's face screwed up in a little pout.

"Do not fret. Everyone considers Jane perfect. Being compared to her is a good thing."

"If you say so."

"Well, I do. You will just have to believe me. Now, I just pray Mr. Darcy agrees with Lizzy not to send me away."

Juliana sat straight. "You cannot be serious. They certainly would not—"

The door swung open again. The Darcys and Mrs. Drummond entered. Lydia and Juliana jumped to their feet and curtsied.

Mr. Darcy towered over them both, straight and serious as always. But there was no tension in his shoulders or jaw, and his eyes held no angry fire.

"The Darcys have invited you to dinner and to stay with them tonight." Mrs. Drummond gave her a stern look. "I have, of course, given my approval."

An invitation to dinner and stay the night? What was Lizzy thinking?

"That is very kind of you, thank you." Lydia dipped her head.

"I have already had a small trunk sent to your room. Juliana, help her pack and be quick. Do not keep the Darcys waiting." Mrs. Drummond clapped twice.

The sharp sound broke through her daze. They curtsied and dashed out.

Juliana leaned close as they trotted up the stairs. "I wonder where they will take you."

"The King's Head is the best inn in town. I am

sure that is where they are staying. But what shall I bring? My head is so muzzy I can hardly think."

"Just sit down and I shall pack for you. You need body linen, a night dress ... a dress for dinner ... and one for tomorrow. Your cloak—" Juliana held up the brilliant red cloak.

Lydia threw up her hands. "Oh pray, not that. You take it. I cannot bear to wear it anymore."

"Why?"

"Mr. Wickham bought it for me."

"But you will be cold."

"Give me your brown wool mantle then. We will both be warm and happy that way."

"Are you sure?"

"Absolutely. Pray help me into my walking dress, the one with long sleeves. It will look very well with the mantle."

Juliana helped her dress, tossed a few last things in the trunk and carried it downstairs.

Mr. Darcy's coachman met them at the foot of the stairs and took the trunk. Less than a quarter of an hour later, Mr. Darcy handed her into the luxurious carriage.

How different things were now to the last time she had ridden in this coach. The springs must be new; it rode so smoothly along the stony road. The squabs were full and plush, covered in buttery-soft leather.

Mr. Darcy sat facing her and Lizzy. He had not been willing to share the space with her the last time. Though he did not look at her, neither did he avoid her. He was simply absorbed in staring at Lizzy.

Was Lizzy aware of the way his eyes lingered over her?

Of course she was. She was aware of everything

around her, but she seemed lost in thought.

What was she thinking?

The carriage was far too quiet.

"I had a letter from Mary just last week. She says Mr. Michaels is due to return from London soon. Mr. Collins will read the banns for them very soon."

"You have been corresponding with Mary?" Lizzy rarely looked so surprised. "She had not mentioned that to me."

"I do not wonder." Lydia gazed at her feet and forced a little laugh. "It is not as if my letters contain anything very important or even interesting. We wrote a bit about gardening and some old songs Mama used to sing. I sent her some drawings of the school. I think she liked them. Oh, she says Mrs. Collins is doing well."

"I am glad to hear that. Her letters have been less frequent recently. But I suppose she has a great deal on her mind."

The carriage stopped nowhere near the King's Head.

Lydia peered out the side glass. "This is Sir Anthony's house."

"He has offered for us to stay here."

Of all places to wish to stay!

"He is not very pleased with me at the moment. I do not think he should want me staying at his home."

"It was his suggestion to invite you." Mr. Darcy sounded like he was merely making a remark about the weather. "He came to Pemberley to extend the invitation himself. Moreover, he has repaired to the local inn whilst we are here—something about not wanting to intrude upon our business."

What business might they be on? Her stomach

churned.

The driver opened the door, and Mr. Darcy handed them out.

"We have a room ready for you." Lizzy slipped her arm in Lydia's.

Lydia's jaw dropped.

"Do not look so astonished. Did you expect we would keep you in the carriage house with the horses?"

Lydia stammered, but Lizzy laughed gently.

"I will show you upstairs. I should think you would like to rest before supper. Would you like some tea and sandwiches sent up as well?"

Lizzy was treating her like a real guest, not a disgraced relation.

She nodded, not daring to meet Lizzy's inquiring gaze lest she understand too well.

Lizzy showed her to a primary bedroom on the second floor. No third floor or attic room for her, this was probably the best guest room in the house.

"It is a lovely room. I have not had a room to myself in a long time. Even when we visited Rosings, Kitty and I shared."

"Who shares your room at school?"

"Annabelle and Juliana. Mrs. Drummond gave permission for us all to share."

Lizzy's eyebrows rose in that all-knowing sort of way she had. "You have merry times together?"

"I suppose … I had not really thought of it that way. More, I think we have needed one another."

The coachman clomped up behind them, trunk in hand.

Lizzy pointed to the far corner of the room. He deposited it and left.

"Now you have your things, I will send your tea up. Best for you to be well-rested for dinner." Lizzy kissed her cheek and closed the door.

That probably meant there was a long conversation in store tonight.

Lydia stumbled to the bed.

She slipped off her shoes and crawled beneath the counterpane, unable to keep her eyes open a moment longer.

.

✤Chapter 16

SHE STIRRED AND opened one eye.

Where … and when was she?

She rose up on elbows and looked around.

Sir Anthony's townhouse with Lizzy and Darcy. She fell back as though by a physical blow.

The pretty clock on the mantle declared two hours had passed. A tea tray perched on the dressing table near the window.

Why had Lizzy invited her here? It was not like Lizzy to offer a pleasant invitation only to turn it into an opportunity to scold and find fault. No, that was something for Papa to relish.

Thank heavens he was not likely to appear.

She rolled out of bed, her feet near silent on the soft carpet. What a luxury compared to the cold, hard floor in her room at school.

Lizzy had not mentioned what time dinner would

be served. Best not tempt fortune by being late.

She sipped the cold tea and nibbled on the dainty sandwich left on the tea tray.

Lydia opened her trunk. Her sketchbook and pencil lay uppermost. How had Juliana packed those without her noticing? And her favorite of Annabelle's dresses too?

Annabelle had probably conspired with her.

Dressing without assistance proved a bit awkward. How accustomed to having Annabelle and Juliana to help her she had become.

It would be so hard when they left.

Best not dwell upon that.

She straightened a few hair pins, tucked a shawl around her shoulders and went downstairs, sketchbook in hand.

Beautiful, soft light streamed through the parlor windows. She sat at a small table near the window and opened her sketchbook. Her pencil took on a life of its own.

What relief to at last be drawing again, even if it was Mr. Darcy's likeness that took shape on the page. He had worn such an astonished expression there in the vestibule at Mrs. Drummond's. Lizzy, too. Her image took shape beside his.

How odd, now away from Papa, Lizzy did not resemble him so much as Lydia had thought.

Lizzy must favor her mother.

"Elizabeth is quite correct. Your drawings are very good."

Lydia shrieked, jumped, juggling her pencil.

Mr. Darcy caught her chair before it fell and steadied the rocking table.

"Pray, forgive me, sir! I had no idea you were

there."

"I beg your pardon. I did not intend to startle you. May I?" He touched her sketchbook.

Every nerve within her screamed 'No!' How could she share something so private? But how could she deny him anything after all he had done for her?

She nodded just the tiniest bit.

"Elizabeth said your drawings told an eloquent tale."

"I … I am not very good with words, sir."

"Nor am I, as my wife will attest. I am fortunate in her ability to discern so much though I might say little." His voice was very soft, and he did not look at her as he spoke.

How strange for such a commanding man.

He took the sketchbook from the table and gestured to the settee.

She followed him, limbs wooden and stomach clenched.

"So, that is how I looked to you this morning?"

Was that a dimple forming in his cheek? Was it possible?

"You did seem quite surprised."

"I suppose so." He flipped slowly through the pages, from end to beginning.

What an odd way to view them.

"Your drawings have become quite accomplished, in a very short time. My sister, Georgiana, has studied drawing for years and is hardly so proficient."

"Miss Honeywell is an excellent teacher."

"And you are an excellent pupil it would seem."

The awkwardness of his voice and posture—he did not offer compliments easily or often.

Her cheeks flushed.

"I am very grateful for the opportunity you have afforded me, sir. I am sorry that I was not sensible of it earlier. And for the grief I caused to bring this all about."

He rose and strode to the windows, silhouette backlit in the afternoon sun.

She held her breath, spine steeled for the lecture that was sure to follow.

His shoulders stooped just a mite, not the posture of a man about to deliver a tongue lashing.

"Did Elizabeth tell you about my sister?"

"No, sir."

"She was nearly duped into running away with Wickham. It was Elizabeth's intervention that saved her. I could not see fit to punish you for the same error. I owed it to Elizabeth to offer the same help to her sister that she gave mine."

"I am grateful."

He turned to face her, eyes so intense she dare not speak.

"I am pleased, and relieved you have taken advantage of the opportunity. I still feel responsible for what Wickham did to both of you. It would be a very difficult thing to bear if only one of my sisters overcame his meddling."

He counted her a sister? She clutched the arm of the settee and swallowed hard. "You gave me a chance, when my father washed his hands of me. I only hope I may—"

"There you are!" Lizzy burst in. "I am glad to see you both ready. Let us go to the drawing room. Our guests shall be arriving shortly."

"Guests?" Lydia gasped. "You must be joking."

Lizzy looked far too satisfied with herself, almost

as though she were ready to laugh.

"Not at all. I have arranged for a small dinner party tonight."

"On such short notice? How?"

More significantly, what was she thinking and why?

"The party will be very good company, I am sure." Lizzy's eyebrow rose in her peculiar little way and the corner of her lips lifted to match. "I cannot vouch for the quality of the food. Sir Anthony finds no fault in his cook, but I have no way to assess his tastes."

"I would have thought it an easy thing for you to discern, Mrs. Darcy." Mr. Darcy's eyebrow matched hers.

Was he teasing? Who would have considered it possible?

"Were it his own home, I am sure I could. But in a house only rented for the quarter, you must grant me that there is very little to go by."

Did he just snicker under his breath?

They entered the drawing room.

Lizzy extended her arm. "You can see how sterile the room is. Nothing personal whatsoever. The only clear thing is that no one actually lives in this place, only stays here."

Lydia glanced about the room. Lizzy was quite right. The room was attractive, but barren of character—like the lifeless backdrop of a fashion plate.

The door knocker pounded and the front door creaked open, admitting muffled voices.

Lizzy gestured toward a chair, and Lydia perched, wringing her hands.

Mr. Darcy stood to one side, face calm, but his clenched hands betrayed him.

The company was not as familiar to him as Lizzy intimated.

His hands were fascinating. Long-fingered and elegant. One index finger bore a long thin scar. What had caused it?

The housekeeper appeared in the doorway.

"Sir Anthony and Lady Annabelle." She curtsied and stepped aside.

"Welcome to *your* home, sir." Lizzy stepped forward, chuckling softly.

"Thank you for the invitation." Sir Anthony sauntered in, Annabelle at his side.

"It is the least we could do to thank you for your hospitality."

Mr. Darcy joined Sir Anthony and Lizzy while Annabelle slipped off to sit by Lydia.

"You look lovely tonight. I am so pleased my dress fits you so well."

"It would have been difficult had it not, as Juliana left me nothing else." Lydia giggled. "I am sorry you did not wear it yourself tonight."

"I do not mind in the slightest."

"It is not as though I am not glad of it, but I am surprised at you being here."

"No more surprised than I am, to be sure. I could not believe it when Sir Anthony told me we were to dine with the Darcys tonight."

"They are not here by chance, are they?" Lydia glanced at the Darcys.

"I do not think so. I only know Sir Anthony went to Derbyshire. It seems he must have gone to Pemberley whilst there."

"I am astonished he would go to such lengths."

"Extravagance seems to be his nature. I suppose I

will have to become accustomed to it."

"Do you know what he told them?"

"You seem ill at ease. Have they been cross with you?" Annabelle's brow creased as though she meant to glare at Lizzy.

"Hardly. I am anxious, for they have been very kind and gracious. It is not the reception I expected from them, given the way we parted."

"I am ever so glad to hear it. I could not bear it if he caused them to be harsh with you." Annabelle squeezed her hand.

"Do you suppose we are to discuss it all tonight?"

"It would be a singular dinner conversation. I do not expect it."

Annabelle was surely right. Though Papa might tolerate such conversations over dinner, Lizzy would not.

"Shall we go in to dinner?" Lizzy called from the other side of the room.

They followed her to the dining room.

Why was the table set for six?

Lizzy indicated Annabelle should sit beside Sir Anthony, leaving Lydia beside the empty chair. Mr. Darcy began carving the meat and the soup course was served, including a soup plate for the empty spot beside her.

Lydia glanced at Annabelle who shrugged. Lizzy only raised an eyebrow over her soup spoon and sipped the pea soup.

Why was Lizzy teasing her so and worse, why did she appear to enjoy it so well?

The knocker rapped against the front door, and Lydia jumped.

"It would seem our final guest has arrived." Lizzy

nodded at Mr. Darcy.

He blinked and the corner of his mouth twitched.

Lydia did not breathe for staring at the doorway.

How long could it take the housekeeper to lead someone—

"Mr. Amberson." The housekeeper curtsied and stepped aside.

"Mrs. Darcy, Mr. Darcy." He bowed. "I beg your forgiveness, for it appears I am late."

Though he spoke to them, his gaze fixed upon Lydia.

She dropped her spoon into her soup, the metallic clink of metal on china echoed like church bells.

"Not at all, sir. I believe the fault is ours. We may have given you the wrong time. Pray sit down and join us. The soup is only just served."

He made his way in, his long stride awkward in the confined space. His hair was tousled as usual, a great shock of it falling over his forehead. The blue of his eyes seemed a little greyer tonight, like the clouds of a dreary afternoon. Little lines that had not been there before creased his forehead and beside his eyes.

Where had he been all this time? Had separation worn on him as much as it had her?

He sat beside her. Though not touching, she could feel him there. Air rushed into her lungs as though she had not truly breathed since his departure.

Perhaps she should say something, but what words might she utter in this company?

She raised her hand to the edge of the table and tapped out a few bars of the music he had written for her. He responded in kind, adding the next measure, and then they played a few notes together.

Could anyone else hear the music?

Sir Anthony stared—no, gawked— at them while Annabelle smiled, eyes glistening. Lizzy shared a knowing glance with Mr. Darcy who nodded.

None of them mattered.

She had been walking with but half her soul and never knew. Now he was here, she was complete, made whole.

"Were your travels from Derbyshire pleasant, Mr. Amberson?" Lizzy asked, signaling the removal of the soup course.

"I … ah … yes they were. One can never appreciate the countryside so well as when one walks it."

It was at least twenty miles to Derbyshire—how much further to Pemberley?

Little wonder he looked worn.

"I am very fond of walking myself. Mr. Darcy is forever losing me somewhere on the grounds of Pemberley. And you, Sir Anthony, what do you say of walking?"

"Not to be disagreeable, madam, but I prefer the view from the back of a horse. Do you ride, Mrs. Darcy?"

"A little, at my husband's insistence. I prefer to drive the lovely equipage Mr. Darcy has placed at my disposal. Lady Annabelle, do you ride or drive?"

"I have not done either since arriving at Mrs. Drummond's, but I very much enjoyed riding at one time."

"Excellent." By the look on Sir Anthony's face, he was already planning a horse for her.

Light conversation continued around her. Thankfully, though, none required her to speak. Mr. Amberson kept his eyes lowered and barely ate. But he slid his booted foot next to hers, not quite touching. He was not ignoring her, and it was enough.

After the sweet course, Lizzy led the ladies to the drawing room. The loss of Mr. Amberson's company ripped at the rawness of Lydia's heart. Would he return with the gentlemen, or would he disappear never to return?

Both seemed equally likely.

"Have you ever seen Sir Anthony's home in Derbyshire?" Annabelle asked.

"We visited his home once whilst touring the area when I first arrived. He was not in residence at the time. The house is quite lovely and his housekeeper very capable. You shall find her a great ally when you take over managing his house."

"You do not think she will disapprove—"

Lizzy chuckled. "Hardly. I believe you will have already won her approbation by your way of managing him."

"I cannot pretend that is unwelcome news."

"Lizzy? Do you mind if I play the pianoforte?" Lydia glanced back at the instrument.

If she did not do something soon, she might just crawl out of her own skin.

"I would love to hear you play. There is music, if you wish, in the cabinet near the instrument."

Lydia sifted through the music without really attending to it. She carried a few sheets to the pianoforte. It did not matter what she played or even if she played well, so long as she did something.

She sat at the keyboard and stared at the black notes dancing on the page. Her fingers though, had plans all their own. Her vision fuzzed and the first notes of Mr. Amberson's duet rang out.

Why was that the only piece she could play now?

She ought to stop, but the music poured out like a spring bubbling from the ground. She closed her eyes against intruders and gave way to the insistent flow.

Someone sat beside her and a familiar elbow tapped hers.

She cracked her eyes open just enough to make out the lanky shadow beside her. Long fingers added in the missing line and the duet became whole. The world around her faded into obscurity as the music embraced her. It filled her senses, completed her soul.

Everything was right in the world, exactly as it should be.

Then it stopped.

A hole as big as the silence opened up within her. Could everyone else see it too?

She looked up, into Mr. Amberson's eyes. The room was empty save him.

He stared into her eyes as no one else ever had—no one else ever would—and raised his hand to her face. He stroked the crest of her cheek with his knuckles.

She leaned into his touch, savoring, locking it into memory in case … in case … oh heavens! Pray let this not—

"I did not want to leave you. You know that, do you not?"

Her throat tightened so only the barest squeak escaped.

"I … I should have told you my plans, but I had not formed them until I was halfway to Derbyshire."

"You walked to Derbyshire?"

"I did."

"Why?"

"It was far less expensive than traveling post."

She tried to giggle, but it nearly strangled her. "Why Derbyshire?"

"Where else could I seek relief for my sufferings?"

"Sufferings?"

"You cannot imagine I felt our separation any less than you."

"I … I did not know."

He winced and screwed his eyes shut. "I have been a fool in so many ways. I should have declared myself more clearly. But you have always understood me so well."

"I … I had hopes, but without words—"

"You had my song."

"I dared not believe … it seemed too much to hope for." She stroked the cool, smooth keys without playing a note.

"Then you understood, just as I knew you would."

"I dared not believe anyone could think such things of me."

"I should have spoken it." He stood and pressed his cheek to the top of her hair. "I had promised my aunt I was reformed, that I would not interfere with her pupils in any way. That was a condition of my employ."

"A very sensible agreement."

"It was, until I met you. I tried to convince myself you were too young; you were my student; you were protected by my aunt. I was not allowed to notice you." He paced the length of the room, hands raking his unruly hair. "How could I help it? I have never met a woman who speaks the language I speak, who understands what I cannot say. How could I turn away from one who seems to have been formed to be my helpmeet, the other half of my soul?"

She bit her knuckle, the breath burning in her chest.

"I was a moth drawn to your flame, a light burning brighter and more alluring than anything I have ever known. Still, I kept my promise to my aunt. At least until that night in the garden. I did not regret that, you know, and I still do not. My only regret is I could not make you an offer that moment." He crossed back to her in three impossibly long steps and dropped to his knee before her.

Lydia gulped as he took her hands and enfolded them in his.

"I have been to see your brother, and there I encountered Sir Anthony. I did not spare him my temper. He well understands the error of his ways. No one shall ever disparage you that way again, at least not while I live and breathe."

Had not Darcy claimed the same for Lizzy?

"I petitioned the Darcys for the privilege to love and protect you all the days of my life. I secured both their blessings and approval of a settlement. Mr Darcy has promised to sign it once I have your approval."

He cupped her face in his hands and kissed her.

She closed her eyes and abandoned herself to his warmth igniting every nerve in her being.

"You are the other half of my soul," he whispered in her ear. "Pray do not force me to go about the world a hollow wraith, withering for the loss of you. Without you I am dry and empty. I have not played a note since I left you, not until just today."

She pressed her forehead to his. "I only picked up

my pencil again this afternoon."

"When the heart finds its completion, it does not function alone ever again. Pray do not insist that I try to go on that way. End my suffering. Do not condemn me to further sleepless nights and purposeless days. Marry me, Lydia."

"The only thing I wanted more than to stay at Mrs. Drummond's was … is to be with you." She laced her fingers in his. "I will be proud to be your wife."

He jumped to his feet, grabbed her by the waist and twirled her around, laughing so deep the windows must have shaken.

"Come, play with me." He seated her on the piano bench and slipped in beside her.

"What shall we play?"

"Just follow me. You will know the song." He pressed his shoulder to hers and raised his hands to the keyboard.

She leaned into him and closed her eyes.

Soft, pleasing chords rose from the keyboard, gentle and warm, beckoning her, laying a clear path for her to follow. She added a line to his music, one chord at first, but soon blooming into a complete part of her own.

The lines intertwined, playing off one another. His, far more complex and full, hers, still shy and hesitant, but complementary and supporting one another. Neither could stand alone, but together they were more than the sum of their parts.

Though his words had been tender, this—this was far and away more articulate, fluently speaking the depth of his feelings in a way words never would. His joy, his commitment, his love.

Oh, his love! How he loved her!

It might have only been twenty miles, but he had walked across England for her. He had not abandoned her, but had fought for her, and strove to make an acceptable offer.

What was more, Darcy had accepted!

Her heart swelled until it filled her throat, nearly cutting off her breath.

Was it possible for one woman to be so supremely happy?

Hot trails trickled down her cheeks and she sniffled.

He nudged her shoulder with his and she opened her eyes. Darcy, Lizzy, Sir Anthony and Annabelle gathered around the pianoforte.

"Are we to wish you joy now?" Annabelle asked.

Lydia barely nodded. Warm arms enveloped her, Lizzy on one side, Annabelle on the other.

Beside them, Sir Anthony pumped Mr. Amberson's hand and slapped his back. Darcy stood half a step away, a slight curve to his lips—a veritable outpouring of joy from him!

"Are you happy, Lydia?" Lizzie whispered in her ear.

"I do not have words to tell you how much. He is the best of men, I do not deserve—"

"He has told us his entire story and I agree. He is a very good man. You both have grown and improved so much. You deserve one another. I am proud to claim you both as family." She kissed Lydia's cheek.

"I believe this good news calls for a toast." Darcy held up the port decanter and waved them to middle of the room.

Mr. Amberson took her arm, escorted her to Darcy and placed a crystal glass in her hand.

"To joy." Darcy lifted his glass.

That was possibly the briefest, most insignificant toast anyone had offered in the whole of England. A year ago, she might have been offended by such meager congratulations, but somehow, tonight, they were exactly right, fitting and proper.

They drank, and she savored the sweet, rich liquid that just barely burned the back of her throat. That flavor would always speak to her of joy.

"How did this all come to be?"

"There is indeed a story to be told. Come, sit and we shall lay it all out for you." Lizzy gestured toward the couch.

Lydia sat between Mr. Amberson and Annabelle, leaning alternately against one, then the other.

How could so much warmth and love surround her?

Sir Anthony pulled a chair close to Annabelle and extended his hand to her. She laid her fingers on his. He closed his eyes briefly and leaned back in his chair. A delicate blush rose on her cheeks.

He had earned her forgiveness.

Lizzy and Darcy shared the settee across from them. Lizzy looked so pleased with herself and even Darcy sported a smug glint in his eye.

"You might well imagine my surprise when Mr. Amberson arrived on Pemberley's doorstep, requesting an audience with me." Darcy stroked his chin with his knuckles.

"I am sure I was quite the sight." Mr. Amberson laughed. "Travel weary and wearing a coat of road dust. I had not even stopped to refresh myself at the local inn. Your butler nearly refused my card altogether. Mind you, I hardly blame him."

"He takes his job rather seriously." Lizzy chuckled. "He *once* tried to keep me from his master's study."

"Only once." Darcy pressed his lips hard, but his cheek dimpled.

Who could have imagined him capable of that?

"I can only imagine your man's regret following that mistake. Thankfully, I was granted an audience. Be certain though, I had alternative plans in mind had that attempt been unsuccessful."

"You would have stalked me like a hound worries a fox."

Mr. Amberson pressed his shoulder against Lydia's. "I had good reason."

"But he brought no letter of introduction, how did you come to believe him?" Lydia asked.

"His name was not unfamiliar. Mrs. Drummond wrote to keep us abreast of your progress."

By the look on Mr. Darcy's face, there must have been many letters.

"You must agree, his story was not one likely to be fabricated, particularly in light of the fact he asked nothing of me, save my approval."

Wickham had demanded, and been refused, ten thousand pounds.

Lizzy nodded slightly. "And Georgiana vouched for his skill as a teacher of music."

"She has studied under many masters and has never spoken so highly of anyone."

"He is a remarkable teacher," Annabelle said softly. "No master ever taught me so much."

"Georgiana pleaded with me to engage him to teach her."

Lydia gasped.

"I expect it was about that time I arrived." Sir Anthony ran a finger along the inside of his collar.

"You went to Pemberley as well?" Lydia gaped.

"Lady Annabelle left me with a charge to fulfill. Where better to begin?" He shrugged.

"It helped that the butler was familiar with your name, and willingly admitted you." Lizzy's eyes twinkled and her eyebrows flashed up.

"Amberson never mentioned Sir Anthony in his discussions with me. I was quite surprised to hear another layer to the affair."

"One rather unexpected I might add," Lizzy said.

"I had to call upon my dear wife's powers of observation to help me sort out the stories—"

"—and petitions of two men eager to make things right with the women they desired to please." Lizzy gazed at Annabelle. "After smoothing over the initial awkwardness—"

Mr. Amberson and Sir Anthony exchanged glances and guffawed.

"What she means is she prevented the encounter from devolving to fisticuffs." Sir Anthony scratched behind his ear.

"I had reason to resent the gentleman's interference." Mr. Amberson snorted.

"A reason I hope is long past and satisfactorily recompensed." Lizzy gave him that look, the warning one that would someday wither her children if they dared disobey.

"Indeed, madam, it has been, far beyond any hope of expectation." Mr. Amberson sat up a little straighter.

"What have you planned?" Annabelle folded her arms over her chest and scowled.

"I think you will be pleased, Lady Annabelle." Lizzy still wore her warning look.

Annabelle shrank back a little.

"With the support of my new patrons—"

Lydia mouthed the word, eyes wide.

"—Mr. Darcy and Sir Anthony, I will establish a school of music in Derby. Miss Darcy and Miss Fitzgilbert—that is Lady Annabelle—will be my first pupils. The gentlemen are also planning to sponsor a series of concerts at the Derby assembly rooms to introduce me to the community."

"Your talent speaks for itself. Once it becomes known, we are certain you will not be in want of pupils."

Now it was Lizzy's turn to look smug.

Sir Anthony turned to Lydia. "I should be honored for you to use the townhouse I have in Derby as your home. Rent can wait until the music school is established."

"Be warned though, we will of course ask for your hospitality when Georgiana visits for her lessons. Perhaps you might host a few teas with the local ladies to entertain us whilst we are there," Lizzy said.

Annabelle squeezed Lydia's fingers.

Sir Anthony leaned close to Anabelle. "Are you assured of my repentance?"

"I am astonished at the completeness of your penance," Annabelle whispered. "This is beyond what I might have imagined."

Lizzy nodded at them. "I applaud you both on the strength of your characters. Despite the unusual nature of your circumstances, I am pleased to count you among our connections."

Mr. Amberson laced his long fingers in hers. "Is this agreeable to you? I have no estate to offer. There are no assurances that I will draw enough students to live comfortably. I appreciate my patrons, but I do not expect continuing charity."

"You are a brilliant teacher, and I am certain we can get by." Lydia's voice was tight in her throat. "I spent many years watching my mother make do on a small income."

Lizzy's eyebrows shot up.

"I know you are surprised, but I did pay attention. I learned a great deal, even though you never saw it. And I am certain you can remind me of anything I do not recall."

"I take that you mean you approve?" Mr. Amberson squeezed her hand.

"Very much." How could she not?

"Then I suppose all we have left is to plan a wedding." Lizzy winked.

⚘Chapter 17

TWO DAYS LATER, after breakfast, Juliana sat on the edge of the bed in their shared room, eyes wide, gaping at Lydia and Annabelle.

"If I did not hear it from your lips, I am sure I would not believe it. It is all so like something we might read in a novel." Juliana hugged herself and rocked a little.

Lydia wrapped her arms around her knees and leaned against the headboard.

"Can you imagine he went directly to Pemberley, with no introduction no less, to ask for her hand?" Annabelle leaned her shoulder into Lydia's. "How romantic—"

"—and courageous! Mr. Darcy does not look like a man any would want to approach without very good reason."

Lydia patted Juliana's hand. "That is his normal

look, but he is really very kind and thoughtful. One must simply overlook how little he speaks and how often he scowls. Lizzy tells me he is uneasy in company and does not know what to say."

"How strange for a man of his consequence. I would never have suspected such a thing." Annabelle shrugged. "But there is no doubt as to the goodness of his character. Sir Anthony speaks very highly of him."

"Sir Anthony! I hardly know what to make of him. Did you expect him to go to Mr. Darcy?" Lydia chewed her lower lip.

Annabelle pressed a knuckle to her chin. "I expected very little from him after what he had done to both of you. At that point, I was very happy to see him gone, though Mrs. Drummond thought me a fool."

"Surely you do not feel that way now." Juliana leaned closer.

Annabelle looked away. "No, I do not."

"I saw signs of a decided preference whilst we were with the Darcys." Lydia tried to catch her eye.

Annabelle's cheeks colored.

"Do not pretend, we can tell. You do like him."

"I … I do. I am not sure I want him to know yet, though. He was so extravagant trying to make things right. I feel that must speak to his true character. For all his stubbornness and quick temper, there is something very good inside him. It is difficult not to like a man who would try so hard to please me when he could simply walk away."

"I think he likes you as well." Juliana reached for Annabelle's hands. "Why else would he go so far?"

"Do you think it possible?"

"There is no doubt he does." Lydia retrieved her sketchbook and handed it to Annabelle. "This is the way he looked when you played the piano for him. That is the look of a man well on the way to being in love."

"It seems too good to dare believe. But, I would not complain if it were true." Annabelle pointed at Lydia, "That is certainly not something you have to concern yourself about. There is no doubt of Mr. Amberson's feelings."

Lydia pressed her hands to very hot cheeks.

A sharp rap at the door made her jump.

"Mrs. Darcy is here," Miss Greenville called through the door.

"Go, go, but you must tell us everything she plans for the wedding and breakfast!" Juliana gave her a gentle shove in the right direction.

Talking to Lizzy never used to make her so nervous. Then again, Lizzy's good opinion had never really mattered until now.

Lydia pulled on her pelisse and bonnet as she hurried down the stairs.

"Be careful! I would not have you tumble down the stairs!" Lizzy peered up from the bottom of the staircase.

"I did not want to keep you waiting."

"We have the whole day for our leisure."

Lizzy led her to the waiting Darcy carriage, and the driver handed them in.

How luxurious not to walk everywhere.

"I know what you are thinking, Lyddie. I do still like to drive, but here it would be unseemly."

"Papa never concerned himself with such things."

"No, he did not, but he should have. And Mr.

Darcy does. It took time for me to become accustomed to it, I confess. We had a few strong words on the matter as I would rather drive myself and do away with a driver altogether. But, Mr. Darcy is correct. It is unseemly in the eyes of society and it is not safe for a lady to travel alone. So, I only drive alone on our estate. Elsewhere, I honor his requests."

"And it does not chafe?"

"Sometimes, but more than anything, I do it because I love him. It pleases him to feel he is taking care of me … and I like the feeling of it as well. It is very different and takes some getting used to. I imagine you will have to accustom yourself to it as well. Your Mr. Amberson would see you well cared for, too." Lizzie clasped Lydia's hands. "Now, I thought we might visit the dressmaker first. I should like to see you married in something new and very pretty."

"I do so hope you like the gown. I designed it."

"Having seen your drawings, I should not be surprised. It sounds like there is a tale to be told. I demand satisfaction."

Lizzy's smile and laugh were so genuine. Is this what she and Jane used to share?

"I suppose it is a bit of a story."

Lizzy listened with rapt attention until the carriage stopped at the dressmaker's, and the driver helped them down.

"Are those your paintings?" Lizzy pointed through the window.

"I had no idea she would display those so prominently!" Lydia covered her mouth with her hands.

Lizzy marched through the door, back straight, chin up, every inch a proper gentleman's wife. She went directly to the framed paintings. Lydia followed several steps behind.

"These look like they might have come from *La Belle Assemblée*. They are extraordinary."

"Those designs are exclusive to our shop, madam." The modiste swept in. "If you should be interested …" She stopped short and stared at Lydia.

"My sister tells me you are preparing a dress for her. I would like to see it and determine if it is adequate for her wedding."

"Wedding? I was led to understand that the other young lady was the bride."

"My sister is recently betrothed. She insists the dress you are preparing will do for her own wedding. I hope to agree with her."

Did Lizzy enjoy the look of confusion and astonishment she engendered on the modiste?

Probably. She never did have much tolerance for superciliousness.

"Yes, yes, of course, madam. If you please, Miss Bennet, my assistant will help you dress."

The modiste waved and the seamstress led Lydia away. The last time she and Annabelle were there, they had been expected to help each other dress.

Was it just her fine gown that made Lizzy's reception so different? No doubt the modiste noticed that first. But it would have been difficult to miss Lizzy's bearing and assurance.

Would she ever carry herself like that?

The seamstress pronounced her ready and ushered her out to Lizzy.

Would she approve of her gown as much as Annabelle had?

Lydia stepped up on the dais in front of three tall mirrors and held her breath.

Lizzy circled the dais, clucking her tongue. "I can certainly see your hand in this and a bit of Mama's influence as well."

Was that a good thing?

"What do you think Lyddie?"

Did she mean a test now? What if her taste was wanting?

"Pray Lizzy, tell me your opinion."

"Does it matter so much to you?"

"Lizzy! It is too unkind of you to tease me so."

"The gown is lovely and perfect for your wedding. Now I have told you what you wish to know, you must answer my question from yesterday. Who is to stand up with you?"

"Is it wrong of me to ask Annabelle instead of Mary or Kitty?"

A little of the bloom faded from Lizzy's cheeks. "I think it a very pleasing choice."

"There is more you are not saying."

"Shall we visit the tea house when we are finished? We might talk there."

How much could there be to talk about?

Lizzy directed the seamstress on a few minor adjustments. A quarter of an hour later they were off.

A serving girl met them just inside the tea house. Lizzy asked for a private space and they were immediately shown to their nicest room. White trim against pale blue walls, and crisp eyelet curtains in a sunny window made the tight chamber feel cool and welcoming. An assortment of tea cups sat on a narrow shelf lining each wall near the ceiling.

"This will do nicely. Bring a full assortment of refreshments." Lizzy sat down as the serving girl curtsied and drew the curtain across the doorway.

They stared at each other, more awkward than they had been since their initial reunion. The silence grew from itchy to suffocating.

Lizzy looked away, blinking rapidly. "I will by no means tell you what you should do for your wedding. You should know, though, Mama and Papa did not attend mine. Jane objected to my decision, but she still stood up with me. Aunt Gardiner was not very pleased with her deportment, though."

"I've never heard anyone displeased with her before." Lydia rolled her eyes.

Lizzy probably would not like the sarcasm she failed to moderate in her tone.

"I have no wish to color your opinion of our sister."

"Everyone goes on and on about how good and lovely and wonderful she is, but that is only true when she is the center of attention. When she is not—" Lydia shrugged and looked away.

"You had such disagreements with her. I used to blame you for that, thinking you merely jealous. I was unfair to you then. I had no idea of the less attractive side of her nature."

"Pray, let us not go to the past, Lizzy. I do not like to dwell upon what was. I have so many regrets. It is all too much sometimes. I would like very much to only look ahead."

"I find I must often do the same."

The serving girl sidled in with their tea, set it on the table and disappeared as quickly as she came.

Lizzy served the tea. "Kitty has been staying with Jane. Mama insisted her prospects are far better in London than in Kent."

"Have they been?"

"I hardly know. The letters from Jane and Kitty are pretty, and proper and very vague. They seem content enough and much as they ever were."

Lydia shivered. "Kitty would not know what to make of me now. I would rather Annabelle stand with me. Kitty will be disappointed but—"

"And our parents?"

"Papa has washed his hands of me." Lydia's throat clamped down, bile burning the back of her tongue.

Lizzy took her hand. "I completely understand."

"Do you think Mr. Darcy might be willing to give me away?"

Lizzy stared and blinked. Thrice.

"I expect he will be very pleased to do so."

"I owe you both so much."

"You have repaid us with your improvement. I am only sorry I did not have more faith in you to do it."

"I am not sure I had very much faith in myself either."

Lizzy laughed softly. "I am glad you will be within such an easy distance of Pemberley and that Georgiana's lessons will often put us in company with one another."

"Miss Darcy did not like me very well in Kent."

"She is very shy like her brother. Once you become reacquainted, I expect you will be very good friends. You have a great deal in common."

Lydia flushed.

"I like to think that you and I shall be great friends now things are so different."

"You mean I am so different."

"I mean both of us. Away from Papa, the world is a different place. A much better place than either one of us might have believed."

Though Mrs. Drummond acknowledged she would miss Annabelle, Lydia and Juliana, she was a practical woman. Their successful launches were a testament to the efficacy of her establishment, one that now had four new openings. Over the next fortnight, she sent many letters to spread the good news. Word of impending visitors began arriving in every day's post. Naturally, every inch of the school had to be scoured and polished to welcome callers.

"What a fine way to send us off, setting us to the most disagreeable tasks possible! Cleaning and polishing the fireplaces? That used to be reserved for punishment. Why it falls to us when we have shown her to her best advantage …" Annabelle rubbed sweat from her forehead with the back of her hand.

"It is a distraction from our anxieties—perhaps not a pleasing one, but distracting nonetheless." Juliana leaned against the wall and panted.

"At least we are nearing the end of the task. Just two more bedrooms and we can hope to never be required to clean another. I shall be much kinder to any maid-of-all-work who cleans my fireplaces. She should have tea and biscuits at the end of it." Lydia draped a cleaning cloth over her arm. "Annabelle, help me move this dresser out of the way. I cannot properly reach with it there."

"I can help you," Juliana said.

"No," Annabelle shouldered her aside. ". I fear it might be too much, and I do so want you to stand up with me. I do not want risk your health. Ready, Lydia?"

Lydia braced her shoulder against the dresser, and they slid it out of the way.

"What is this?" Juliana retrieved a piece of paper from the floor.

Annabelle peeked over her shoulder. "It is a letter, I think—yes, it is addressed to Amelia."

A shiver slid down Lydia's spine, the one that always accompanied thoughts of Amelia.

"Look here." Juliana pointed to a spot midway down the dusty, creased paper.

Neither Papa nor Mama is impressed with the so-called accomplishments you have gained at your school. They are not inclined to sponsor your come-out anytime soon and perhaps not at all.

"Did she not say she had been presented at court?" Lydia whispered through her hand.

Annabelle sniffed. "I knew that story was rot, but I did expect that she was at the very least out."

"There's more …" Juliana pointed at another line.

I must be honest with you, sister; your headmistress reports she is not impressed with your improvements. Papa is in high dudgeon. He told Mama he had no intention to continue support if you remained bent on your ruinous ways. He will give your headmistress leave to send you off as a servant before he takes you back unreformed.

If your young man still wishes to marry you, then do everything you can to further the alliance, and do it soon. It would be good for you to be married, even to a plain man, before Papa loses all patience. Mama has quite given up hope and does not even argue in your favor anymore.

"So that's why Mrs. Drummond set her as a maid in Mrs. Harrow's house." Annabelle fell back against the wall and slid down to the floor.

Lydia and Juliana joined her.

"I am ashamed at how many of her stories I believed," Lydia said.

"I wonder if Joan knew." Juliana folded the letter along its previous creases.

"I doubt it."

"How difficult it must have been for her, carrying those secrets." Juliana wiped her eyes.

Lydia hugged her knees. "Her situation was no more dire than the rest of ours."

"She is right. Think about it. Until just recently you were set to be an apprentice with Mrs. Harrow. Lydia and I were here only on the good reports of Mrs. Drummond. Had I refused Sir Anthony, I would have been looking for a position right now."

"Still though, I am sure Amelia made all this worse by keeping it to herself."

"She did." Lydia leaned her head back against the wall and closed her eyes.

"It is hard to improve if you do not admit you have something to improve. One cannot do that well whilst pretending to be the envy of everyone else."

"Perhaps Mrs. Drummond will allow us to go to her. We could tell her we know, encourage her—"

Annabelle and Lydia exchanged glances.

Juliana really was far too sweet.

"Would any of us have listened to such a speech?" Annabelle's lips wrinkled into a characteristic frown.

"No, I suppose not. I just feel like we should help her somehow."

"The situation is of her own making."

"But it is kindness that changes the heart."

Lydia rubbed her fist against her lips. The old

midwife had insisted on christening Juliana's son. It was as important for Juliana, as it was for the boy, she had said. She was right. Little else had given Juliana so much peace as that and the boy's burial in the churchyard.

"Mrs. Harrow is very kind, and wise. Perhaps Mrs. Drummond believes Mrs. Harrow will be able to reach Amelia when she could not."

Annabelle cocked her head and stared.

"Perhaps you are right. I had not thought of that. Yes, yes that sounds like just the thing Mrs. Drummond would arrange." Juliana sniffled and blotted her eyes with the edge of her apron. "Thank you, that was exactly what I needed to hear."

Annabelle blinked rapidly. "Yes, it was."

On Saturday morning, Lydia sat in the schoolroom for the last time, easel fixed with paper and paints ready. Sunrise dappled the back garden with light and color, and she had to capture it one final time.

"I will miss finding you here, painting and drawing," Mrs. Drummond said softly from the doorway.

"I will miss it, too. It is hard to believe that I will be leaving here."

"I shall miss you, all of you." Mrs. Drummond entered, eyes bright. "I have something for you. I thought you should have a reminder of your time with us."

She handed Lydia a small band box, covered in a delicate patterned paper.

Lydia's hands trembled as she set down her paintbrush and took the box.

"Go on, open it."

She slid the lid open and gasped. "Mr. Birch! You found him in the garden?"

The little sailor was a bit weather-beaten and dusty, but still very much the same as when she first crafted him.

"I have known about him for quite some time. In fact, James—"

Lydia blushed at the mention of his name. She had only just reconciled herself to calling him that in the last few days. Oh, how his eyes shone when she did…

"He told me about it and his suspicions about your talents shortly after he encountered you in the garden."

She probably should make a reply, but words remained stubbornly out of reach.

"Although you both made it difficult for me, I am pleased you will be his wife. You shall do very well together."

"Thank you."

"Is your painting nearly finished? It is almost time for you to dress."

"It is done, but it must dry. May I call and pick it up during the week?"

"I think it would be instructive to the girls to see how I receive a proper young lady."

"Ever teaching, are you not?"

Mrs. Drummond shrugged. "Will you be traveling to Derbyshire with Sir Anthony?"

"Yes. We shall stay at his townhouse here this week. After his and Annabelle's wedding, we shall travel with them to Derby. Lizzy has offered to arrange things for our arrival."

"Then it seems all is ready. Come, I will help you

all to prepare."

Lydia flung her arms around Mrs. Drummond's waist, and buried her face in her shoulder. How could so much strength and wisdom be held in such a tiny frame?

"You already have, madam, you already have."

"They are ready." Mrs. Drummond led Lizzy into their room. "Her trunks have been sent along."

Lizzy picked her way through the crowded room and took Lydia's hands. "You are beautiful!"

"Is not her gown perfect?" Annabelle fluffed out the skirt.

"I shall have to ask you to design my next ball gown. Truly Lydia, this is stunning."

"Lydia designed mine as well." Annabelle twirled just fast enough to swirl her skirt around her.

"I told her she should not wear her wedding dress to stand up with me." Lydia crossed her arms over her chest.

"I see no reason why not. It is by far the prettiest dress I own. Why should I not wear it to stand up with you? Were you not going to wear your new gown to stand up with me?"

"That is different. That was the purpose of my gown from its inception."

"You look very lovely too, Miss Morley. Did Lydia have a hand in your dress as well?" Lizzy asked.

Juliana blushed and plucked at the bodice trim. "She did, madam."

"We pulled apart some of our older dresses. With the three of us working together, we crafted this in just a few days. I must say, I am impressed with what we could do ourselves." Annabelle straightened the ribbon bow at Juliana's waist.

"You have done a beautiful job. Are you ready to go?"

Lydia gulped and wrung her hands. "I thought I was."

"Leaving is often difficult, and so is beginning, but they are both often very worthwhile." Lizzy stepped closer and played with a stray curl dangling by Lydia's ear. "I found it so and I am certain you shall as well."

Lydia sniffled and nodded.

"Shall we?"

Mrs. Drummond led them out.

Mr. Darcy waited for them with the coach. He handed them inside and climbed up onto the box with the driver.

Lydia giggled. Four ladies dressed for a wedding were too much company for him. But who could blame him? It was gracious of him to come for them himself.

Annabelle took one of her hands and Juliana the other.

"It is good of Mrs. Drummond to allow all her students to attend your wedding." Lizzy said.

"I am sure she sees it as a way of reminding them of what good can come from improving oneself." Annabelle smirked.

Lydia's cheeks grew hot. "It is difficult to believe she could consider mine an example to follow."

Lizzy gazed at her with such a peculiar, misty-eyed look.

The coach rolled to a smooth stop before the church. Mr. and Mrs. Weatherby met them halfway to the door.

"The girls did such a lovely job decorating the chapel. Thank you for your assistance, Mrs. Darcy." Mrs. Weatherby said.

"Lizzy?" Lydia stared at her, jaw dropped.

"You know I cannot be idle. Besides, it seemed like Mrs. Drummond would welcome having her charges gainfully occupied and out of the house for a little while. Come and see." Lizzy linked arms with Lydia and escorted her into the chapel.

A waft of fresh, sweet perfume greeted her first. The bower of cut flowers became visible only after she stepped all the way in.

"So many blossoms!" Juliana peeked over her shoulder. "How did you come by them all?"

"Mr. Darcy finds them a very appropriate accessory for a wedding. Since your dress was already acquired …"

"He did this?" Lydia's eyes burned and the room went a bit blurry.

Lizzy squeezed her arm. "He is a very generous man. It is his way of celebrating a sister he is pleased to claim."

Juliana pressed a handkerchief into Lydia's hand.

"We ought to take our places, come."

Mrs. Weatherby showed each of them to their places. Mr. Darcy joined her at the back of the chapel.

How fine he looked, so tall and somber. He was a very well-looking man. So was James, but in a very different sort of way. Where Mr. Darcy always seemed so well ordered and constrained. James was sharp awkward angles, tousled and rumpled around the edges. Their eyes shared a similar warmth and their voices both had a warm, fuzzy character that tickled the depths of her heart. They would do well as brothers.

No doubt Mr. Darcy agreed. Why else would his lips lift at the corner?

"Thank you, sir, for everything. Without you, none of this would have been possible."

He nodded slowly, his eyes crinkling with a widening smile. "You are very welcome, sister."

How could one word have the power to shatter her composure so?

He pressed a handkerchief into her hand.

How many would she collect before the day was out? She might have to spend her first whole day as a married woman returning them to their owners.

She giggled and dabbed her eyes.

From her place in the pews, Lizzy nodded at them, sharing a meaningful glance with Mr. Darcy. What must it be like to be married to a woman who missed nothing?

Mrs. Drummond, the teachers and the girls arrived, followed by Sir Anthony who was to stand up with James.

He must be at the church as well.

Lydia's heart fluttered.

Mr. Weatherby took his place at the front of the church.

Mr. Darcy offered her his arm and James took his place at the front. He looked back at her and her knees melted.

Oh, the expression in his eyes! She clung to Mr. Darcy's arm, staring hard to capture that gaze in her memory so she could transfer it to paper.

That drawing would be for her alone.

Mr. Darcy held her steady until she regained her

strength. He shortened his step to allow her to walk easily with him down the aisle of the church.

Lydia smiled at each of her friends as she passed. Only Joan turned aside, but the blush on her cheeks suggested more self-recrimination than ill-will.

Annabelle and Juliana offered happy little squeaks as she passed and Mr. Darcy placed her hand in James's.

Mr. Weatherby began to speak.

She nodded and spoke where required barely aware of the words.

James slipped a ring on her finger, a beautiful fili-greed band of gold and tiny pearls.

"It was my mother's."

She sniffled and blinked hard. He should have prepared her for that!

Mr. Weatherby joined their hands, slipping a handkerchief into Lydia's palm as he did so.

Great heavens!

"For as much as Lydia Bennet and James Amber-son have consented together in holy wedlock, and have witnessed the same before God and this company, and thereto have given and pledged their troth either to other, and have declared the same by giving and receiving of a Ring, and by joining of hands; I pronounce that they be Man and Wife together, In the Name of the Father, and of the Son, and of the Holy Ghost. Amen."

"Amen."

The rest of the wedding passed in a flash.

Lizzy and Mr. Darcy escorted them to the waiting

carriage.

"They will join us at the town house. All the well-wishing can take place much more comfortably there with breakfast." Lizzy arranged Lydia's skirts out of the way of the men's boots.

James slid his arm around Lydia and slid closer next to her. Lizzy's brows pulled together in a bit of a scowl, but Mr. Darcy slipped his arm around her shoulders and pressed closer to her.

Did he just wink at James?

From the corner of her eye, she caught James winking.

Gracious goodness! Were the two already on their way to being friends?

Given Mr. Darcy's connections with Mr. Bingley, it was clear he welcomed friends from spheres outside his own, so it was possible.

She leaned into James' shoulder. Would today's surprises never cease?

Lizzy opened her reticule and removed several letters. "Here, these are from the family. Forgive me, but I took the liberty of reading the one from Papa and Mama. I know it was not proper of me at all, but I could not bear the possibility of him being cruel to you on your wedding day."

"And?"

"What she means to say is that *I* read his letter." Mr. Darcy grumbled under his breath.

"I have given him the liberty of reading all of Papa's correspondence before I do and deciding if it is needful for me to read it."

Mr. Darcy's lip curled back as though someone steeped his tea in vinegar. "A great deal of it is not."

"And I am better by far for not having seen it. I

hope you will forgive us taking that liberty for you as well." Lizzy bit her lip.

"I would suggest, Amberson, that you might consider taking such an approach when dealing with Bennet. Lydia, you may well wish to ask him to read your father's letter first and convey to you its relevant messages."

"You would have me read my bride's post and decide if she needs to be bothered with it?"

"Only that which comes from her parents. Read this one letter and see if you agree with me."

"You have never met our father, James." Lizzy said very softly.

"Perhaps she is right. At least this once, I think I would like you to do that, if you are willing." Lydia handed him the unsealed letter.

James nodded and took it from her. He unfolded it, and she turned away slightly.

His face grew dark and his neck corded with tension. His left hand worked in and out of a fist. Slowly, carefully he refolded the letter and handed it back to Lizzy.

"He and your mother are ... pleased at the news of your marriage."

"That is all he said?" Lydia asked.

"That is the only gainful thing he said. I believe the Darcys have excellent advice in this matter. If you agree, my dear, I should like to follow that from this day forward."

Lizzy nodded vigorously. "Trust me, Lydia, it is truly for the best. Only for Papa's letters, to be sure, but it is best."

James squeezed Lydia's hand and looked at Darcy, brows drawn low over his eyes. "You and I need to have a talk before you leave for Derbyshire."

"I am at your disposal." Darcy nodded sharply.

"I will trust you then, all of you." Lydia glanced down at the other letters in her hands.

"Go ahead and read the others. I am sure Mary's letter will be very pleasing," Lizzy said.

"Shall I read it aloud?"

"I think that an excellent way to pass the time." Mr. Darcy settled back into the squabs.

The wedding breakfast included many of Lydia's favorite foods. Her favorite flowers decorated the table, and the cake was all that she ever hoped it might be. Had Mama planned it, not nearly so many of her preferences would have been honored.

Lizzy's warm hospitality kept the guests lingering, but Mrs. Drummond insisted it was time for the girls to return to the school. Sir Anthony departed as well, leaving Lydia and James standing awkwardly in the vestibule with Lizzy and Mr. Darcy.

"Perhaps, this would be a good time for you gentlemen to have that discussion you mentioned earlier. There is an excellent bottle of port waiting in the study for you, courtesy of Sir Anthony."

Darcy tipped his head toward James. "That, I believe, is a subtle hint our presence is no longer required. I have learned it is not a suggestion one should ignore."

"I shall defer to your wisdom, sir." James's eyes lingered on Lydia, though.

Butterflies filled her stomach and her cheeks heated.

Lizzy slipped her arm into Lydia's. "A sisterly chat before Mr. Darcy and I depart for Derbyshire?"

It was not a question, but she nodded as though she agreed because it seemed she should.

They climbed the stairs in perfect step.

"I thought you would prefer these rooms. I had them made up for you." Lizzy opened the door and warm sunlight poured out.

Bowls of flowers filled the spacious chamber with color and fragrance.

"They are beautiful. Everything has been beautiful. I cannot thank you enough. I never imagined …"

Lizzy entered and sat on the edge of the bed. "Nor did I. Perhaps that is why it was so very pleasing to be able to do it for you. Save Mary, I have had so little connection to our family since my marriage."

"Do you miss them? I know Papa …"

"Yes, I miss even him. It makes no sense at all, not even to me. It probably never will."

"Did you hope he would be pleased to hear of the success of Mr. Darcy's efforts on my behalf?"

"I am a fool, but I did."

"I would have liked that too." Lydia sat beside Lizzy. "They are settled now in Derbyshire, are they not? At Matlock? Is that very far from Pemberley?"

"Not at all, especially by carriage. We could see Mama and Papa quite regularly."

"But you do not."

"No. Mr. Darcy does not permit Papa on Pemberley grounds and Mama will not come without him. When we visit Matlock, he is not permitted to come to the house. His patient prospers under his care, but the Earl is not like Lady Catherine."

"You suggest we follow your suit?"

"It is entirely up to you. You must make your own way."

"What of Jane and Kitty?"

Lizzy rose and leaned her cheek against the bed-post. "It is difficult to know what to say of them. Kitty has been with Jane for months now. But I do not think either very happy. It is more what is not said in their letters than what is."

"Jane is no longer the center of attention and she is unhappy with that, I suppose. Her new life must make many demands on her that she finds taxing."

"Enough of that. Is there anything you wish to ask me?"

Lydia laughed, but it had a bitter aftertaste. "I am not untouched. And he …"

"He was honest with us as to his past. Still, you are not at all anxious?"

"I love him, but this is so different to …"

"It will be different, but remember what he has promised with that ring you wear."

Lydia stared at the unexpected ring on her finger.

His mother's ring.

He thought enough of her to put his mother's ring on her hand.

Lizzy grasped Lydia's hands firmly. "It takes time to become accustomed to being loved ardently. Be patient and do not assume things are as they were in Papa's house. You may speak with me about anything you wish, at any time. Darcy and I will be there to support you both. I think I hear the gentlemen on the stairs."

She kissed Lydia's forehead and slipped out the door.

Lydia clutched her hands tight in her lap.

Thoughts and feelings swirled around her, threatening to overwhelm. If only they would slow down so she might catch them, recognize them for what they were.

But how?

She scanned the room. Someone had piled her trunks neatly in the far corner.

She flung open the topmost trunk. Her notebook and pencil case lay in the top tray. How soothing they were in her hands, just the weight of them.

Did Lizzy put the dainty table near the window just so she could draw there? It would be just like her.

She fell into the chair and opened her notebook. The dusty, woody fragrance of the paper—better than any flower might impart—quieted her soul. Her pencil fit into her hand, an extension of her voice, more eloquent than any words.

So many images floated in her mind, where to begin? Her pencil flew, roughing out faces, Lizzy's, Mr. Darcy's, Mrs. Drummond's, James's. That moment during the ceremony, the one she must not forget, took shape on the paper before her.

"I knew you would put that to paper." He whispered behind her.

She set her pencil down and turned.

He was so tall, all length and angles with hair that insisted on falling into his eyes. That was how he had always been and would never change. When she had first seen him though, he had not been handsome.

When had that changed?

"I wish I had your skill, to allow you to see how you look to me." He laid a hand on her shoulder.

She rose and stood very close. "But you can, in a melody. You must write the song of our wedding."

He cradled her cheek in his palm and stroked it

with his thumb. "I will, but do not be surprised if it is something that should not be played in company."

She looked up at him and he slowly, tenderly removed a pin from her hair.

How could he make such an action so incredibly intimate?

Long fingers plucked a single curl from its elaborate styling. He wound it around his fingers and brought it to his lips.

She swallowed hard, lips trembling.

He leaned close to her ear and hummed. The music—or were those his fingertips—trailed along the nape of her neck, leaving heat and passion in their wake.

His cheek pressed closer, his lips near her ear, barely touching, but the song flowed on, surging with longing, but not lust, the sound of love.

Gentle fingers entwined with hers and led her to the fulfillment of both their desires.

Hours later, she lay nestled in his arms. He breathed deep and slow, slumbering. Though languid and satisfied, sleep eluded her. Being with him was nothing compared to what she had expected. Nothing could have prepared her to feel so … so … treasured, so complete.

He rolled to his side and tucked an arm around her waist. "What are you thinking about, Mrs. Amberson?"

Oh, how it tickled when he nuzzled her neck like that!

She squirmed in his arms.

"I was wondering what you and Mr. Darcy spoke of."

"All manner of manly secrets, my dear. Apparently, you Bennet women require special care and handling. As the local expert on the art, he saw fit to impart his impressions upon me."

"And what did you learn from him?"

"I am a very fortunate man and must remind you of that constantly for you have never been shown your true worth."

The words fell hard and heavy on her chest, so heavy she could not draw breath.

He sat up and pulled her up beside him. "I know your past, and you mine. Neither one of us wants to return, so let us promise to leave it behind. We will not be perfect, but let us make a pact to make entirely new mistakes, our own, not the ones of our ancestors or ones we have already made."

She stared at him, silhouetted in the moonlight. "I am not certain if that is brilliant or utterly daft."

"I am not sure myself, but promise me we shall find out together."

"We will."

⚜Sneak Peek

Don't miss the first book in the series:

Mistaking Her Character:

LADY CATHERINE LOOMED in the parlor doorway, her features gathering into her darkest, most menacing scowl. "A word, if you please." She turned on her heel and disappeared into her lair.

Elizabeth dropped a small curtsey and rushed into the parlor to brave the dragon in all her fury. If only she had remembered to bring her sword in her workbag.

Lady Catherine ascended her throne, a stony mask of creases, gnarls and shadow firmly in place.

Was that the scent of burning sulfur in the air?

"Your ladyship?"

"You think I am ignorant of what you are about, young woman?"

"I have not the pleasure of your meaning, madam."

"None of your cheek here, girl. I know. Oh, I know." She shook her finger toward Elizabeth. "You have ambitions beyond your station, beyond all propriety and decency."

"Excuse me?" Elizabeth grabbed the back of the nearest chair to shore up her liquid knees.

"It is written upon your face—clear in that indecent display I just walked in upon."

"Mr. Darcy?" She gasped. "You assume far too much. I only met him yesterday."

"Entirely long enough to form designs upon his person and fortune. You spurned Mr. Collins—I am sure—in the hopes of someone of greater consequence whom you have now found in the person of my nephew."

The upholstery tore a tiny bit beneath her fingernails. "I assure you, madam, I never considered such a thing. Mr. Collins and I … our temperaments are so different. We could never have made a good match. I am entirely convinced he has a much happier situation with—"

"Are you suggesting happiness may be found in disobeying me?"

"By no means."

"Then turn your attentions to Mr. Wickham. He studies at the Inn of Courts—."

"He does not, nor is he likely to, having offended a very influential member."

She flushed puce.

That could not be healthy.

"Where do you come by this information?"

"Mr. Darcy—"

Lady Catherine slapped the arms of her chair and heaved to her feet. "What were you doing talking to my nephew?"

"We met on the road this morning."

"While you were driving, unchaperoned, as I have expressly forbidden."

Her shoulders drew up and she tucked her elbows close into her sides. "Yes, your ladyship."

One, two, three steps. Lady Catherine stood so close their skirt hems touched. She waved her bony finger under Elizabeth's nose. "I will make this very plain to you, young woman, so that even you, in all your cleverness, cannot pretend to misunderstand me. Darcy is for Anne. From their cradles, they have been promised to one another. It was the fondest wish of his mother and me. No upstart like you is going to interfere with those plans."

"What am I compared to Miss de Bourgh?"

"What are you—exactly! Exactly! But do not play coy with me." She circled Elizabeth, a hungry cat stalking a bird. "We both know you have arts and allurements to distract him from his duty to his family. You have no delicacy, exposed to the basest things of life—of men."

How did one respond to such raving? Perhaps best not.

"Have you considered why I have been trying to find you a match? Even with your connection to me, few decent men will ally themselves with a woman like you. Despite your youthful airs and arrogance, I have had—and will continue to have—your best interests in mind—unless—" She stabbed her sharp finger into Elizabeth's chest.

Elizabeth jumped back.

"—unless you insist on preying upon Darcy. You are not his equal and would bring shame upon his name and all his family."

"Shall I leave Rosings?"

"No, Anne requires your presence. I will not deny her any comfort, no matter how little I fathom it."

"Then shall I ignore him? Turn my back as the servants do when he approaches?"

"You are not … not … a servant."

"How am I to behave?"

"With every civility, but nothing more."

"As you wish, your ladyship."

"I will be watching you, Miss Elizabeth. Do not think you can escape my notice if you disobey. Now leave me."

She curtsied and strode away, fists balled so tightly her arms shook.

Two steps into the corridor, Mr. Darcy blocked her path. She stopped short and barely held back a tiny shriek. How tall he was, towering—or was that, hovering over her.

"I hardly know what to say, my aunt—"

She raised an open hand. "Pray forgive me, sir, but I am truly in no state for conversation at the moment."

"Will you speak with me later?"

"I do not know, sir. Excuse me." She curtsied and hurried away.

Acknowledgments

So many people have helped me along the journey taking this from an idea to a reality.

Jan, Ruth, Anji, Debbie, April and Julie thank you so much for cold reading, proof reading and being honest!

And my dear friend Cathy, my biggest cheerleader, you have kept me from chickening out more than once!

And my sweet sister Gerri who believed in even those first attempts that now live in the file drawer.

Thank you!

✣ Other Books by Maria Grace

Given Good Principles Series:
Darcy's Decision
The Future Mrs. Darcy
All the Appearance of Goodness
Twelfth Night at Longbourn

Queen of Rosings Park Series:
Mistaking Her Character
The Trouble to Check Her

Remember the Past
The Darcy Brothers
The Darcys' First Christmas
A Jane Austen Christmas: Regency Christmas Traditions (non-fiction)
A Spot of Sweet Tea: Hopes and Beginnings
(short story collection)

Short Stories:
Four Days in April (free on all platforms)
Sweet Ginger
Last Dance
Not Romantic
To Forget

Available in paperback, e-book, and audiobook format at all online bookstores.

On Line Exclusives at:

www.http//RandomBitsofFascination.com

Bonus and deleted scenes
Regency Life Series

<u>Free e-books</u>:
Bits of Bobbin Lace
The Scenes Jane Austen Never Wrote: First Anniversaries
Half Agony, Half Hope: New Reflections on Persuasion
Four Days in April
Jane Bennet in January
February Aniversaries

✠ About the Author

Though Maria Grace has been writing fiction since she was ten years old, those early efforts happily reside in a file drawer and are unlikely to see the light of day again, for which many are grateful. After penning five file-drawer novels in high school, she took a break from writing to pursue college and earn her doctorate in Educational Psychology. After 16 years of university teaching, she returned to her first love, fiction writing.

She has one husband, two graduate degrees and two black belts, three sons, four undergraduate majors, five nieces, six new novels in the works, attended seven period balls, sewn eight Regency era costumes, shared her life with nine cats through the years and published her tenth book last year.

She can be contacted at:

author.MariaGrace@gmail.com

Facebook:
http://facebook.com/AuthorMariaGrace

On Amazon.com:
http://amazon.com/author/mariagrace

Random Bits of Fascination
(http://RandomBitsofFascination.com)

Austen Variations (http://AustenVariations.com)

English Historical Fiction Authors
(http://EnglshHistoryAuthors.blogspot.com)

White Soup Press (http://whitesouppress.com/)

On Twitter @WriteMariaGrace

On Pinterest: http://pinterest.com/mariagrace423/

22227203R00209

Printed in Great Britain
by Amazon